PRAISE FOR

The Boyfriend of the Month Club

"A novel as quirky as its main character, *The Boyfriend of the Month Club* delivers comedy, romance, and a little bit of literature . . . immensely sexy, immensely satisfying and humorous." —*Portland Book Review*

"There's nothing like a satisfying chick lit book on a blah winter's day or on a sunny day at the beach. The machinations of friends and family in a cozy setting while the main character falls in love with the perfect guy becomes the chocolate bar for the soul . . . *The Boyfriend of the Month Club* is such a nugget of pleasure." —*All About Romance*

"*The Boyfriend of the Month Club* is the perfect book to grab on vacation or while relaxing over the holidays when you want a quick, funny read with lovable characters." —*Philadelphia Women's Fiction Examiner*

"This book is a straight fun-read girls' book. No other way to put it." —*Celebrating the Southern Written Word*

"This is a hysterical novel about a woman trying to find the perfect man. Grace's close-knit family and friends serve as great secondary characters that add so much humor and love to this novel." —*Chicklit Club Review*

"This is a good romantic comedy story of literary heroes versus modern men, and the mistakes of modern relationships. Grace is a fun character with a lot of spirit. She's the perfect romantic comedy heroine." —*Parkersburg News and Sentinel*

continued . . .

"The action is fast, the characters are smart in addition to being sassy, and the one-liners never stop." —*Romance Junkies*

"A funny look at love and relationships." —*Southern Pines Pilot*

"There are plenty of laughs, great characters, and romance. *The Boyfriend of the Month Club* is just plain great fun! Enjoy!"
—*Reader to Reader Reviews*

"This book is a quick, entertaining read that will keep you smiling until the end." —*Two Lips Reviews*

"Style-wise, think Dorothea Benton Frank meets *My Big Fat Greek* . . . er, Cuban *Wedding*. It's a happy day when I read something that wouldn't ordinarily end up on my to-be-read pile and end up loving it. Maybe you'll get your hands on *The Boyfriend of the Month Club* and love it too!" —*What Women Write*

"A lighthearted and fun read, I would definitely recommend *The Boyfriend of the Month Club* to chick lit fans."
—*ChickLit Plus Reviews*

"Geraci fills the . . . enjoyable story with literary references and her leading lady is endearingly flawed. Romance readers will revel in the Austen-perfect happy ending and the warm friendship among members of the club." —*Publishers Weekly*

"The first thing that comes to mind with this book is the unique and fantastic humor that is found from the beginning and just doesn't end . . . I absolutely loved it and hated to put it down . . . If you need a good laugh about the dating scene or just like to read about some fun characters, pick up *The Boyfriend of the Month Club*. It's a terrific way to relax and learn not to take things too seriously as characters look for love and find it where they don't expect it. (Or maybe they do.)"

—*Night Owl Reviews*

a girl like you

Maria Geraci

BERKLEY BOOKS, NEW YORK

BERKLEY BOOKS
Published by the Penguin Group
Penguin Group (USA) Inc.
375 Hudson Street, New York, New York 10014, USA

Penguin Group (Canada), 90 Eglinton Avenue East, Suite 700, Toronto, Ontario M4P 2Y3, Canada
(a division of Pearson Penguin Canada Inc.) • Penguin Books Ltd., 80 Strand, London WC2R 0RL,
England • Penguin Group Ireland, 25 St. Stephen's Green, Dublin 2, Ireland (a division of Penguin
Books Ltd.) • Penguin Group (Australia), 250 Camberwell Road, Camberwell, Victoria 3124, Australia
(a division of Pearson Australia Group Pty. Ltd.) • Penguin Books India Pvt. Ltd., 11 Community
Centre, Panchsheel Park, New Delhi—110 017, India • Penguin Group (NZ), 67 Apollo Drive,
Rosedale, Auckland 0632, New Zealand (a division of Pearson New Zealand Ltd.) • Penguin Books
(South Africa) (Pty.) Ltd., 24 Sturdee Avenue, Rosebank, Johannesburg 2196, South Africa

Penguin Books Ltd., Registered Offices: 80 Strand, London WC2R 0RL, England

This is a work of fiction. Names, characters, places, and incidents either are the product of the author's
imagination or are used fictitiously, and any resemblance to actual persons, living or dead, business
establishments, events, or locales is entirely coincidental. The publisher does not have any control over
and does not assume any responsibility for author or third-party websites or their content.

Copyright © 2012 by Maria Geraci.
Cover design by MNStudios.
Cover photos by Shutterstock.

PUBLISHING HISTORY
Berkley trade paperback edition / August 2012

Library of Congress Cataloging-in-Publication Data
Geraci, Maria.
A girl like you / Maria Geraci.
p. cm.
ISBN 978-0-425-24780-8
1. Women journalists—Fiction. 2. Stock car drivers—Fiction.
3. Florida—Fiction. I. Title.
PS3607.E7256G57 2012
813'.6—dc23
2012005213

PRINTED IN THE UNITED STATES OF AMERICA

10 9 8 7 6 5 4 3 2 1

For Mami,
who always loves me no matter what kind of sandwich I am.

acknowledgments

First off, thank you to Deidre Knight, my wonderful agent and friend for believing in this story. And to my editor, Wendy McCurdy, for giving me the freedom to write this without knowing how it was going to end. I'd also like to thank her assistant, Katherine Pelz, and the rest of the team at Berkley.

Thank you, Rosanne Dunkelberger, my Bunco pal, and the editor of *Tallahassee Magazine*, for answering all my questions and for the tour. A special thanks also goes to Alicia Miles for reading portions of my manuscript. I really hope I got everything right.

Thanks to my pal Melissa Francis for all the brainstorming, and to Jamie Farrell for the great critique, and, last but not least, to Beth Spooner for being my beta reader. I'd also like to thank my daughter, Stephanie, for giving me the initial feedback that started the novel.

As usual, I'd like to thank the awesome nurses in labor and delivery at Tallahassee Memorial Hospital, my home away from home. And of course, to my family: my parents; my sister, Carmen, whose support means so much to me; and of course, my lovely husband, Mike, who eats way too much takeout when I'm in writing mode. I love you all.

Ugly Friend: A friend a person brings with him/her to a gathering/event in order to make him-/herself appear more attractive in comparison.

—THE URBAN DICTIONARY

chapter one

· · · · ·

It was a dark and stormy night . . .

I open the door to Captain Pete's, the new "it" club in Ybor City, and am immediately reminded of that famous bar scene from *Star Wars*. Except in this scenario, I am the alien and everyone else is normal.

"Why is your hair wet?" Torie asks the second she sees me.

Kimberly stares at me in horror. "You look like a drowned rat."

The bar is incredibly crowded even for a Friday evening and I have to strain to hear them above the noise. Someone male and reeking of Hugo Boss bumps into me but doesn't stop to apologize.

"In case neither of you noticed, it's raining outside," I say.

"*Emma,*" Torie says, "that's what valet parking is for."

"It's no biggie." I pull the ends of my dark hair forward to wring the water out. "I'm exhausted, so I'm only staying for one drink."

"One drink?" Torie frowns at me and gives Kimberly a look I can't interpret except to say that they are both up to something, which usually does not bode well for me. Torie and Kimberly are terrific friends, but they are constantly trying to fix me up because they don't think I'm aggressive enough to find a guy on my own.

I signal the bartender. He ignores me and moves to another customer before finally taking my order.

The guy who bumped into me earlier finagles his way onto the edge of our group. He points to the nearly empty beer in Torie's hand. "Looks like you need a refill."

Torie smiles brightly. "Thanks, maybe later?"

This is Torie's standard spiel. She never shoots a guy down completely, because as she likes to say, "You never know."

Hugo Boss smiles back. Disappointed, but not discouraged.

Stuff like this happens a lot to Torie. Unlike Kimberly, Torie is not a classic beauty, but she gets hit on more than Kimberly and me combined. I think this is because while Torie is pretty and has a great figure, the real attraction is that she exudes a combination of confidence and accessibility. Only the really cocky guys make a play for Kimberly. As for me, I admit to getting a lot of their leftovers.

"Don't I know you from somewhere?" Hugo Boss asks me.

See? Leftovers.

I really shouldn't reward him by validating this cheesiest of all pickup lines but I can't help but be sympathetic to his plight. While he's not exactly cute, he's not a dog either. Plus, we *are* here to meet men.

"Somewhere sounds a little generic," I say, trying to give him an in. "Maybe you could be more specific?"

Before he can respond, Kimberly pulls me away. "Thanks, but she's not interested," she says over her shoulder.

Hugo Boss shrugs, as if to say *no biggie*.

"Kimberly," I hiss, "that's kind of rude."

"Forget about him! We dropped by your office on the way here."

Let me tell you about my job.

I work for Dunhill Publications, which owns *Florida!* (yes, with an exclamation point) magazine, where I've been employed for the past six years as a journalist. *Florida!* is a high-end publication dedicated to celebrating the beauty and uniqueness of the Florida lifestyle (that's our tagline). I worked as a freelancer for almost four years before I was hired full-time. It might not sound like a dream job, but I love it. Each magazine is a like a work of art. Great photos, great stories.

"You came by the office? Where was I?"

"*Ben*," Kimberly says, emphasizing my boss's name in a way that makes me twitchy, "said you were out running errands."

Torie sniffs. "Without an umbrella, obviously."

I ignore Torie's little barb. Up to now, neither Torie nor Kimberly had met Ben, who only joined the staff at *Florida!* six months ago. Ben came to *Florida!* from *Newsweek*. He's lived in New York and has traveled all over the world. How he ended up at *Florida!* I'm not sure, because although *Florida!* is an awesome magazine, it certainly can't compare to the glamour of a publication like *Newsweek*. But whatever made Ben land here in Tampa, I'm grateful. Ben is a brilliant editor and I've really grown under his tutelage. I'm dying to ask the girls what they think of him, but I bite my tongue.

"We invited your sexy boss to go out with us tonight," says Torie. "He should be here any minute."

This seemingly benign statement causes my beer to go down the wrong way.

"Are you okay?" Kimberly slaps me on the back.

Hugo Boss turns around to see me choking and slips into the crowd without looking back. So much for chivalry . . .

"Raise your arms above your head," instructs Torie.

What this will do, I'm not sure, but it works. I take a deep breath and try to calm myself. I've been secretly in love with Ben Gallagher since the day he told me his favorite word was *ubiquitous*.

This is how it happened.

Ben had been working at *Florida!* for about a month. The two of us were alone in his office discussing an article, when out of the blue, I blurted, "What's your favorite word in the whole world?"

Without blinking, skipping a beat, or even pausing to frown, he turned to me and said, "Ubiquitous." He then continued talking about the article as if we'd never had the exchange. I know this might sound dumb, but put in that same scenario, 99.9 percent of the population would have looked at me and said, *"What?"* for going off subject like that. But not Ben, because he totally gets me.

Ben is everything a guy you hope to fall in love with should be. He's handsome (but not too handsome), smart, has a great laugh, and is kind to animals. I know this last part because a couple of months ago a stray cat wandered off the street into our office. The cat was kind of mangy and looked like he hadn't had a meal in days. Richard, a fellow journalist at *Florida!* (more on Richard later) immediately called Animal Control, which took the cat away. The next day Ben called the shelter and asked them to notify him if they planned to put the cat down, which, of course, is exactly what they were going to do. Ben drove to the shelter and adopted the cat, even though he is not a cat person. The cat's name is Lucky (pretty appropriate if you ask me). Personally, I think the whole cat adoption story speaks volumes on Ben's character.

Ben is also originally from Boston, which I totally love. While this might not sound exotic, for me, a rube from small-town

Florida, cities like Boston and New York and Chicago hold some mysterious appeal. I've been to New York a few times. Once with my moms after I graduated high school, and a couple of times with Torie and Kimberly for a girls' weekend. I don't think I'd want to live there, but I'd love to say that I'm *from* there. It sounds so much more sophisticated than saying I was raised in Catfish Cove, Florida.

I envision my first date with Ben like this: He picks me up at my town house in his Toyota Prius (Ben is a member of the Sierra Club, another thing I love about him) and we go to a quaint little restaurant no one has ever heard of, but where the food is terrific. The owner greets Ben by name because Ben has discovered this fabulous restaurant that no one else knows about and the two of them have become chums. He orders the second-least-inexpensive bottle of wine on the menu and we begin a three-hour dinner that seems to go by in minutes because our conversation is so enthralling.

Afterward, we hit an independent bookstore where we peruse the aisles—poetry for me, natural history for Ben. Next, we take a walk along Bayshore Avenue. In the middle of the walk, Ben stops. He tenderly takes off my glasses, cups my face, and says, "Emma, is it all right if I kiss you?" While this might sound corny, it's something I've always dreamed of a guy saying to me, so it's definitely included in my perfect date scenario.

Even though we are surrounded by people, we kiss like we don't care who sees. Ben then whispers that he's *dying* to sleep with me (this is something else I've always dreamed a guy would say to me), only he won't because he doesn't want us to rush things, and I agree. I don't sleep with Ben until our fifth date and it's utterly perfect. He proposes on our tenth date and—

Okay, maybe I'd gotten a little ahead of myself.

"I hope you don't mind about Ben," Kimberly says, snapping me back to reality.

"Mind? Why should I mind? It'll be fun."

"Admit it, Emma, you have a crush on him."

Torie playfully punches me in the shoulder. "And we're going to help you do something about that."

"I do not have a crush on him!"

Torie and Kimberly stare me down.

After about four seconds, I sigh because it's pointless. They have always seen right through me. As a matter of fact, anyone who knows me for more than a minute can see right through me too. I have the kind of face that mirrors exactly what I'm feeling. Please, don't ever take me to Vegas.

"You could have warned me you invited Ben to go out with us." I came here straight from work, so I have on the same khaki pants and sensible black flats I've worn all day. I'm not going to stand out among the push-up-bra-and-stiletto crowd. I'm pretty sure Ben is above all that, but still, it couldn't hurt to have changed into something more flattering.

"How were we to know you'd come here with wet hair?" says Torie. "And ditch the glasses."

Frankly, I'm not too worried about my hair. It's my best feature. It's shoulder length and straight, but it's thick and dries pretty much the same as if I'd spent a half hour blow-drying and styling it. Plus it's a shade of brown that's very in right now. Think Sandra Bullock hair. The rest of me, though, is kind of average. I probably fall somewhere between a five on a bad night and a seven when I'm really working it. Ben is a solid seven (remember, he's handsome, but not too handsome), so he's on the higher end of my scale, but I don't think I'm totally out of his league. I know Torie called him sexy, but I'm pretty sure he's not the kind of guy who walks into a bar and has women fall all over him.

I'm about to go to the bathroom to freshen up my makeup when I spot Ben. He sees me and heads our way. I've never seen Ben outside of work before. He's wearing jeans and a black polo shirt. I watch as he cuts his way through the crowd with confidence. Men step to the side to let him through, and women . . .

Crap. I was wrong.

Ben is not a seven. He's not even an eight.

Ben is an undisputable nine.

chapter two

· · · · ·

I whip off my glasses and stuff them inside my purse.

"Hey," Ben says with his slight Boston accent that sends a tingle down my spine. "Thanks for letting me tag along."

He orders a Heineken and the bartender does not ignore him. Kimberly and Torie get refills. I order a cosmopolitan, and despite our protests, Ben picks up the tab for all our drinks. So far, so good.

He takes a sip of his beer and gazes around Captain Pete's. "So, Frazier, is this how you spend your Friday nights?"

Ben calls me by my last name. It's kind of cute, really. I like to imagine myself as the Rosalind Russell to his Cary Grant (think *His Girl Friday*), except I thought that since we're outside the office, he'd call me Emma. Maybe I should rethink my kissing fantasy, because "Frazier, can I kiss you?" doesn't sound so romantic. But surely by the time we reach that point, he'll be calling me by my first name.

"I have to do something to relax," I say. "You should meet my boss. He's a real slave driver." I know this sounds dumb but I'm too nervous to think of anything cleverer.

Ben smiles and my knees go wobbly. He seems genuinely happy to be here and pays just the right amount of attention to

Torie and Kimberly, but his focus is on me. Not too much to make it obvious, though. This is just a couple of friends having drinks after work. It is *not* a setup (well, it is, but he doesn't seem to be making a big deal of it and that's good).

I think I owe Torie and Kimberly big for this. I should buy their drinks for the rest of the night. Maybe even for the rest of forever.

Everything is going fabulously until Torie's friend Amy shows up. Amy is an attorney at Torie's firm and every once in a while she joins us on our Friday nights out.

Amy hugs me like we're long-lost friends and generally makes a big production out of her entrance, like, *Now that Amy's here, let the party begin!*

I'll be honest, Amy rubs me the wrong way, but it's not because she always has to be the center of attention. There's something else about her that I don't like but I've never been able to pinpoint what it is exactly. Torie says that Amy is a killer in the courtroom, but because I've only seen Amy in the barroom, the only thing I've seen her kill are appletinis and I can tell she's already murdered a few tonight.

I am forced to introduce Ben to Amy, who immediately picks up on Ben's Boston accent. This is when I discover that Amy is a graduate of Harvard Law School.

Wait. Why did I never know this before? I must have heard wrong.

I shout above the grinding music, "Amy, did you just say you went to Harvard Law?"

She smiles and nods and bats her eyelashes, and Ben looks mightily impressed, but I am now speechless. Amy has never struck me as the modest type. If I graduated from Harvard Law, I think I would shout it from the rooftops. Ben graduated from

Columbia, and despite the fact he doesn't mention this to Amy, I am beginning to feel slightly inferior with my little journalism degree from the University of Florida.

As if things aren't bad enough, before I know it, the two of them are talking about the Boston Red Sox, and I can tell this excites Ben because he starts to get really animated, the same way he does when he's just read something well written. I listen to them yap about how much they hate the Yankees and Amy is saying things like "wicked cool" (I have never heard her use this expression before), and how weird is it to discover that at one time they only lived a few blocks from each other. Imagine that!

I'm at a complete disadvantage here because (a) I've never been to Boston, and (b) baseball is about as exciting to me as a root canal. I could hate the Yankees too, if I thought about it enough.

But what makes me nervous is that Amy is what our friend Jason calls smokin' hot. It suddenly occurs to me that Amy is a triple threat. Attractive, smart (I mean, she graduated from Harvard Law, so she has to be, right?), and most people would say she has an engaging personality.

I decide this is a good time to regroup and touch up my makeup. I excuse myself and Torie and I weave through the crowd to hit the bathroom, which is blessedly quiet compared to the chaos out in the club.

"So what do you think?" I ask once the two of us are alone.

"He's awesome!" Torie says. "And he likes you."

"You think?"

"*Definitely.*"

"You . . . you don't think he's into Amy?"

"No! Little Miss Drunken Two-Shoes totally shoved her way in there. He's just being nice."

"I don't know," I say, wanting more of Torie's opinion. I'm not fishing, I'm really not. It's just that I don't always trust my take on these types of situations while Torie is usually spot-on.

"Emma, I've been watching him. The whole time she's been monopolizing him, he's been sneaking looks at *you*."

This perks me right up, but then I look in the mirror and cringe. Tonight, I'm lucky if I'm a five. The minimal eye makeup I wear to work wore off long ago, so my muddy-brown eyes seem lost, and even though it's June, I'm pale from lack of sunshine. I do the best I can with the weapons at my disposal, which is some borrowed blush from Torie and a swipe of mocha-colored lipstick. I hand-tousle my hair, which is beginning to dry, and I immediately feel better. Then I go into the stall to take care of business. That's when I hear the bathroom door open. A sudden blast of techno pop music is still not enough to drown out the *clickety-clack* of Amy's stilettos.

"Oh my God, Torie, he's *fabulous*. Where did you find him?" I hear Amy say.

"Find who?" Torie responds coolly.

"Boston Ben!"

"Hands off. He belongs to Emma."

"Who? You mean your ugly friend?"

My hand freezes on the stall door. Silence engulfs the little bathroom. I almost think I must have imagined Amy's remark, but then I hear Torie demand in a strangled whisper, "What the fuck did you just say?"

Amy giggles nervously. "Oh, chill. I *love* Emma. I really do. But you have to admit, she's your ugly friend."

My first reaction after the shock is anger and I think about opening the stall door and going all *Jersey Shore* on Amy's ass. I know I'm not beautiful. I'm not even close. But *the ugly friend*?

Torie says something to Amy in an angry tone and I strain to listen. It doesn't take a genius to figure out that Torie is telling Amy I am right here in the bathroom listening to every word they are saying and that she needs to shut the hell up. All this serves to calm me down.

Torie is right. Amy is drunk.

I've also just figured out why I don't like her.

Amy is an obnoxious bitch.

I'm so above her petty, junior-high-school antics.

I muster up as much dignity as I can and calmly open the stall door.

The two of them turn to look at me. Torie looks part mad, part worried, and Amy looks appropriately guilt-stricken, although I can also tell it's an act on her part.

"Hey!" I say as brightly as I can. I have decided to take the high road and pretend I didn't hear anything. "Do either of you have gum?"

They both tear into their purses, and after a few seconds of fumbling, Amy produces a breath mint.

"Thanks!" I pop the breath mint into my mouth.

Amy is so dumb (sorry, but I think Harvard Law was scraping the bottom of the barrel here) that she buys this. Apparently along with thinking me unattractive, she also thinks I'm deaf. She comments on my "fabulous" shoes, then *clickety-clacks* her way out the bathroom door.

"I hate that bitch," Torie mutters.

I guess Torie and Amy are not the good friends I thought they were, which relieves me.

"Don't worry about it."

"Emma, you don't believe what she said, do you?" I hesitate just long enough for Torie to add, "You're *beautiful,* and smart, and generous, and you have a great personality. Any guy would be lucky to get you."

Let me tell you about Torie.

I've known Torie Jacobs since I moved to Tampa after graduating from the University of Florida ten years ago. She was a friend of a friend of a friend and at the time neither of us could afford our own apartment, so we were roommates for about two years. Until the Great Tuna Fish Incident. Which we can laugh about now, but at the time was pretty traumatic.

One day, while cleaning our apartment, we found an opened, half-eaten can of tuna fish hidden beneath a stack of towels in the linen closet. Yes, I know. Pretty gross. Neither of us admitted to knowing how it got there, except I suspected (and still do) that Torie opened that can of tuna fish after coming home drunk and in some bizarre lapse of consciousness stuck the can in between those towels. She accused me of something similar and this all led to one of those roommate free-for-alls in which all the stupid things that bug you about the other person come out, the end result being that Torie and I split up. By then I could afford my own place and Torie had decided to quit her job and go to law school, so it all kind of worked out anyway. But then, after law school, she came back to Tampa and we got together for dinner, and after a bottle of wine we made up and we've been best friends ever since. Torie is a *much* better friend than roommate.

So while I think calling me beautiful is definitely overkill on Torie's part, this is just one of the many reasons I am so happy we were able to get over the Great Tuna Fish Incident. Everyone should have a best friend like Torie.

"You forgot talented," I say.

"Don't go overboard," Torie says, and we both laugh.

I'm feeling better but then we get back to the bar area and I see that Amy is gone. Which is awesome. Until I realize that Ben is gone too. Kimberly must have sensed my angst because she points to the back of the room, where Ben and Amy are playing darts.

Amy throws a dart and doesn't even hit the board.

Is it safe playing darts while you're drunk?

What if she accidentally spears someone?

Visions of Amy being hauled off to the Hillsborough County Jail for negligent homicide, followed by the disgrace of her disbarment and the subsequent stripping of her Harvard Law degree, almost make me smile. But what really makes me smile is that while Amy is blabbing in Ben's ear, he turns around and gazes through the room as if he's looking for someone. He catches my eye, and even though my vision is somewhat blurry from not having my glasses on, I'm pretty sure he gives me what Amy would now say is a *wicked* smile.

I knew it!

I have not been deluding myself these past months. There is something more between Ben and me other than just my overactive writer's imagination.

I'm still smiling to myself when Brian comes along. Brian is on my overthirties soccer team. We play on Thursday nights and we're not half bad. Brian is an investment banker and every girl on the team has a crush on him, except me. He's never seemed interested in me before, but boy, does he now. He offers to buy me another drink, which I refuse because I'm still nursing the cosmo Ben bought me. Brian introduces his two friends to me, one of whom, coincidentally, is Hugo Boss, whose real name is Cameron.

I know Torie will not be pleased that Cameron has wiggled his way into our group, but we can't blow him off anymore because he's with Brian, who I can't ignore since I know him from soccer.

Everyone introduces themselves to one another and we settle into the small talk/banter/flirtation that always makes me feel weird in these situations (hence my alien sensation from earlier). I wish I was home in bed curled up with a good book. Or with Ben. Yes, I could definitely be curled up in bed with Ben.

I glance back to the dartboards, only this time instead of looking bored, Ben laughs at something Amy says. She is standing so close to him she's practically on top of him. Amy might be drunk, but she radiates sex on a nuclear scale and few men can resist that sort of energy. I try through mental telepathy to force Ben to look over at me again, but he doesn't. I think about taking matters into my own hands and marching over there and snatching him away from Amy. But something stops me from doing this, although I'm not sure exactly what that something is.

"So, Emily, how do you think we'll do against the Strikers?" Brian asks, referring to our next week's opponent.

I think about correcting him and telling him my name is Emma, but instead, I reply, "We'll kick their ass!" because this is our team mantra and it's what he's expecting me to say.

"Hell, yeah!" He raises his beer and laughs but I can see him lean in to try to listen to whatever it is Kimberly is saying to his friend.

The hairs on the back of my neck rise.

I glance back to the dartboards. There is no sign of Amy and Ben.

Did they leave?

Surely Ben wouldn't leave without saying good-bye to me.

And surely, *God no,* he wouldn't leave with Amy.

Or would he?

I think back to what Amy said in the bathroom. Obviously, she has the hots for Ben and she thinks I am no competition. There is no doubt that Amy is flashier than me and she certainly has a much better body. My size-twelve (sometimes fourteen) ass cannot compete with her size-four pertness.

My head begins to throb.

Brian is blatantly ogling Kimberly's cleavage now. It's like I don't exist anymore. I'm tired and I want to go home but I have to find Ben first, and just as I think this, I see him. He's walking out of the bar with Amy. At least I think it's Ben and Amy. I pull my glasses out of my purse and put them back on to make sure it's really them, and it is. She tugs on his arm. Then he kisses her hard on the mouth and whisks her out the door.

I stare at the door for what seems like the longest time. I think a part of me is expecting Ben to walk back in and yell "Gotcha!"

But that doesn't happen.

Everyone around me is laughing and talking but I don't understand a word they are saying. It's as if they are speaking some foreign language that everyone took in high school except me. Slowly, I begin to fill with the sort of clarity that comes from being the alien in the room full of Others.

Brian is Cameron's wingman and I am the fat friend he's forced to suck up to so his friends can meet the hot chicks they've been lusting after all night. The fact that Torie and Kimberly are oblivious to this (or are they?) is not important. It's just the way it is. I'm a five and they are tens. Who said life was fair?

Maybe the reason I was able to hold it together in the bathroom is that on some subconscious level I've always known I was the ugly friend. Although no one has spelled it out for me as explicitly as Amy (I guess she *is* smart enough to get into Harvard Law, after all). But I can truthfully say that I have never been one of those women who obsess endlessly because their butt is too big or their boobs are too small. I was raised by two women, one of whom believed intelligence is the most important quality a woman can possess, and the other of whom placed kindness, good manners, and an appreciation of poetry even above the intelligence. But neither intelligence, kindness, nor even good manners will make much of an impression at Captain Pete's. Or with Ben either, it appears.

It is high school all over again. Only this is worse, because here we all are, a bunch of thirtysomething professionals acting just like we did almost two decades ago. This is supposed to be real life. The scary part of all this is that I think it is real life.

Despite the fact I've only had half a beer and a few sips of my cosmopolitan, I think I'm going to be sick.

I have to get out of here.

I hand my drink to Kimberly, who looks confused when I tell her I'm leaving, and before I know it I'm making a mad dash out the front door.

chapter three

· · · · ·

I arrive at my town house and my cell phone dings, telling me
I've just received a text message. It's from Ben.

Amy too drunk to drive. Am taking her home. Have fun.

At least he has the courtesy (audacity!) to let me know what's
going on.

Torie and Kimberly arrive five minutes later demanding to
know what happened. I hate that I ruined their night, but I am
glad they followed me.

"Ben took Amy home," I say in a voice that sounds surprisingly devoid of emotion.

"Maybe it's not what it seems," says Kimberly. "She was
pretty drunk. He's probably just doing a good deed and making
sure she gets home safely."

I tell them about the kiss and Torie looks surprised. "Good
deed, my ass! I can't believe I was wrong about him." Torie prides
herself on being able to "read" men, and although I know 99
percent of her indignation is all on my behalf, there is 1 percent
that is miffed for herself.

Driving home, I had time to evaluate the situation. Ben might
be a great guy, but he's just a guy and the temptation Amy presented was too much to overcome. I've seen Amy in action before.

This is her modus operandi. She gets drunk and uses it as an excuse to do whatever she wants. Frankly, I don't care. If Amy wants Ben and Ben wants Amy, they can have each other (it seems they are in the process of doing just that).

I break out the Absolut from my freezer and we end up having a girls' slumber party. By the time we fall asleep somewhere around three a.m., we have concluded that Amy is a skank, and that we all hate Ben's guts.

Neither Torie nor Kimberly mentions the ugly girlfriend thing, although I know Torie had to have told Kimberly what Amy said in the bathroom.

It is like the big five-hundred-pound gorilla in the room that no one wants to go near.

It's Monday morning and I always bring donuts to work on Monday, so I make the trip to the Krispy Kreme on West Kennedy. I'm in luck because the "Hot Now" sign is out and the donuts are so much better when they are fresh. Three years ago I brought donuts in for the weekly Monday staff meeting and everyone loved them so much I kept doing it.

The editorial headquarters of *Florida!* magazine is located on Howard Avenue, which is near, but not too near, downtown Tampa. The office is a one-story remodeled Craftsman with dark hardwood floors and cream-colored crown molding. Framed prints of the magazine's best photos spanning its forty-year history cover the sage-colored walls. There are only two private offices—Ben's, and the one that the sales team uses when they're in-house. There's also a conference room, and one open room that houses four tiny cubicles. This is where the rest of us work, including Ben's assistant, Lisa. Jackie, Richard, and I are the only full-time writers on staff. The rest of our articles are written by freelancers, and Ben communicates with them by phone or e-mail. The sales team, photographers, and the rest of the production staff work out of Dunhill Publications' main office, located sixty miles away in Orlando. But here in Tampa, at *Florida!* magazine's editorial home base, we're one small happy family.

I take the donuts to the conference room, which is currently empty. I can tell that Lisa is here because the coffee is made. I pour myself a cup and open the donut box to pull out a hot, delicious Krispy Kreme. I bite into it, savoring each and every warm sugary nibble.

I confess, I briefly thought of going cold turkey on the donuts this morning. But then I remembered reading somewhere that Frenchwomen do not get fat. And it isn't because they are constantly dieting. It is because they practice moderation. They enjoy themselves without worrying about every little thing they put into their mouths. Their reward for this is a happy and fulfilled life with a natural-looking body admired worldwide by connoisseurs of good living.

Although I've never been to France, I'm feeling very Parisian today. I'm wearing my gladiator sandals along with my favorite denim above-the-knee shirtdress cinched with a brightly colored scarf to accentuate my waistline. Yesterday I got a pedicure and let them paint my toes red. My dark hair is pulled back in a purposely sloppy (but hopefully) chic-looking knot at the nape of my neck. Besides the red nail polish, I'm also sporting red lipstick (a shade I've never worn to work before) and have purposely worn my glasses. I usually wear my contacts only when I play soccer or go to the beach because they make my eyes itchy. I feel much more "me" in my glasses and I am perfectly happy with that, just like I am perfectly happy about everything this morning.

Unlike most people, I happen to *like* Mondays. Mondays are about beginnings and new possibilities. I have decided the hell with Amy. She and her flying monkeys can take a hike. As corny as it sounds, today is the first day of the rest of my life.

A person's a person, no matter how small.

Yes, I am quoting my favorite poet of all time: Dr. Seuss.

I have my pride. I might not be a beauty queen, but I too am a person (even though there is no arguing that I am not small). No matter how plain I might be, I am deserving of love. I refuse to pine after any man. Not even Ben Gallagher, who has certainly fallen in my eyes.

I'm just finishing off my donut when Ben enters the conference room. He's wearing a suit and tie, something he used to do daily when he first came to work here, but now only wears on special occasions. It didn't take Ben long to figure out that most Floridians only wear a suit if they're going to court. I don't think Ben has killed anyone, so he must have big plans for today.

Like all men, Ben looks great in a suit. He eyes the Krispy Kremes and moans. "Frazier, I think I love you." He reaches over and pulls a donut from the box.

I point to his tie. "What's the occasion?"

"Lunch with T.K."

T. K. Bennet is our publisher, so either Ben is driving to Orlando to meet him or T.K. is coming to Tampa. As far as I know, Ben has never met T.K. for lunch on a Monday before and I'm instantly curious. I wait for Ben to say something else about his lunch, but instead he says, "So, did you get my text?"

I could be coy and pretend I didn't, but we Parisians are very frank. "Yep. Thanks for letting us know Amy got home safely."

"Did you have a good time Friday night?"

I roll my eyes and make the "God, yes!" face. "I always have a good time at Captain Pete's," I say cheerfully (so maybe occasionally I might have to revert to some American chicanery).

Ben clears his throat, something I know he does when he's nervous. He looks like he's about to say something more, but then Jackie walks in. She takes one look at the donuts and lunges.

Jackie is forty, fashionably thin, wears only designer clothing, and religiously avoids sweets except for the Monday-morning donuts (or so she says). Jackie used to be a buyer for Ralph Lauren until she started writing for *Glamour* magazine. She ended up in Tampa a few years ago after she got married and she's a good writer. *Florida!* was lucky to nab her. Jackie and her husband, Chris (who is a plastic surgeon), have been building their dream home on Davis Island for what seems like forever. I call their future home the Death Star because Jackie has been keeping the details on the q.t. (as in super hush-hush). She won't tell anyone exactly where it's being built or how big the place is or anything. Jackie says the secrecy is because she's part Armenian and Armenians are superstitious about this kind of stuff. Personally, I think it's because she just wants to wow us with a big unveiling when the whole thing is done.

She inhales a donut, then stares at me hard like she's trying to figure something out. "Nice lipstick," she says finally. I don't think Jackie has ever complimented me before on my appearance. I vow then and there to always wear red lipstick.

Richard, as usual, is the last one to arrive. He immediately pulls out two donuts. Richard is thirty-three, eats more than anyone I know, and never gains an ounce. He has the metabolism (as well as the hormones) of a sixteen-year-old boy. Today, he's sporting a tan, which is pretty cheeky, if you ask me.

I don't know if Ben has caught on yet, but since February Richard has called in sick every fourth Friday, which effectively gives him a three-day weekend each month. Richard has worked for *Florida!* the longest of anyone in the Tampa office—almost eight years—so he probably has a lot of sick time stashed away. Still. It's not very professional of him, which kind of disappoints me. Richard is a good journalist but he tends to cut corners. I'd love to see him live up to his potential, but I'm not his mother, so there's not much I can do about that.

"You're looking awful healthy for someone who was dying of the flu on Friday," I say to him.

"Aw, Emma, were you worried about me?"

"You know I was."

Richard grins in response.

This sort of meaningless banter between Richard and me is another Monday-morning tradition at *Florida!* magazine. I have sat less than ten feet away from Richard five days a week for the past six years, long enough to know that if a paper bag walked into the room wearing a skirt, Richard would flirt with it too.

Lisa sets up her laptop to take notes, and before you know it, the donuts are gone. Honestly, these people would probably die without their donut fix. Krispy Kreme is their crack and I am their dealer.

Richard points to Ben's suit. "Who'd you kill?"

Lisa giggles the way she always does at Richard's jokes, whether they are funny or not.

Ben ignores Richard's quip and dives right into a recap of the September issue, which, thank God, we've just put to bed.

As per the magazine's forty-year tradition, September is our "Life Beneath the Water" issue. A few months ago the staff drew straws to determine who would be the lucky writer assigned the task of writing the feature article celebrating the beauty and uniqueness of this year's selected topic, the Florida manatee.

If you guessed me, then you'd be right.

I admit, at first I was bummed. Despite that I am usually the one who writes the nature and environmental pieces, a two-thousand-word article on the migratory and mating habits of the manatee seemed like a surefire way to put our readers to sleep. But after some extensive research (and a little imagination) I found an angle that elevated my story to the next level.

It seems there was an old female manatee nicknamed "Susie" who died earlier this year. Susie used to hang out at the Manatee Viewing Center at Apollo Beach, which is sponsored by TECO (that stands for Tampa Electric Company). TECO pumps warm water into the river and this attracts the manatees during the cold-weather months, only Susie liked hanging out there year-round. Now the biologists who keep track of the manatees at Apollo Beach have noticed an older male named "Sam" who has broken off from the pack. He swims in circles all day long and no one can figure out why. I think Sam must have known Susie (in the carnal way). I think this is where they met and I think Apollo Beach was their special spot. What makes the whole thing pretty amazing is that manatees are indiscriminate breeders. In other words, the males will go for just about anything that's in heat (similar to their brethren mammal—the Homo sapiens).

I think the fact that Sam is pining for Susie is very romantic. Currently, there is no scientific evidence to back any of this up but I was able to word it in such a way that this was my own personal version of what *might* have happened.

To my surprise, Ben passes a copy of my article around the table. "This is an example of a really great piece. Not that I'm buying this manatee love stuff, but hey, Frazier basically took a crap assignment and made it into something fun to read." He catches my eye. "Good work."

Richard and Jackie mumble something similar under their breaths, but I can't tell you exactly what they are saying because my heart is pounding so loudly it's causing my ears to buzz. I've told you before that Ben is a brilliant editor, but he is not the kind of boss who goes around blowing smoke up your ass. A simple "I like it" from Ben is worth a million "love its!" from anyone else.

I am still riding high on Ben's praise when he goes to agenda item number two, which is to brainstorm stories for future issues.

Richard immediately pipes up. "What about a sports piece?" Richard played baseball in college and always tries to work a sports story in whenever he can. He was a relief pitcher for Florida State and played in the minors for a couple of years, until a rotary-cuff injury shut down any hopes he had of making it to the pros.

"What do you have in mind?" Ben asks, but before Richard can say anything Ben warns, "No more fishing articles."

This is obviously what Richard had in mind because he looks visibly deflated. "Okay, so how about something on college football?" Richard tries again. "We could showcase all the big ex-players."

"I want something sexier," Ben says.

I sit up straight. Ben has never said anything like this at a staff meeting. The words reverberate in my head. *I want something sexier.* I cannot help but think he is talking about more than just the magazine.

Richard snorts. "You do know this is *Florida!*, right?"

"How about NASCAR?" Lisa says.

"Is that even a sport?" asks Jackie.

Lisa looks insulted. "It's just the most popular sport in the country."

"Go on," says Ben.

"How about something on the Daytona 500?" suggests Richard.

Ben frowns. "Didn't the magazine do a piece on that last year?"

And this is when my big idea occurs to me.

Ben wants *sexy*? I'll give him sexy.

"How about a day and a night in the life of a NASCAR superlegend? More specifically, Trip Monroe."

Everyone turns to look at me.

"Yes!" Jackie says. "Now, *that's* sexy. And he's a Florida native."

Ben ponders this over for a few seconds. "I like it."

"Trip Monroe is an impossible interview," says Richard. "My buddy at *Sports Illustrated* did a piece on him last year. He basically says nothing. Just spouts the party line over and over." Richard breaks out into an exaggerated southern drawl: " 'Thank God that Jesus and all the angels were with me tonight when my car almost blew up!' "

Lisa begins to giggle again.

Okay, this kind of gets me mad. I have a tiny drawl myself that Richard has made fun of upon occasion. Richard is a native Floridian, but he's from Fort Lauderdale and Florida is one of those states where the farther south you go, the more northern you sound. "Trip's accent isn't that heavy," I say.

"How do you know?" Richard asks.

"I know because I actually *know* Trip Monroe. We went to high school together."

"Get outta here." Richard appears startled and I take a secret glee in this because Richard always thinks he knows everything. Which he usually does, so it's kind of satisfying to rock his boat a little.

"Yep. Catfish Cove High. Home of the Fighting Crusaders."

"How come you never mentioned this before?" he asks suspiciously.

Jackie and Lisa start talking at the same time. Ben asks in a low voice so that only the two of us can hear, "How well do you really know this guy?"

God help me, but I cannot control myself. I hold up two intertwined fingers.

"Trip Monroe and I are like this."

Ben looks both impressed and skeptical. "Do you think he'll consent to an interview?"

"Sure!" I hear myself say.

"Okay," Ben announces. "Trip Monroe and NASCAR it is. Frazier's on it. We can feature him as the top headliner in the October 'Famous Floridians' issue."

"I thought that was going to be my piece on the guy who's opening up all the new strip malls near Whispering Bay," says Richard.

"You mean the guy who's ruining the beaches?" I say.

"You mean the guy who's shaking up this crummy economy with actual jobs?" Richard shoots back.

"Oh yeah, that guy. What's his name again?" Jackie asks.

Richard slumps in his chair. "Point taken."

I almost feel bad for taking Richard's feature spot away from him. Normally, the same writer doesn't get the magazine's feature slot two months in a row, but Trip Monroe definitely trumps this guy whose name nobody can remember.

"Trip Monroe is gorgeous," Lisa gushes. "I can't wait to see what kind of cover we come up with."

"Maybe Trip will consent to go shirtless," Jackie says with a giggle. I don't think I've heard Jackie giggle before and this suddenly worries me.

"Is he as handsome in real life as he is on TV?" Lisa asks.

"Um, sure," I say.

It just occurs to me that I have promised my boss I could get an interview with someone I haven't spoken to or seen in over fourteen years. Worse is that now that I think about it, I don't remember *ever* talking to Trip Monroe. But that can't be possible. My graduating class had fewer than a hundred students. I would have had to talk to him at some point.

Ben goes on to talk about the Christmas magazine and this involves more Jackie than me, which is a blessing because I can just sit back and keep my mouth shut. Which is probably what I should have done in the first place.

I glance over at the empty Krispy Kreme box and silently curse Richard for taking the last donut. Practicing French moderation is all good and fine, but right now I could use a good old American sugar high.

I close my eyes for a second and take a deep breath. What am I getting so worked up about? Trip Monroe is a superstar. He gives interviews all the time. For argument's sake, let's say Richard is right and they are boring interviews. I am *not* just any journalist. I am a fellow Catfish Cove Crusader. Trip and I are bonded by the threads of high school angst, and if there is anyone that Trip will spill his deepest, darkest secrets to, it will be me. Compared to all the tedious research I had to do on the manatee article, Trip Monroe should be a piece of cake.

chapter four

· · · · ·

It's four o'clock and Ben still isn't back from his lunch with T.K. Is this a good thing or a bad thing? I'm not sure. The one thing I am sure of is that with the exception of Lisa and myself, no one knows where he is. Jackie has been grumbling since two p.m., saying that she needs to talk to him about a big idea, and why isn't he here or answering his cell? Richard is too busy Tweeting and playing on Facebook to even notice that Ben is gone.

For the first time today I am worried. The I-4 stretch between Orlando and Tampa is worse than maneuvering the Daytona 500. What if Ben got in an accident? I might hate Ben's guts, but I don't want to see those guts splattered on the highway. I send up a silent prayer. I'm not religious, but when I was a little girl Mama J taught me that if you ever have a bad thought, it could be nullified by sending up a personal request to God. I'm not sure how that works, but I feel better after doing it.

After this morning's meeting I got the number for Trip's PR firm and called to request an interview. The firm is in Dallas and a woman with a thick Texas accent tells me she will be happy to send me some "materials." When I explained that I wanted a live interview and not a press kit, she told me I needed to put the request in writing, and although I hated sounding all schmoozy,

I had no choice then but to mention that Trip was a personal acquaintance of mine. She still didn't budge. So I whipped out what I thought was a pretty fantastic e-mail and sent it to the PR firm and I'm still waiting to hear back.

Meanwhile, I decided to spend the day doing background work. It's amazing how much information you can pull off the Internet. I Googled Trip's name and got like a gazillion hits. Trip is basically the Mother Teresa of NASCAR. He's given away hundreds of thousands of dollars to charity, which is commendable. But what makes Trip interesting is that he's gorgeous and apparently modest as well. A couple of years ago, he was named *People* magazine's Sexiest Man Alive. Lisa is somehow able to get a print copy of the two-year-old issue. (She later admitted to having it hidden in the bottom drawer of her desk.)

According to the article, Trip has dated several Hollywood actresses, an assortment of models, and it was even hinted that he was once secretly engaged to Carrie Underwood, although Trip denied this, saying, "Carrie and I have always been good friends." Trip goes on to say that his "playboy" image is all a facade and that he's looking for a girl "as sweet as his mama to raise a passel of kids with."

I hate to admit it, but as usual, Richard is right. Trip is a boring interview. Although it doesn't matter much because the photos in the piece are first class. Lisa, Jackie, and I spent considerable time salivating over them. The best one is of Trip wearing one of those one-piece mechanic outfits with the top half zipped down to his navel, exposing what has to be the most perfect six-pack ever.

Richard glanced over my shoulder to study the picture. "That's airbrushed."

"I don't know," Jackie said. "I've seen him in a few commercials and he looks pretty buff."

In the photo Trip is leaning back on his race car and it's . . . well, I had no idea he was this sexy. I'll be honest: I can barely remember Trip from high school. The last time I saw him was on graduation day. He didn't come to our ten-year reunion, which disappointed everyone since he is our only celebrity alumni and it would have been cool to have him there.

I decided to jostle my memory by doing some personal research. So during my lunch break, I drove to my town house and searched my closet until I found my senior yearbook, which is both fun and slightly painful to look through (I had forgotten I was president of the glee club). Even though Trip and I weren't what you'd call friends, I do remember talking to him now, as well as other things about him.

He was a member of the basketball team his freshman and sophomore years, but after that there is no listing of any extracurricular activities. This is because the summer before junior year, Trip's daddy died of a heart attack and he went to work at his uncle Frank's auto repair shop after school to help his mama make ends meet. We were in the same English class our senior year and he sat one row over from me. We worked on some kind of English project together, although I can't remember the details. He was quiet and a decent student and didn't stand out much. He wasn't even that cute. He was tall and skinny and always in bad need of a haircut. Plus, he had acne. Boy, has Trip changed. Another thing I had totally forgotten was that Trip signed my yearbook.

My senior year I won the poetry contest. I never meant to win, because I never meant to enter, but my English teacher submitted a poem I had written for my senior literature portfolio. I found out the day before the end-of-the-year awards program that I was a finalist. I could have withdrawn, but I'm glad I didn't.

The poem was about my two mothers and about my father. Or

rather, the male person who provided half my DNA. Mom used a sperm donor to get pregnant. She has never tried to hide this from me, so I've never had any big angst over it, but writing that poem released a lot of emotions I never knew I had. I'll never forget the look on her and Mama J's face when they heard my poem for the first time (along with the rest of the student population at Catfish Cove High). It turned out to be the best day of my teenage life.

Back to Trip.

This is what he wrote in my yearbook:

Emma,

I liked your poem. Good luck in the outside world.

Trip

Not exactly eloquent, but when you consider this was written by a seventeen-year-old boy, it's not half bad either. Short and to the point. I wonder what I wrote in his yearbook.

I'm still thinking about this when Ben returns. All in one piece. *Thank you, Mama J.*

He disappears into his office and a heartless Jackie (can't she see how tired he looks?) follows him inside shooting off question after question. After about fifteen minutes, Jackie leaves Ben's office looking decidedly unsatisfied. I'm tempted to go ask him how the lunch went (and more importantly, what it was about), but I want to give him space.

I'm ready to leave work when Ben comes to my desk. "Frazier, got a minute?"

I follow him back to his office and settle into the sofa, where I always sit when I go into Ben's office, which is my dream office. The room itself isn't particularly special, but there's a private door that leads to a small enclosed patio that boasts some pretty tropical landscaping, an Adirondack chair strategically placed to get the best afternoon sun, and an outdoor fountain. Stuart, my old boss and Ben's predecessor, used to smoke out there. That patio was totally wasted on him, but not on Ben. When the weather isn't oppressively hot, like it is now, Ben likes to sit out there and write, and I'm totally jealous of this. I would also love to sit in that chair with my laptop propped on my knees, listening to the soothing trickle of water gurgling from the fountain, instead of sitting in my cramped little cubicle with the chair that wobbles, trying to ignore the pounding beat of Richard's hard-rock radio station.

I sneak a peek at the wall behind Ben's desk. This is something I always do too. Why I do this, I'm not sure, but I can't help myself. Hanging in a brown frame is his diploma from Columbia and next to that is a picture of Ben rowing crew. Ben is thirty-four, so the picture is at least twelve years old, but Ben hasn't changed much. He's still got the same broad shoulders and crooked grin he had in college.

I look away from the picture. "How was your meeting with T.K.?"

"Fine." Ben loosens his tie and settles back in his chair. "About Friday night . . . I liked your friends."

Yeah, well, they hate you.

"They liked you too," I lie.

I will admit that Friday night was the last subject I expected Ben to bring up. Might as well get it over with. "So did you and Amy hit it off?" My mind goes back to that kiss. Of course they hit it off. What a stupid question.

"Amy? Oh yeah, sure." He shrugs and I take this as a man-yes. I guess that answers that.

Neither of us says anything for a few awkward seconds.

I wish I could control myself and stop from asking, but I can't. "Are you going to see her again?"

Ben clears his throat. "We're having dinner this weekend."

"That's great! Amy's a terrific girl. She's really smart, you know."

"So . . . we're okay?"

"Well, of *course* we're okay. Why wouldn't we be okay?" He looks so uncomfortable that I can't help but feel sorry for him. "About the Trip Monroe article," I say, directing us back to business. "I think I found an angle."

Ben looks surprised by my change of subject but nods at me in encouragement. "Go on."

"In high school, Trip was basically a nobody. But now, besides being this big sex symbol and superstar on the track, he's also this reluctant playboy with a heart of gold. He's the embodiment of the American Dream. It's Zero to Hero. Everyone knows about the Hero, but there's not much written about the Zero. I'm going to focus on Trip's roots and what made him the man he is today." My voice rises in excitement. "I'm going to find out what makes Trip Monroe tick and I'm going to write the best damn juiciest article on NASCAR's golden boy of the tracks that's ever been written." Pause. "While still keeping to the magazine's high journalistic standards of course."

Ben chuckles. "That's my girl."

And in this, he is partially right, because no matter how much I would like to hate him, I can't. He has shitty taste in women, but he is still the best boss I've ever had. As far as work is concerned, I will always have his back.

It's Thursday morning and I'm trying not to panic. I've received an e-mail from Trip's PR firm in Texas refusing my request for an interview. I call and get the same secretary I talked to on Monday.

"Mr. Monroe's schedule is completely booked for the next six months," she says in her twangy accent. I grew up in north Florida, where the accents are twangy too, but in a different way. Why didn't the Yellow Rose of Texas tell me this when I talked to her on Monday?

"But there has to be an exception. This is *Florida!* magazine, and Trip grew up here in—"

"I suggest you call back at the end of December or perhaps January."

December? I know a brush-off when I hear one. I ask if there is anyone else I can speak to who might help but she basically hangs up on me, although not before wishing me "a blessed day!"

I go back and do more research. The *Sports Illustrated* "interview" done by Richard's pal was a runaround piece à la "Frank Sinatra Has a Cold" only it is not nearly so clever. There is just one little quote from Trip, but everything else in the article is information garnered from other sources, which, as far as I can tell, aren't even that close to Trip.

As impossible as it is to believe, Trip Monroe has not done a real, honest-to-God interview since his Sexiest Man Alive piece came out in *People,* which, interestingly enough, was their biggest-selling issue *ever.* Everything that has been written about him in the past two years has either been speculation, information from an unauthorized third-party source, or taken off his bland press interview, which basically says nada (even though I didn't request it, Yellow Rose sent it to me). Getting an exclusive interview with Trip would be like hitting pay dirt. The only thing I can imagine that would sell more magazines would be an interview with Princess Diana from the grave.

I now want this interview more than ever.

That evening I go to soccer, where despite my bravado of the other night, it's the Strikers who kick our asses. Brian barely speaks to me. The hell with him.

Friday morning comes and Ben is acting as if everything is status quo, but I can pick up a tenseness in him that wasn't there before his lunch with T.K. Jackie is running on hyperactive mode, which means she's probably back on her diet pills (obviously Jackie is not French). Richard is his same self-absorbed self, and I've broken out in a rash. If I don't get a lead on this interview soon, I'm going to have to tell Ben that I basically lied to him about my close relationship with Trip.

It occurs to me that my best shot at connecting with Trip lies back in Catfish Cove. I call Torie to tell her I can't make Friday-night drinks.

"This isn't because of last weekend, is it?"

"What part of last weekend are you referring to? The fact that I'm apparently the ugly friend or that Ben hooked up with Amy?"

"You are not the ugly friend!"

I notice Torie doesn't deny the fact that Ben and Amy slept together. Did Amy tell Torie about it at work? Did she give Torie a play-by-play at the watercooler? If she did, I never want to hear about it. I've already told Torie and Kimberly about my idea to interview Trip Monroe but they don't know I'm having trouble making a connection, so I fill Torie in on what's been going on. Now that she knows I'm not purposely ditching Friday-night drinks, she stops harassing me and wishes me luck.

I toss some clothes in my weekender and head north on I-75. I haven't been home since Christmas and it's long past time I paid a visit to my mothers.

chapter five

· · · · ·

Although Mama J is not related to me by blood, she is as much my mother as my biological mother is. She is the softer side of our little family and the first person I go to if I need consoling. My mom met Jennifer Brewster when I was five. I remember that time clearly because Jenny lived in Jacksonville and we only saw her on weekends. The first time I met her she bought me an ice-cream cone and read me a story and asked me to call her Jenny. I fell in love with her instantly. After she came to live with us, it seemed like the most natural thing in the world to call her Mom. But it got kind of confusing, so I started calling her Mama J and the name stuck.

I get to the outskirts of Catfish Cove and immediately slow down to thirty-five miles an hour. Like small towns everywhere, we take the speed limit seriously.

Let me tell you about Catfish Cove.

It has a population of seven thousand, and besides being the birthplace of a NASCAR superlegend, it is the annual home of "The North Florida Monster Truck Rally for Jesus." My house is on the north edge of the city limits, so I have to drive through our little downtown, which consists of just a few blocks. The buildings all date to pre–World War II and the streets are paved in brick. There are three restaurants, as well as a converted movie theater where the Catfish Cove Community Theatre group performs three plays a year (this past spring they did *Guys and Dolls* and it was a huge smash). There's also an upscale boutique, two antiques shops, a few novelty stores, some professional offices, and Carpe Diem aka Mama J's bookstore.

It's almost eight p.m. and it's getting dark. White lights illuminate the majestic oaks that line Main Street and along the sidewalks are giant terra-cotta planters filled with bright red geraniums. It's all very quaint and pretty, like something out of a movie set. My mother's medical office is located in the more "modern" part of town, next to the Piggly Wiggly and the Ace Hardware store.

Walmart Corporation has not yet discovered Catfish Cove.

I hope they never do.

I pull up to the house I was raised in, a modest one-story brick ranch, and park my car behind my mother's 1997 Volvo, which has fewer than sixty thousand miles on it. Mom is one of two practicing medical doctors in town. Most days she rides her bike to work and she rarely takes a vacation. She could easily afford a new car, but her mantra is "if it ain't broke, don't fix it."

I walk in through the back door to find my moms arguing over how long to cook the pasta. Neither of them is a good cook, but they both like to be the boss of the kitchen.

Walt is the first one to spot me. He's a four-year-old golden retriever named after Mama J's favorite dead poet, Walt Whitman. He barks loudly, thumping his tail in joy. Mom drops the wooden spoon in her hand, causing marinara sauce to splatter over the stove top. "Well, look who's here!"

Mama J spins around and lets out a squeal and runs to hug me. Mom comes up behind me and entwines her arms around

Mama J's, cocooning me in what, when I was a little girl, I used to call the "mommy sandwich."

"What kind of sandwich are you today?" Mama J asks.

Walt barks enthusiastically (I think this is his way of participating).

The game always plays out the same. It is now my turn to tell them what sort of filling I am. Like peanut butter and jelly, or ham and Swiss cheese, or if I'm in a really good mood, my favorite sandwich of all time, turkey with cranberry relish. No matter what I say, Mom then responds with, "Yummy. That's my favorite!"

I have long since outgrown girlhood but I always play along. It would break their hearts if I didn't. But when I go to speak, my throat feels tight. Tears well up in my eyes. I have done such a great job of keeping it together all week long, but now, surrounded by the love of my family, I become a wuss.

My moms step back in alarm. Walt slinks to the ground and places his head between his paws.

"Oh no, here comes the drama," Mom mutters. Mom hates tears. When I was a little girl, if I ever started to cry, she always chucked me under the chin and told me to "buck up, little cowgirl!"

Mama J, on the other hand, looks ready to cry herself.

"What happened? Did you lose your job?" Mom asks, cautiously optimistic.

While losing a job would seem like a catastrophe to most parents, my losing mine would not so secretly thrill Mom. She has always wanted me to go to law school, which was my original plan after graduating from college. But I loved writing so much, I just couldn't do it. I know Mom is still harboring a hope that I'll change my mind. She envisions me living in Washington,

D.C., working for the ACLU righting wrongs like a caped crusader. But if I ever did become a lawyer, I'd want to be like one
of those kick-ass prosecutors from *Law & Order* who puts the
bad guys away in jail.

"Sheila, those are man tears," Mama J says, gently correcting Mom.

Mama J is right. I'm ashamed to say that I'm crying over the
loss of Ben. Or rather, the loss of the *dream* of Ben. I really
thought he was the guy for me. I'm thirty-two years old. I want
to be married. I want to have kids. Preferably in that order. But
more importantly, I want to find someone to spend the rest of
my life with. Someone who'll argue with me over how long to
cook the pasta.

Mom pulls up a stool and hands me a glass of red wine and
a box of Kleenex.

I swipe away my tears. "Stupid female hormones," I lie.

Neither of them looks as if she buys this, but they don't push
it. We finish making dinner and polish off a bottle of wine and
some mediocre spaghetti and I fill them in on my idea about the
article on Trip.

"Honestly, Emma," says Mom, "of all the interesting people
in the world, why would you want to interview *him*?"

"He's a big celebrity."

"He drives a car around in circles."

"Emma's right, Sheila, NASCAR is big," Mama J points out.

"Plus, he's a Florida native and he's donated a lot of money
to charity. Right here in Catfish Cove too." I found this out
through my Google search.

Mom immediately softens her expression. She is a sucker for
anything or anyone related to this town. My great-grandfather
was one of Catfish Cove's first residents and my grandfather

George was the town's only medical doctor for over thirty years. He also served in the Korean War and is buried in the veterans' section of the city cemetery. There's even a street named after him—George Frazier Boulevard, which is more a dead end really, but it's where the elementary school is located. Other than the time she spent away at college and during her residency, Mom has always lived here. Despite this being a politically conservative town, no one other than a few dumb rednecks ever give my moms a hard time anymore. They might be lesbians, but they are "our lesbians," if you know what I mean.

Mom goes to the linen closet and hands me fresh towels. "How long do you plan to stay?"

"Do you want to come to the store tomorrow?" Mama J asks hopefully.

Whenever I'm in town I always help Mama J out at the bookstore. It's something I love doing and I know she loves having me there, but it's not in my agenda this weekend.

"I was kind of hoping to spend tomorrow doing research on Trip," I say.

"But you're staying through till Sunday?" Mom asks.

"Well, sure."

"Excellent! Tomorrow night the Lutheran Church Day Care is sponsoring cow-chip bingo. The whole town will be there. You're not going to want to miss that."

Mama J claps her hands in glee. "We've been looking forward to it for weeks. Now it will be extra fun if you're there too."

Cow-chip bingo. Great. I put on my biggest smile. "Sounds like fun."

My moms both grin in agreement.

For two women as educated as my mothers, you'd think they were talking about the opera.

*   *   *

After an evening playing Scrabble and a good night's sleep in my old bed, I wake up at the crack of dawn with a stratagem. Trip Monroe is no different from any other subject of any other story I've written. There is a way to get to him. I just have to be creative. I decide to start at the root of the subject—Trip's family. The first thing Trip did after making it big was build his mama a mansion. Unfortunately the mansion is not in Catfish Cove. It's in a private gated community near Naples. But Trip's uncle Frank still lives in town and this seems like an excellent place to start.

I put on some shorts and sneakers, pull my hair up in a ponytail, and grab a bottle of water from the fridge. It's not even eight yet, but I can tell it's going to be a scorcher. Walt looks at me with longing in his eyes. "Sorry, big boy, I'll take you for a walk when I get back." I'm going on a Trip Monroe Scavenger Hunt and scavenger hunts are best done on foot and alone.

Two miles later I'm standing in front of Monroe's Auto Parts and Repair and I'm already sweating. I open the door and am hit with a blast of cold air conditioning and a plethora of Trip Monroe. There isn't a space of wall that isn't covered by a picture of Trip. There's a poster of Trip holding up a trophy after winning the Indy 500. Another one of Trip standing next to his race car with a helmet in his hand. There are personal pictures too. Trip graduating high school. Trip playing basketball. Trip wearing mechanic's overalls standing next to a car. The one I like best is more recent. An adult Trip is wearing jeans and a T-shirt, his forehead smudged with grease, with his arm slung around his uncle Frank's shoulder. The inscription at the bottom says simply, *To Uncle Frank, Love, Trip.*

"Can I help you?" asks the guy behind the counter. He's in

his early twenties and clean-cut with a toothy grin, the epitome of small-town southern friendliness.

"Is Frank Monroe here? I'd like to speak to him."

"Who's askin'?"

"My name is Emma Frazier. He probably doesn't remember me, but I went to high school with Trip." I point to a picture, which suddenly strikes me as dumb. As if this kid needs a visual aid to remember who the mighty Trip Monroe is.

His expression turns unfriendly. "Sorry, I can't help you."

"But I'm a personal friend of Trip's and I was wondering—"

"If you're a personal friend, then you don't need my help finding Frank. Do ya?" He gives me a quick up and down and clearly finds me lacking.

The kid has a point. No problem. I'll just look Uncle Frank up in the directory. I spot a phone book in the waiting room but there is no listing for Frank Monroe. I guess I'll have to ask my moms, which is probably what I should have done in the first place. Frank Monroe is close to their age and has lived here all his life. They must know his address. I whip out my cell phone and am about to dial home when the door to the shop opens and in walks one of Catfish Cove's finest. Nick Alfonso, sheriff's deputy.

It appears Nick is currently off duty because he's wearing shorts and a Bonnaroo T-shirt. I went to high school with Nick Alfonso. He was the most popular boy in our class. Captain of the football team, homecoming king, and overall stud. Like every other girl at Catfish Cove High, I had a huge crush on him. Nick never looked at me twice in high school. Not because he was stuck-up; there were just better options. Nick dated Shannon Dukes, the prettiest girl in our class, captain of the cheerleading squad, and a former Miss Dixie Deb (I was actually a Dixie Deb too, but that's another story). Nick and Shannon got married two years after graduation and were divorced six years later. Nick and I talked for over an hour at our ten-year reunion. Ever since then, whenever I'm home and run into him, it's like we're long-lost friends.

"Emma Frazier," Nick says in a slow deep drawl, "you sure are lookin' good."

chapter six

• • • • •

Even though I suspect he says this to every woman under the age of ninety, I still feel myself blush.

"Hey, Nick." I give him a quick hug.

"What are you doing in town?"

"I'm here to visit my moms."

Nick smiles. He's been a big fan of Mom's ever since she saved his life.

This is what happened.

While Nick was still married to Shannon, he went to see Mom for a sharp pain in his lower abdomen. He was nauseated and running a fever. Mom immediately diagnosed him with appendicitis. She tried calling Shannon so she could take him to Tallahassee asap (the nearest city with a hospital), but Shannon's phone kept going to voice mail. So instead of wasting time trying to call more relatives, Mom put Nick in the backseat of her Volvo and drove him all the way to Tallahassee herself. By the time they opened Nick up, his appendix had burst. He spent three days in the ICU. Nick found out later that the reason Shannon wasn't picking up her phone was because she was having a midday quickie with Nick's now ex–best friend, Ed, a revelation that no doubt led to Nick and Shannon's subsequent divorce.

It occurs to me that Nick could help me. He's lived here all his life and he's a cop. He has to know where Frank Monroe lives.

"Hey, do you have a few minutes?" I ask him.

"For you? I have a whole morning. Let's grab a cup of coffee." He tosses a set of keys to the kid behind the counter. "Can I get an oil change, Toby?" Although it's a question, Nick is not asking.

"Sure thing, Nick." Toby, who has become all friendly smiles again, tells Nick his truck will be ready in thirty minutes.

Nick and I go next door to Ruth's coffee shop, where the waitress seats us, but not before she spends a considerable amount of time batting her lashes at him. It appears that not much has changed since high school. Nick Alfonso is still King of Catfish Cove. The waitress brings us coffee and asks if we'd like to see a menu, and coffee quickly turns into breakfast. Nick orders pancakes and I order the chocolate chip waffles.

"I need a favor," I say.

"Name it." Nick's brown eyes smile back at me. Despite the air-conditioning I suddenly feel warm all over.

I tell Nick about my idea to interview Trip and how I'm having trouble getting in touch with him. "You wouldn't know how to get ahold of Trip, would you?"

"Nah. We were never close in high school," Nick says, which I already knew but it never hurts to ask.

"I tried to get some information from the kid back at the auto shop but he wouldn't budge."

"Toby is pretty protective of Trip. Frank too. You'd be amazed at the number of groupies who come sniffing around here trying to get to Trip through Frank. Being the sexiest man alive must be a bitch."

"I don't want to have Trip's baby."

Nick leans back in his seat and grins. "Whose baby do you want to have?"

If I didn't know any better, I'd think Nick Alfonso was into me. "Nobody's at the moment, thank you."

Nick laughs.

The waitress brings us our food and I begin to eat my chocolate chip waffles. In moderation, of course. "So . . . back to that favor. Do you think you can get me Frank Monroe's address?"

"That's the favor?"

"Well, yeah."

"I can do better than that. I'll take you by Frank's place after we finish breakfast."

"That would be awesome. Thanks!"

I am so happy that I ran into Nick Alfonso this morning. Not only has he solved my Frank Monroe problem, but he's also good company. We catch up on each other's life and Nick tells me he's just bought a house by Otis Lake, which, coincidentally, is near Frank Monroe's place. Nick hasn't remarried since his disastrous marriage to Shannon. I tell him about my job and the people I work with, omitting any mention of my boss.

"So, Emma, are you seeing anyone?" Nick asks.

This question takes me completely off guard. If Nick hadn't used my name, I would have turned around to see who he was talking to. "Nope. I'm free as a bird."

There is no longer any doubt that Nick Alfonso is flirting with me.

Me. Emma Frazier!

It's my wildest high school fantasy come true.

Something must be wrong with the universe.

I gaze around the diner expecting to see galactic chaos, but everything appears in order. There are a few high school kids eating at the counter and an older couple seated in the booth behind us. The waitress comes by to refill our coffee and lingers over Nick's cup. He thanks her and she breaks out into a smile, revealing tobacco-stained teeth. She's probably only in her late twenties, but I can tell she's led a much harder life than I have.

It occurs to me that while I might be a five in Tampa, here in Catfish Cove, I'm a definite seven. Maybe even an eight. There are two options for most girls in Catfish Cove after high school graduation. You either go to college, in which case you rarely ever come back, or you get married and start having babies. I'm currently available, have never been married (which means I have little to no baggage), have all my teeth (straight and white, thank you), and some pretty fine childbearing hips. Jeez. I might even be a nine.

We finish our breakfast and walk back to the auto shop, where Nick's truck is waiting for him. He puts on the local country-western station and we swing by Otis Lake. Nick points out the house he bought. It's a two-story brick with a private dock. The windows are outdated and the yard is overrun with weeds but I can see the potential in it. It's a house for a family, not a bachelor. I guess Nick is getting all his ducks in a row.

We drive around to the other side of the lake and he parks in front of a sleek one-story wood house.

"This is Frank's place," Nick says.

We walk up the driveway and I start to get nervous. What if Frank Monroe considers this an invasion of his privacy? By now I have figured out that his phone and address are unlisted in order to ward off nosy reporters. Technically, yes, I'm a journalist, but Trip wished me good luck in the outside world in my yearbook and what better way to ensure my good luck than by giving me an exclusive interview?

Nick knocks on the door and an attractive woman who appears to be in her late fifties answers. "Nick Alfonso, I sure hope you're not here to arrest me," she flirts outrageously.

"Only if you deserve it, Julie."

She laughs, then sobers instantly at the sight of me. "You're Sheila and Jenny's girl, aren't you?" I nod and she smiles. "I've seen pictures of you at the store. You sure have grown up pretty."

While I know this is just small-town small talk, I can't help but smile back. I wish I could remember this very nice lady named Julie who finds me pretty and who obviously patronizes Mama J's bookstore, but unfortunately I don't. I make a mental note to ask my moms about her.

"We're looking for Frank," Nick says.

"Frank is gone for a couple of weeks fishing down in Naples. I'm watching his place while he's gone."

"Is there a number where we can reach him?"

Julie glances my way. "What's this about?"

"Emma needs to get ahold of him for some research for an article on Trip."

I am almost expecting another shutout, when Julie says, "Oh!" She frowns for just a second, then nods. "Sure, hold on." She also invites us to come inside the house.

We wait in the foyer while Julie writes down the number. "I have to warn you, Frank isn't keen on giving out information to reporters about Trip." She pauses. "But . . . seeing as how you're a local girl, maybe that will make a difference."

"Thanks," I say, hoping Julie is right.

"You two going to cow-chip bingo tonight?" she asks.

Nick meets my gaze. "I'm planning on it."

"Apparently my moms have bought half the squares. So yeah, I'll be there too."

We say our good-byes and get back in Nick's truck. Since I've gotten the information I need, there's no use traipsing all over town anymore. If Frank Monroe can't get me in with Trip, then no one can.

Nick drops me off in front of my house, but before I can open my door, he's already done it. "See you tonight, then?"

"Sure."

Cow-chip bingo suddenly takes on a new appeal.

I wait till Nick drives off and I dial Frank Monroe's number, which goes directly to an automated voice mail. I hang up, think about the message I want to leave, and try again.

"Hi, there, Mr. Monroe, this is Emma Frazier. You probably don't remember me but I grew up in Catfish Cove. I'm Sheila Frazier and Jenny Brewster's daughter. I was wondering if you could please call me back. I have something I need to ask you, and well . . . it's kind of important. Urgent, almost."

I leave my number and hang up. Seeing as how Frank Monroe is so protective of his nephew's privacy, I'd already decided I wasn't going to mention anything about Trip or the magazine on a voice mail. I'll work up to that later.

chapter seven

· · · · ·

Half the town is in Grovers Field tonight for the Fifth Annual Lutheran Church Day Care Cow-Chip Bingo fund-raiser. Mama J bought a hundred dollars' worth of tickets. There's no telling how many Mom bought but I bet it's twice that much. We have a cooler full of sodas and a bucket of fried chicken from the deli at the Piggly Wiggly, as well as two cans of insect repellent. A live band is playing at one end of the field and an inflatable moonwalk is set up at the other end. There's a face-painting station and a clown walking around making balloon animals plus the obligatory bake-sale booth, a soft-boiled peanut stand, and an entire row of food vendors, selling nothing that hasn't been fried or dipped in powdered sugar (or both). Saturday night in Catfish Cove does not get any better than this.

We find a place along the crowded sidelines and set up camp. At least two dozen people wave to us and several more come up to ooh and aah at me.

"Sheila, that girl of yours is even prettier than the last time I saw her!"

"Jenny, tell Emma she has to visit me before she heads back to Tampa. I'll make her that rice pudding she used to love so much. She still eats, doesn't she? She's gotten so *skinny*!"

These things are all said as if I'm not present. Only in Catfish Cove is size twelve (sometimes fourteen) considered emaciated.

I spot Nick out of the corner of my eye heading our way. As usual, he looks great. He's wearing shorts, a Florida State T-shirt, and a grin that (as my grandpa George used to say) could melt the ice off an igloo. I'm glad I took a little extra time getting ready tonight. My hair is braided so that it falls over my left shoulder and I'm wearing the diamond earrings my moms gave me for my college graduation. I have on khaki shorts that hit just a few inches above my knees and a snug bright blue T-shirt. I'm also wearing red lipstick, which I now consider my signature lip color.

Nick makes nice with my moms and asks if he can join us. Of course we all say yes. He sets up his folding chair next to mine and hands me a cold beer from his cooler. A hush settles over the noisy crowd as the cows are led onto the field.

"Howdy, folks!" booms a male voice over the loudspeaker. "Welcome to Grovers Field and cow-chip bingo!"

The crowd roars in approval.

"Proceeds tonight go to benefit the All Saints Lutheran Church Day Care, so I hope y'all have been generous buying tickets!"

The crowd roars again.

Nick shakes his head and grins at me. There is an absurdity to it all that makes me grin back and a familiarity that tells me to prepare for a night of unrivaled fun.

Mama J pulls out her tickets and hands me one. "B4 is your lucky square, Emma." Not to be outdone, Mom gives me two of her tickets. I now have three squares I'm rooting for.

We settle back in our chairs and attack the fried chicken. I know fried chicken is probably public enemy number one on the Parisian food pyramid, but I haven't eaten since breakfast and I'm famished. Plus, I'm sure if faced with either eating a piece of fried chicken or passing out from hunger, the typical French-woman would pick the fried chicken every time. Along with moderation, they are also pragmatic.

At least a good half hour goes by without any of the cows doing their "business," but everyone is too busy having fun to notice until someone in the crowd yells, "Didn't anyone feed those heifers?"

Everyone laughs good-naturedly but there is now a current of undisguised impatience. The band starts to play "Sweet Home Alabama," the national anthem of small-town southern fairs, and the crowd is instantly soothed. Disaster averted.

"Wanna dance?" Nick asks.

Mom looks at me with interest and Mama J's eyes pop. I know they are both dying to ask me what is going on with Nick Alfonso. I'm sort of dying to know myself.

We head over to the dance area. Nick is not a great dancer, so we sway more than anything else and end up laughing a lot. This is not the first time I've danced with Nick Alfonso. I wonder if he remembers the other time as clearly as I do. I sure hope not.

I decide to forget the past and concentrate on the here and now. The glorious smell of roasting hot dogs and sweet funnel cakes blends with the sharp tang of freshly mown grass. The music is loud, the company is excellent, and for the first time this week I feel almost happy. I haven't thought of Ben all day (well, not hardly).

When the song is over, Nick takes me by the hand to lead me back to our spot and that's when we run into Nick's ex and her new husband, Shannon and Ed Norris.

Talk about awkward.

I have not seen Shannon and Ed for ages. They missed our ten-year high school reunion because they were honeymooning in Greece. Whether or not they timed it that way on purpose, I'm not sure, but it was awful considerate of them.

Shannon must be two years' pregnant, her belly is so big. Shannon's huge belly is an illusion, however. It only looks so big because the rest of her is so teeny tiny. At thirty-two she still has the same tight, size-two cheerleader body and tanned, toned legs she had in high school. Ed has not fared as well. His blond hair is thinning and he has the start of a slight paunch going on. Ed works for his daddy, who owns Norris Corporation, a local business that makes circuit boards. It employs about two hundred people and Ed is the plant "manager." I'm not saying Ed doesn't deserve the job, but I heard Mom say once that her patients who work for Norris Corporation grumble that Ed spends more time playing golf than actually managing the plant.

"Well, hey, Emma!" Shannon says, her smile overly bright. "It sure is good to see you!"

The four of us exchange strained hellos.

Shannon's gaze zeros in on my hand, which is still clasped with Nick's. I can practically see her brain shorting a fuse trying to figure out why Nick Alfonso is wasting his time with plain ol' Emma Frazier. I have to confess, although I felt like a nine at the coffee shop this morning, I'm feeling very five-ish right now. Even though Shannon is fully pregnant, I probably outweigh her by a good thirty pounds.

"So are you still livin' in Tampa?" she asks me.

"Yep. I'm just up for the weekend."

The weirdness of it all has now reached a boiling point. Nick says we have to go and pulls me away. I can't help but feel sorry for him. A vision of Shannon and Ed screwing while Nick is writhing in pain with his burst appendix makes me angry. I hope Shannon gets stretch marks and all of Ed's hair falls out.

Luckily, it is at this moment that the crowd begins to hoot and holler, telling me that something big is about to happen and we forget all about Shannon and Ed.

Let me tell you about cow-chip bingo.

It is exactly what the name implies. Basically, you mark off a large field of grass into squares. Then you get some well-fed cows and wait until they do their business. If their business lands on a square you've bought, you win a prize. In this case it's cash. Half the cash raised from selling the squares goes for prizes and the other half goes to the charity of choice. It's a win-win situation for everyone. Cows included.

Right now one of the cows is straddling two squares, and by the way she's acting, it's showtime. I stand on tiptoe to see over the crowd that has now gotten on its feet. The cow patty could fall in either square B4 or B5.

This must be a diva cow because she is taking her sweet time. The impatient crowd roars louder. If this is meant to encourage her, it's not working. Not that I blame her. If someone was yelling at me while I was trying to do my business, I think I'd be constipated.

Finally, after what seems like forever, she lets go and it lands on . . . B4!

I let out a whoop of joy. Nick has been solemnly quiet since the run-in with Shannon and Ed, but he now comes to life. He picks me up and twirls me around. You'd think I'd won the lottery. In reality, I've won ten dollars and I'm thrilled. Nick sets me on my feet, leaving me feeling a little dazed.

Now that the field has been baptized, the rest of the cows go into action. By the end of the night, Mama J has won forty dollars, Nick and I have won twenty dollars apiece, and Mom's squares stand empty. The cows are led off the field and everyone starts to pick up after themselves. My moms say their good-byes to Nick and scurry back to the car to give us what is obviously meant to be some "privacy."

"I had a good time tonight," says Nick.

"Yeah, it'll be hard to find anything as exciting as cow-chip bingo back in Tampa."

He smiles. "You're a funny girl."

I've heard this line before. It's the cousin to "You're a nice girl, but . . ."

Only Nick doesn't add the "but." Instead he takes my hand again and says, "Tell your moms I'm taking you home."

His confidence is both a turn-on and a little annoying. But I'm more turned on than annoyed, so I say okay. We get in his truck, but instead of taking me home, he drives by Otis Lake and parks in front of his house. He takes a blanket and a small cooler from the backseat and hands me a flashlight. All this is done without once asking me if I'd like to spend more time with him.

"Do you always get your way or did you just assume I wouldn't say no?"

For a second Nick looks confused, then he shakes his head and laughs at himself. "Sorry, I thought . . . well, *shit*. Do you want me to drive you home?"

I glance out the window into his dark yard.

"I meant it earlier, when I said I had a good time. I was hoping we could talk a little more. That's all," he says.

Talk about cosmic weirdness. Fifteen years ago I would have given my right leg for this moment. It's late and I probably should be getting back home, but I've had a good time tonight too and I don't want it to end just yet. "Sure, Nick. I'd like that."

He smiles and we make our way to the end of the dock. Nick places the blanket down and we sit with our legs dangling over the edge. The water is just a foot below. The coolness of it rises up to bring relief to our overheated bodies. We sip bottled water and talk, and though I'm loath to bring it up, I sort of feel like I have to.

"It must suck to have to run into Shannon and Ed all the time."

Nick shrugs. "Shannon was a long time ago."

"But you haven't . . . you know—"

"Haven't what? Moved on? Just because I haven't remarried doesn't mean I haven't moved on. I'm just taking my time, is all. I'm not making the same mistake again," he says tightly.

I wonder exactly what he means by that, but before I can ask, Nick says, "Did you get ahold of Frank Monroe?"

To tell you the truth, I haven't thought about the Trip Monroe article all night, which is kind of significant because there's a part of me that's always thinking about work. "Not since the last time I checked my messages."

"You'll hear soon. Frank's a good guy."

I tell him a little more about the article I plan to write and then we end up talking about Nick's job. He has to be at work at seven in the morning. I feel guilty for keeping him up late but he's in no hurry to leave, and honestly, neither am I. I've enjoyed Nick's attention more than I like to admit. Despite my Monday-morning bravado, last weekend totally blew my confidence. Having Nick flirt with me has helped restore some of my battered self-esteem.

We both turn to say something to each other at the same time. But instead of laughing about it, we just stare at each other for a long second, and before I know it, I'm flat on my back and Nick is kissing me.

Let me tell you this. Nick Alfonso is an excellent kisser. This is a rumor I heard all the way back in high school but I never once dreamed I'd find out firsthand. If my seventeen-year-old self could see me now, she'd think she'd died and gone to heaven.

We kiss for what seems like forever. His hand snakes inside my T-shirt to cup my breast. I know I don't have much in that department but what I do have immediately responds. It's been an embarrassingly long time since I've had sex and my poor body is starved. I can feel Nick's erection against my thigh and I automatically rub myself against it. Nick breaks off our kiss and drops his face into the crook of my neck. He lets out a strangled moan and rolls to his side.

I'm so embarrassed, I could die. I have practically begged Nick Alfonso to take me right here on the dock in his backyard.

What must he think of me?

I sit up and straighten my T-shirt. My braid has come partially undone. I pull out the rubber band that's holding what's left of it in place and try to smooth my hair out while I wait for Nick to speak.

"I like you, Emma," he says after what seems like forever.

"I think it's pretty obvious I like you too."

"No, I mean I *really* like you." The way he says this sounds as if he's surprised. He stands and holds his hand out to help me up.

Nick drives me to my house and walks me to the front porch, all in silence.

I'm confused. What just happened back there on the dock?

"When are you coming back to Catfish Cove?" he asks.

"I hadn't planned to come back anytime soon," I admit.

"In that case, can I visit you in Tampa?"

"Sure, you can visit anytime."

Nick reaches out to playfully tug on the end of my hair. "I mean as in visit you to take you out."

Nick Alfonso wants to drive over two hundred miles to take *me* out on a date? I have to admit, I thought this was just a weekend flirtation for him. Something to pass the time because there wasn't anything better around. I'm so flustered I can't think of what to say.

Thirty minutes ago I was ready to have sex with Nick, but that was my body talking. Now my mind is in control and my mind tells me that a relationship with Nick Alfonso could end in disaster. For starters, it was just a week ago that I was dreaming of a relationship with Ben. If Ben suddenly snapped out of his Amy trance and declared his undying love for me, what would I do?

The answer makes my heart sink.

I'm so not over Ben.

But Ben doesn't want me. And it's not as if Nick is asking me to marry him. He just wants to visit. Anything can happen. We could hang out for a weekend and have a good time as friends and that would be the end of it.

Or we could start to date and I could fall madly in love with him. In which case there's every probability that Nick will break my heart for the second time in my life. No matter how confident he seems and how many years it's been, I'm not sure he's completely over Shannon. Plus, I highly doubt Nick sees me as potential wife material. Sure, he says he "likes" me but I'm pretty certain I'm not his long-term type, and while I'm really jumping the gun here—

"It's just a date, Emma." Nick leans down to kiss me. It's slow and sweet and at the same time so hot that I forget my name, let alone anything else I've just hashed out in my head. Nick is right, it's just a date. But I can't help it. I have a tendency to overanalyze things. It's both my greatest strength and my greatest weakness.

We make plans for next weekend and I open the front door

to find my moms sitting on the living room couch waiting up for me. Walt is nestled between them, his big tail thumping happily.

"Well, well, well," Mom says. "Break out the champagne. Looks like Emma has finally snagged herself a man."

"I've always liked that boy," says Mama J.

Walt joins in with a bark.

"Were you three spying on me?"

"It's two o'clock in the morning, missy; we were worried sick about you. Crime in this town has gotten out of control. Just last week someone stole a shopping cart from the parking lot at the Piggly Wiggly." Mom's eyes are sparkling as she says this. It's obvious both she and Mama J approve of Nick Alfonso.

I always thought Mom would want someone smarter for me. Not that Nick isn't smart, but a small-town cop is probably not what she had in mind for my perfect mate. Maybe she's beginning to feel the pinch of thirty-two just like I am. I know she and Mama J want grandkids. They started hinting when I turned thirty.

"You two are getting way ahead of yourselves. Nick and I are just friends."

"Yes, I could see just how friendly you two are," Mama J says.

"I'm going to bed," I say, heading down the hallway to my room. "Good night!"

"Good night!" they shout back, giggling like teenage girls.

I'm too tired to wash my face or brush my teeth. I throw off my clothes, pull an oversize T-shirt over my head, and flop into bed. My last thought before I drift off to sleep is that I came home Friday night in tears and am going to bed Saturday night with a smile on my face.

It's funny how your life can change in just one day.

chapter eight

. . . . .

I leave Catfish Cove early Sunday afternoon and meet up with Kimberly and Torie for sushi. I wasn't going to say anything about Nick Alfonso, but I can't help myself. The whole story spills out, including our high school make-out session on the dock.

Kimberly squeals and jumps out of her seat to hug me. For Kimberly, who is usually so cool about men, this is more emotion than I've seen from her in a long time.

Let me tell you about Kimberly Lemoyne.

She is also from Catfish Cove, only there she is known as Kimmy Petis. I've known her since grade school, although we never hung out together as kids because she's three years younger than I am. She was raised by a single mom who worked for minimum wage on the assembly line at Norris Corporation. Despite her humble origins, Kimberly is smart and elegantly beautiful. If there is such a thing as an eleven, then Kimberly is one. But she's also intensely private. Even with Torie and me. Once upon a time Kimberly was briefly married to Jake Lemoyne, whose family owns half of Florida's west coast (or at least the half anyone cares about) and she's determined to remarry up. Which is going to be impossible because filthy-rich handsome types like Jake Lemoyne don't just drop out of palm trees. After her divorce,

Kimberly decided to keep her married name, and I don't blame her, because it opens up a lot of doors for her.

"Emma, Nick Alfonso is like . . . gorgeous," Kimberly gushes. I have to remember that Kimberly was a freshman when Nick and I were seniors, so her view of Nick is based on a fourteen-year-old perspective. Not that I don't think Nick is gorgeous too, but I'm a little surprised by her reaction.

"Calm down," I say. "More than likely nothing will come of it."

Torie throws down her napkin. "Why are you always so negative?"

"I'm not negative. I'm cautious. There's a difference."

"Well, I like this Nick already," says Torie. "He sounds like a great guy. Much smarter than that Ben Gallagher person."

"Speaking of that Ben Gallagher person," I say in what I hope is an uninterested tone, "any news on him and Amy?"

Kimberly and Torie exchange a look.

"I know they had dinner plans for Friday night," Torie says, "because she talked about it all week long ad nauseam. She has absolutely no class."

Since Ben already told me about the dinner, this comes as no surprise. I take a bite of my California roll. Over the weekend I have concluded that the Amy-Ben thing is for the best. We have such a great dynamic going on at the office that I would hate to ruin it with a romance gone bad. Knowing that Ben is unavailable will make it easier for me to move on, which is exactly what I plan to do.

It's Monday morning and I'm standing in the line at the Krispy Kreme debating whether or not to call Frank Monroe again. I don't want to be a pest. It's only been two days since I left him a message and he is on a fishing trip. Maybe he's on one of those deep-sea excursions where they have no cell-phone access. I decide to wait another few days. If I don't hear from him by Thursday, I'll call again.

I pick up the donuts and drive to work. Ben is already waiting in the conference room, which is unusual. Besides Lisa, I'm always the first one here on Monday.

"Good morning!" I chirp in an upbeat voice. Partly, this is because I love Mondays, but also partly because I can't help but overcompensate. I don't want Ben to think that just because he dissed me for Amy, I hold a grudge against him.

"How was your weekend?" he asks.

I tell him about Catfish Cove and cow-chip bingo and how the cows took their sweet time doing their business, and I embellish it just enough that Ben laughs so hard his eyes water. Nowhere in the story do I mention Nick Alfonso.

"Frazier, you're making this up."

"Am not."

"Okay, the next time that town of yours does one of these cow-chip bingo things, I want an invite."

Luckily, at this exact moment, Jackie and Richard both walk in, so I'm saved from responding. I know Ben is not serious about wanting to visit Catfish Cove. It's just one of those things people say, but it still rattles me.

"Cow-chip bingo?" says Richard, crinkling his nose in disgust. "Is that what I think it is?"

My cell phone pings. I glance at the screen and my heart speeds up. It's Nick! Sometime during my dinner with Torie and Kimberly, he left a message on my cell phone. I called him back and we talked for over two hours. We also texted till three in the morning. I should be exhausted from lack of sleep, but I'm not. I've discovered that Nick likes to fish (something I'd already assumed, since every baby boy in Catfish Cove is born with a fishing pole in his hand), is into country-western music (didn't take a genius to figure this one out either), hates cauliflower (me too!), and his favorite movie is *300*. (No one is perfect.)

I also found out Nick likes to read. Which greatly relieves me because I just don't know if I could ever date a guy who didn't read. Nick's favorite author is John Grisham (I can live with this) and his favorite book of all time is *Of Mice and Men* (yes!).

I read his message. *Have a great day. Can't wait till Friday.*

Back at ya, I text.

Part of me is thrilled and excited and another part of me is scared and leery. I'm not used to guys giving me this kind of rush. Up to now my relationships have always started out timid toe in the water, not cannonball dive.

Lisa joins us in the conference room, and after a few minutes of personal conversation about what everyone did over the weekend, the donuts are gone and it's time for our Monday-morning staff meeting. I set my cell phone on vibrate.

Ben glances my way, all business now. "Frazier, how are things going with the NASCAR article?"

"I'm in the process of setting up an interview." This is not a lie, but it's not the whole truth either. I fill them in on the other articles I'm working on, but neither of them is as "sexy" as the Trip Monroe story. I *have* to get this interview.

Ben ends the meeting by once again reminding us to post a daily contribution to the magazine's Facebook page and to Twitter, but although he's addressing all of us, he's really only talking to Richard.

I'm headed to my cubicle when my cell phone vibrates. I look down hoping to see another text message from Nick, but I've just received a voice mail. I click over to my messages and instantly recognize the number. It's from Frank Monroe. Finally! Now I can set up my meeting with Trip. Can my day get any better?

I listen to Frank Monroe's message. Then I listen again another three times just to make sure I'm hearing it right.

"This is Frank Monroe, returning your call. I have a pretty good idea why you want to speak to me and the answer to your question is no. Please don't call again."

His tone wasn't rude, but it wasn't friendly either.

I spend the next hour stewing, thinking about exactly what I said in my message that might have put him off. The only thing I can figure out is that Julie must have warned him that I wanted to interview Trip. I understand why Frank Monroe would be protective of his nephew's privacy, but I can't believe that he wouldn't at least talk to me. Then I remember Toby's hostile reaction when all I did was inquire about Frank, and I chalk the whole thing up to celebrity paranoia.

I camp out in my cubicle and begin to attack the Trip Monroe story from another angle. After two hours on the Internet and another call to the Yellow Rose of Texas in which I basically suck up to her, I get her to send me a copy of Trip's public itinerary. In three weeks Trip Monroe will be in St. Petersburg for a cocktail party, hosted by one of those tony charity groups, that is being held to honor celebrities who have given lots of bucks to local organizations. The event will be covered by a few select local media. *Florida!* magazine, unfortunately, is not one of the select few, but for a thousand dollars I can purchase a ticket.

Great. I can feel myself itching all over again. Not only does

Florida! not have that kind of budget, but there is no way I can justify a thousand-dollar expense on the *possibility* of getting an interview. Lisa would laugh me out of her cubicle.

I do, however, know someone whose firm *does* have that kind of budget. I go to my computer and find the Web site of the charity organization hosting the cocktail party. Just as I'd hoped, listed among the names of local businesses attending the event, is the Yeager Agency.

I call Kimberly and tell her I need to see her about business, something I've never done before. She's instantly curious and tries to wheedle me into giving her information, but all I tell her is that I'm working on something that will be mutually beneficial to us both. After a few minutes she gives in and tells me she has an opening at four, which is perfect. I work through lunch and by three-thirty I've researched and written a proposal I'm secretly calling "Ambush Trip Monroe." In reality the proposal's title is "The Benefits of Signing on with the Yeager Agency." Which is really boring, but I'm way out of my comfort zone here and this is just meant to get Kimberly's creative juices flowing.

I touch up my red lipstick to boost my confidence, say goodbye to everyone for the day, and head downtown. The Yeager Agency is one of the most prestigious advertising and public relations firms in the Southeast. Their Tampa office takes up an entire floor of one of those high glass numbers that make up the downtown skyline. I park my car in the garage across the street and present myself to the receptionist. The Yeager Agency is as sleek and modern as the *Florida!* magazine office is homey and low-key. All the men look like they stepped out of *GQ* and the women look like they belong on the runway at Bryant Park.

Kimberly meets me at the reception area and escorts me to her office, which is small, but has a great view of the city. She is wearing a pencil-thin skirt that I could never wear in a million years because my hips are too big. She's also got on the most uncomfortable-looking pair of cockroach killers I've ever seen. Her honey-blond hair is swept up in a sleek knot at the nape of her neck and her makeup is perfect. I've never been envious of her, but I can't help but feel frumpy wearing my dark blue pants and my sensible ballerina flats.

"Want a cappuccino?" Kimberly's restraint is admirable. I know her well enough to know she's dying to find out what I'm doing here.

I glance around her office. "You have a cappuccino machine in here?"

She shrugs impatiently. "There's one in the break room."

This is tempting. But I'm too excited to put this off any longer. "No thanks." I hand her my brief, two-page proposal. "Read this and tell me what you think."

Kimberly pulls out a pair of black, designer reading glasses that only serve to make her more attractive. She skims the pages. "Where did you get all this?" Her voice is tempered, but I can see by the look in her eyes that her mind is already racing with possibilities.

"Off the Internet, so I'm sure it's not all completely accurate."

The proposal includes a list of all the endorsements Trip Monroe has been involved in over the past few years. Seeing that he is NASCAR's current superstar and the poster boy for clean living, his endorsements are all grade A. I knew they would be, of course, but it's nice to have things spelled out on paper for you.

"Don't you think it's terrible that a Florida boy like Trip is using an out-of-state PR firm when there are so many fabulous firms right here in Florida?"

"It's downright sinful," Kimberly agrees, letting her voice

revert back to the natural Catfish Cove twang she's worked so hard to get rid of. "But how does this involve you?"

"I need an interview with Trip Monroe. Which, I'm pretty sure I can get if I ever talk to him in person." I tell Kimberly about the charity cocktail party in St. Petersburg and this is when she informs me that her firm has purchased four tickets for the event (which of course, I already knew).

I offer her a simple deal. A ticket for the cocktail party in exchange for an introduction to Trip Monroe. Because Trip was such a nobody in high school, plus the fact that Kimberly is younger, she's never actually met him.

"I have to clear this with Murray." Murray is Kimberly's boss and we both know this is just a formality. Murray (and probably every other guy who works here) is infatuated with Kimberly. If Kimberly asked him to jump off the top of the building, he'd at least consider it.

Although it is just the two of us in the office, Kimberly lowers her voice. "This is top secret, but we're really close to getting the Dr Pepper account. The advertising division would be my bitch forever if I could get them Trip Monroe."

"Trip Monroe, shirtless, holding a can of Dr Pepper to his lips," I say.

We both envision this and let out a dreamy sigh. I don't even like Dr Pepper, but an ad like that would make me buy it by the cartload.

We strategize for over an hour and Kimberly promises to get back in touch with me as soon as she talks to Murray. She cautions me not to get my hopes up because anything can happen.

Thirty minutes later, she calls to tell me I'm in. Murray is impressed with my chutzpah and has arranged for two of the Yeager Agency's tickets to go to me and Kimberly.

chapter nine

· · · · ·

It's early Friday evening, and in exactly one hour, give or take a few minutes, Nick Alfonso will be at my door. For the next two nights we will be sleeping together under the same roof, less than twenty feet apart from each other. We skirted around this issue all week, and then last night he finally said, "Any clean, cheap hotels close to your place?"

This is how I answered him: "It seems kind of silly to waste your money on a hotel when I have a perfectly good guest room with its own bathroom."

Now that that's been established, I've come up with the following ground rules.

A. I will not sleep with Nick Alfonso until I'm sure our relationship is going somewhere.
B. No matter how great his kisses are, I will absolutely positively NOT sleep with Nick Alfonso this weekend because it is way too soon and I definitely don't want to blow our budding relationship with premature sex.

And finally . . .

c. I will not sleep with Nick Alfonso until I've lost
twenty pounds.

To reinforce all this, I write it down on a sheet of paper and
tape it to a secure spot where I am confident Nick will never see it,
but where it will be a constant reminder to me, lest I forget myself.

I read through the bullet points again. I think A and B are pretty
self-explanatory; C, however, is a bit trickier. It's not that I'm
ashamed of my body. I know I can never compete with the Shan-
nons and Amys of this world, nor do I want to. I just want to look
and feel my best and my best is probably about twenty pounds
lighter. Of course, seeing that I've been trying to lose the same
twenty pounds for the past ten years, I might never have sex with
Nick Alfonso, but I have to set some kind of standards for myself.

Nick arrives promptly at eight-thirty. He's wearing jeans and
a T-shirt and has one small overnight bag. Along with a dozen
red roses. I can't remember the last time a guy brought me flowers,
and although red roses seem a bit clichéd, I'm touched. I put them
in water, and even though I know Nick must be tired after driving
for three and a half hours on top of working all day, he still insists
on taking me out to dinner. We go to a little Cuban restaurant
that has the best *ropa vieja* I've ever tasted. Nick admits to not
having had much Cuban food before, so I order for him and he
eats everything on his plate, which really pleases me.

We're sitting at the table, drinking our *cortaditos,* when Nick
asks me how the Trip Monroe article is going. I tell him about
Frank Monroe's voice mail.

Nick frowns. "That doesn't sound like Frank."

I tell him about my plan to meet up with Trip at the charity
cocktail event, including how I finagled the ticket through my
good friend Kimberly's public relations agency. Although Kim-

berly certainly remembers Nick, he does not remember Kimberly, which is not unusual, given the age difference. Nick seems properly impressed by my tenacity.

After dinner we go back to my place, order a movie on pay-per-view, and snuggle on the couch, where we basically have another make-out session. I'm not sure who broke it off first, Nick or me, but the fact that he didn't push for anything more leads me to believe that he has also established a few ground rules of his own.

I go to bed, well kissed, thoroughly aroused, and definitely alone. If this is not a recipe to make sure we have sex sooner rather than later, I don't know what is.

The next day we sleep till ten and I make us breakfast. We decide to drive to the beach and this is where I start to get nervous. I think my bathing suit is flattering. It minimizes my butt and maximizes my chest, but it's not a tiny bikini and I don't want Nick to be disappointed with my body. I wish I didn't feel this way but I can't help it.

We get to the beach and set up our blanket and chairs near the water, and then comes the moment of truth. He pulls off his shirt and I slip out of my loose sundress and we discreetly eye each other's body out the corners of our sunglasses while pretending to be interested in something else.

Nick is a beautiful swirl of tanned pecs and hard abs. I, on the other hand, must be a cloudy haze of cellulite-puckered thighs and pale skin.

I reach into my tote bag and pull out a tube of SPF-50 sunscreen. I wish I could use a lower SPF level and actually get a tan, but when one of your mothers is a medical doctor, you've listened to the dangers of skin cancer enough that you don't dare take the risk.

Nick takes the tube from my hand. "Turn around," he orders. He rubs the sunscreen over the tops of my shoulders and down my back, pausing at the skin above my bathing-suit bottom. He finishes rubbing in the sunscreen then surprises me by giving me a playful swat on my butt.

If Nick is disappointed in my body, he certainly isn't acting like it.

I take the tube of sunscreen and offer to do the same for him, making sure I get the tops of his shoulders and the back of his neck. And then (because I can't help myself) I slap his butt right back. He laughs then sits down in his chair and I sit in mine.

And then the second moment of truth comes.

I pull a book out of my tote bag and prepare to do what I like best at the beach, and that's read. And while this might not sound like a big deal, the thing is, I'm kind of a boring person and this is something Nick needs to know right away. I like nights like last night, where we stay in and watch a movie. I like hanging out in a beach chair, watching the clear Gulf water lap onto the shore while sipping a drink and reading a good book. Don't get me wrong, I like hanging out with my friends and having a good time, but sometimes I just like being quiet too.

Nick leans his head back in his chair like he's settling in for a nap.

My cell phone rings.

"What are you doing?" Torie asks.

"I'm at the beach."

"With Nick?"

"No, I left him back at my place."

"Ha ha. Which beach are you at?"

I freeze. I really don't want Torie to crash my beach date with Nick. Torie in a bikini is not the kind of landscape I want Nick exposed to. At least not this soon in our relationship—

Wait. Where did that come from?

I have never *once* thought of hiding my more attractive girl-friends from a guy I'm interested in. Until now.

Amy's ugly friend remark has done more than just shake up my confidence. I hate her for saying it, but I hate myself more for continuing to hear it over and over in my head. Maybe I need to go to one of those guys who hypnotize you to stop smoking. Only what I need is someone to wipe out the memory of that night at Captain Pete's.

But if Nick is going to dump me for someone more attractive, shouldn't I know this right away, before we get more involved?

"You still there?" Torie asks.

"We're at Clearwater Beach. Want to join us?"

Nick raises his sunglasses to look at me. He's curious, and not completely pleased that I've just invited someone to tag along on our date.

"Hell no. I just want to know where you are," says Torie. "So Kimberly and Jason and I are going to that pizza place we ate at a couple of weekends ago. Do you and Nick want to come?"

"Let me call you back." I click off my phone and turn to Nick, who appears to have gone back to his nap. "Want to go out to eat with my friends tonight?"

"Sure," Nick says.

I call Torie back. "What time?"

"Around eight."

"Okay, see you then."

The beach date was a complete success. I read over sixty pages of my current novel, Nick got in a much-needed nap, and we even took a swim, all without getting sunburned.

Nick has that olive complexion that often comes with dark

hair and dark eyes but I'm pretty pale, so a day at the beach is tantamount to smoking three packs of cigarettes on the cancer meter. But Nick did a good job with the sunscreen. Instead of looking like I'm radioactive, I now have a subtle, healthy glow. I spend some time thinking about what I'm going to wear and I decide on a yellow cotton halter dress that shows off a good portion of my back, and some strappy sandals. Tonight I'm a definite seven and I'm feeling pretty good.

Nick and I are the last to arrive at the restaurant. Torie and Kimberly hug me and I introduce them to Nick. Our friend Jason is also here tonight.

Let me tell you about Jason.

He's our favorite guy friend. He's also Torie's ex. They dated for almost a year and I really thought he was going to pop the question but then they got in a big fight and broke up (I'm pretty sure their fight didn't involve tuna fish). But instead of avoiding each other like most ex-couples do, within two weeks of the breakup Jason was hanging out with us as if he and Torie had never been serious. It should be awkward, but it isn't, and I'm glad because I really like Jason.

Jason is a prime example of how plain-looking guys can get hot girls. Jason is a five even on a good night. He's on the short side (but taller than Torie) and has an Ed Helms kind of smile that makes it hard to take him seriously, although, apparently, plenty of women do. I asked him once how he did it. Jason told me he credits his success with women to the three Ps: personality (yes, he certainly has plenty of that), persistence (as well as the ability to know when to back off), and podiatry.

You'd think the last one would almost be a turnoff. Jason is a podiatrist and I can't think of a goofier medical specialty than feet. But apparently women don't care what kind of doctor you are. Just having the word *Dr.* in front of your name adds at least three points on the attractiveness scale. Torie also told me that Jason gives a foot massage that will make you have an orgasm. I'm not sure how that works but I'll take Torie's word for it.

I don't care how many conquests Jason has made in the two years since he and Torie split up. I'm convinced that he's still in love with her. It's kind of sad really, because I don't think Torie feels the same way.

Jason and Nick shake hands and immediately ask what the other does for a living. This is something I think guys do because they want to find some common ground. I'm worried that Jason and Nick aren't going to have much to talk about, then Jason finds out Nick is a cop and his eyes light up like a little kid's and he starts grilling Nick for "cop" stories.

The pizza and beer arrive and we all dig in.

Jason wants to know what's the weirdest thing Nick has ever seen as a cop and Nick obliges him by telling us a story about a woman he stopped for speeding on the outskirts of Catfish Cove.

"It's pretty late, like two in the morning, and I walk up to the car and there's this blonde behind the wheel. She rolls down her window and I ask for her driver's license and registration," Nick begins.

"First things first," says Jason. "Was she hot?"

Nick takes a long swig of his beer before answering. "Yeah, she was pretty hot."

Jason leans forward in his seat.

Nick looks my way and winks. "I can tell she's just come from a bar because she's pretty dolled up. And she starts giving me this story about how she lost her driver's license and she's slurring her words, so I ask her to please step outside the car—"

"Let me get this straight," interrupts Jason. "You're alone and she's alone and she's hot and she's drunk?"

"Yep."

Jason grins. "I think I'm gonna like this story."

Torie shakes her head. "Is sex all you think about?" she asks Jason.

Kimberly sighs. "The average man thinks about sex every seven seconds."

"I'm hardly average," says Jason. "For me, it's every three."

We all laugh and Jason waves at Nick to continue.

"So then I ask her if she'll take a Breathalyzer test and she panics and tears off running down the road in four-inch heels."

"What did you do?" Kimberly asks.

Nick looks playfully insulted. "I ran after her, of course." He pauses. "That's when she starts taking off her clothes."

"Wait," says Jason. "She's running and stripping at the same time?"

"Yep," says Nick. He takes another sip of his beer to draw out the moment. Nick is a great storyteller, very relaxed and natural. It's a side of him I haven't seen and I like it. A lot.

"First, she throws her shoes at me, one at a time, and she's got great aim. A pair of four-inch stilettos hit me right here," Nick says, pointing to his right temple. "Left a bruise for a week. Then off comes her panty hose."

"She was wearing panty hose?" I ask.

"It takes a while to take off panty hose," Kimberly says. "And you *still* hadn't caught up to her? Are you that slow a runner?"

"I was calling for backup," Nick explains with mock indignation. This is twice now that Kimberly has questioned his cop actions and I can tell he is both amused and slightly irritated by it. "You obviously have no idea how much damage a pair of four-inch stilettos can do to a man." He gives Jason a sly look and the two of them grin knowingly.

Torie punches Jason in the arm. "I never threw my shoes at you!"

Jason stares her down for a few seconds, then Torie's face turns pink and she starts to giggle.

At first, Nick looks confused by Torie and Jason's exchange, but then he seems to get it. Kimberly and I are used to Jason and Torie making private jokes like this. These are the times when I start to think that maybe Torie still harbors a secret thing for Jason, but then the moment will pass and I think I'm just reading more into it than I should.

"She's running fast, like she's high on something, but she still manages to take off her dress," Nick says, continuing with the story. "And she's not wearing underwear."

Jason's jaw drops.

"Then she takes off her bra and I almost trip over it but I keep going. I'm just a few feet behind her and I'm ready to tackle her ass to the ground when I can see there's something not right about her."

I meet Nick's eyes and immediately know where this story is going. I want to laugh but try my best not to so that I don't give anything away.

Jason frowns. "Not right like how?"

"Not right 'cause she's got a package. Only I don't put two and two together until I'm completely on top of her. Or rather, him."

"So . . . you're like . . . on top of a *naked* guy?" Jason asks.

"Turns out the guy likes to hang out at a tranny bar near Tallahassee. He starts crying about how he can't let his wife and kids see him like this and how it was the first time he'd dressed in drag. Poor schlep was more afraid of being outed than he was of a DUI charge.

"I tell him he has about three minutes till my backup gets here and if he wants to change then he better hurry. So he pulls off his wig and starts wiping off his makeup, only he's so drunk he can't remember where he left his guy clothes, so I give him the dirty clothes from the gym bag I keep in back of the cruiser and he takes it like it's manna from heaven."

Jason is now laughing, and while, yes, it's funny the way Nick tells it, it's also kind of sad. I'm glad Nick gave the guy a chance to "right" himself before being hauled off to jail.

"So while this guy is trying to get into my dirty gym clothes, he's begging me to get rid of the 'evidence,' as he calls it. And I feel kind of sorry for him, so I take his clothes and his wig and his stilettos, which, by the way," Nick says, playfully rubbing his temple to elicit sympathy, "are like a men's size thirteen, and stuff them in my gym bag. Then my backup gets there and we haul this guy's ass down to headquarters and charge him with a DUI, and the whole time he's thanking me, and my buddies think he's seriously whacked. By this time it's early morning and my shift is over, so I go home. And I forget all about my gym bag sitting in the back of the cruiser."

Jason starts chuckling again.

"The next day I get off work and I head to the locker room to change out of my uniform and I find the gym bag with the tranny's girl clothes hanging on the handle to my locker with a great big sign that says"—Nick glances around the table with a grin—"'Nice outfit, Nicole.'"

We all burst into laughter and Jason orders another pitcher of beer.

I couldn't have wished for a better evening. Nick has fit in perfectly with my friends, something both Kimberly and Torie make a point of telling me while we're in the bathroom.

"Emma, he's perfect," Torie says.

Kimberly nods. "We're so happy for you!"

"We've only been dating a week," I remind them. "It's no big deal."

"Oh, it's a big deal," says Torie. "He's the one. I can feel it."

Eleven p.m. rolls around and the pizza place prepares to close for the night. Jason yawns and says he has to get up early but Torie wants to go dancing. At first, Jason balks, but then Torie wraps her arm around his and whispers something in his ear, causing him to grin. Game on. They convince Kimberly to join them. Jason calls a cab and urges us to join them as well, but Nick and I politely and unanimously decline. We are not interested in clubbing. We drive back to my town house. The mood between us is almost electric.

I wish I could say where our relationship was going. I wish I could say I'm patient enough to take things slowly and not ruin everything for a little instant gratification. And I certainly wish I could say that I've miraculously lost twenty pounds today. But none of that matters right now because I am definitely going to sleep with Nick tonight. I think I made up my mind while he was telling the tranny story.

First off, I'm incredibly attracted to him. Sure, I had a huge crush on him in high school, but this is different. This is grown-up-I-want-you-and-you-want-me attraction at its finest. I've been attracted to lots of guys before but I would never dream of sleeping with them after just a couple of dates. For one thing, unless you've been set up by a friend who knows the guy really well, you can never tell if someone is a whack job or not, and before you know it, it's looking for Mr. Goodbar all over again. But I've known Nick over half my life. He's what Mom calls "good people."

Second, if there was ever a test to see if a guy was worthy of my affections, then Nick has passed it. He just spent three hours in the company of my beautiful friends and never once looked at them the way he was looking at me all night.

I think I must have been looking at him the same way, because the minute we get in my town house, he takes my hand and leads me straight to my bedroom, where we stay until Nick has to leave Sunday evening to head back to Catfish Cove. I think we hit the kitchen once for food. I'm not sure. And in case you're wondering, yes, Nick did find my bullet-point list of reasons why I should not sleep with him (what was I thinking when I taped it to the mirror in my bedroom?).

He got a big kick out of reasons A and B. But he got very quiet after reading reason C. "Seriously, you weren't going to sleep with me until you lost twenty pounds?"

"Well . . . this was just sort of a general guideline, you know?" I smile, but Nick is astute enough to know that I'm embarrassed.

He sighs and tucks a strand of hair behind my ear. "Emma, I like you just the way you are. Okay?"

Maybe Nick has seen *Bridget Jones's Diary,* or maybe not. It doesn't matter, because even if he has ripped off this best-line-ever from Colin Firth's Mark Darcy, it's the most perfect thing for him to say.

The sheets on my bed are still warm when I call Torie and Kimberly, who both squeal with happiness for me. Now that my two best friends have been informed, I go to my computer and open my Facebook account to change my status.

It's official.

I am now in a relationship with Nick Alfonso.

chapter ten

· · · · ·

For the second Monday in a row Ben has beaten me to the office. He's waiting in the conference room sipping his coffee when I walk in with my box of donuts. I used to live for moments like this, but for the first time ever, I wish we weren't alone.

"How was your weekend?" he asks like he does every other Monday, only this Monday his question feels like a grenade ready to explode in my face.

"It was . . . great." Visions of Nick and me writhing on my bed dance through my head. I don't know why I suddenly feel guilty about sleeping with Nick. I can feel my face go red. I wish I could help it, but I can't.

Jackie, Lisa, and Richard all arrive at this exact same moment, so I don't have to elaborate on just how great my weekend was.

Richard is not here two seconds before I wish he'd called in sick. "So, Emma, how's your relationship going?"

Everyone turns to look at me.

"Emma has a new boyfriend," Richard announces. "His name is Nick Alfonso and he's my latest Facebook friend."

Richard prides himself on having more Facebook friends than anyone else in the office. He's up to four thousand eight hundred and fifty-two (correction: apparently that number is now four thousand eight hundred and fifty-three). Personally, I think Richard trolls Facebook in search of potential victims to friend, because he couldn't possibly know that many people. Could he?

"Nick friended you? How did that happen?"

"I woke up this morning to update my Facebook status with some clever little quip, the same way I do every day, and I started browsing. Imagine my surprise when I discovered that our very own Emma Frazier is now in a relationship with this Nick Alfonso character. Being the conscientious friend that I am, I had to look him up and make sure he wasn't sketchy. So I sent him a friend request. Told him you and I worked together, how we were great pals, you know, the usual. He accepted an hour ago." He pulls out his laptop and gazes around our little group. "Wait till you get a load of this guy."

Everyone is rapt with attention. Including Ben.

Lisa slides her chair next to Richard. "Show us," she urges.

Richard doesn't need any more encouragement. He types in his user name and password and his Facebook page pops up. "By the way, Emma, you really need to update your photos."

"How did you get to my photos? I'm pretty sure I marked those private." Private as in only a few of my friends can see them, Richard not being one of those. Not that I have anything against Richard seeing my photos, but I heard once that you should block your photos from everyone you work with in order to keep your professional and private lives separate.

"Check your settings. Everyone in the world can see them. Rule Number One: If it's on Facebook, then it's not private unless you make it private."

I send Ben a pleading look. "Don't we have work to do this morning?"

But instead of breaking up the shenanigans like he would

normally do, Ben gets out of his chair to stand behind Richard so he can get a better view of the computer screen.

I grit my teeth because there is nothing I can do to stop this without looking like a great big party pooper. I have only myself to blame. But my relationship status on Facebook has read "single" for so long I just couldn't help myself. Plus, what's the use of having a boyfriend like Nick if you can't show him off?

Richard pulls up Nick's Facebook page. Everyone stops talking.

Jackie stares at the photo for a few long seconds, then turns and looks at me as if she's never seen me before.

"Wow!" Lisa says finally.

I know exactly what everyone is thinking. How did a girl like me land a guy like Nick? I have to admit, I've been thinking the same thing myself.

Richard proceeds to read Nick's statistics with an obvious relish. "Works for the Catfish Cove Police Department."

"He's a *cop*?" Lisa says. She makes the overused *bow chicka bow bow* porn sound and she and Jackie laugh. Why women equate cops with sex, I have no idea. I guess because they think cops are sexy, which Nick definitely is, but if you could see the majority of the rest of the cops on the Catfish Cove Police Department, you'd quickly change your mind on that one.

"Religious views," continues Jackie. "Catholic."

"Uh-oh," says Richard. "Emma's an atheist."

"I am not an atheist. I'm an agnostic. There's a difference."

"For him," says Jackie, pointing to Nick's profile picture, "you can convert."

In his profile picture Nick is wearing a baseball cap and a grin that makes my cheeks burn. I *know* that grin. Intimately. I saw it twice Saturday night and twice more on Sunday. Richard zips through the rest of Nick's pictures and each one is better than the one before.

"Birth date: March twenty-fifth. That makes him what? Pisces?" asks Jackie.

"Aries," corrects Richard. "I'm one too." Richard's birthday is April first, something we have joked about in the past.

Lisa claps her hands like a little girl who can't wait to open her presents Christmas morning. "Let's see if Emma's sign is compatible with Nick's! You're a Gemini, right, Emma?"

Lisa knows well and good that I am a Gemini because we just celebrated my birthday a few weeks ago and she "read" my palm for me. It's like the three of them—Richard, Lisa, and Jackie—are on a mission to embarrass me in front of Ben. Damn it. I thought these people were my friends. I bring them donuts every Monday. What have I ever done to warrant this kind of shoddy treatment from them?

"Yep, I'm a Gemini," I say, forced to play along with their little game.

Lisa takes back the laptop and minimizes the Facebook screen. She goes to Google, where she punches in some information and comes up with a Zodiac "love compatibility chart." She hits the information for Gemini and Aries.

"Oh my God, Emma. You're a perfect match. 'Aries'—that's Nick," Lisa points out as if we don't already know, " 'lives for a challenge, and Gemini'—that's you," she unnecessarily points out again, " 'is drawn to Aries' sex appeal. Aries is drawn to Gemini's intelligence and humor, both big turn-ons for the fiery Aries. Sex between these two signs will be *hot* and love will be *very* possible.' "

"If things don't work out with this guy, Em, remember, I'm an Aries too," says Richard.

He waits for my comeback, but I have absolutely nothing to

say to this because I'm so frazzled. This is the first time in the six years I have worked with Richard that I have failed to come up with some cleverish retort to one of his taunts.

Richard, one.

Emma, zero.

Lisa scrolls down the chart. "Good thing Nick isn't a Pisces like I *originally* thought. Listen to this: 'Pisces will see adventure in Gemini, but Gemini will tend to ignore Pisces' deep emotions and not take Pisces seriously. Better skip this one or someone could walk away heartbroken.'"

Jackie shudders dramatically. "God, Emma, I hope you never date a Pisces. It all sounds so . . . *doomed*."

This has now gone past the realm of strange and into the country of bizarre. Jackie has never expressed any sort of interest in horoscopes or palm reading or the zodiac or anything else woo-woo.

It is at this point that Ben mercifully brings everything to a swift and abrupt halt. "Okay, people, let's get to work," he says.

Everyone sighs good-naturedly and we get down to what it is we came to do. Jackie complains about her latest article, saying that she didn't have enough time to do a proper interview, and Richard tries to score a fam trip to a new golf and tennis resort that is trying to get the magazine to write a review. After an hour of the same old, same old, we go to our separate corners and begin the work of putting together a magazine.

As I'm settling down to finish edits on a piece that's due tomorrow, I can't help but reflect on the irony of this morning's playtime. I know for a fact that Ben is a Pisces (everyone else knows this too). His birthday is March 19 and Lisa decorated his office with tiny cutout cardboard fish. Although only six days separate his birthday from Nick's, apparently Nick is my celestial dream and Ben is my star-crossed nightmare. I could have saved myself months of heartache if I'd just paid attention to my horoscope.

Later that afternoon, Kimberly calls to ask me what I plan to wear to the charity event in St. Petersburg.

"It's not till next month," I say.

"Three weeks and four days," she corrects.

"Um, my black cocktail dress?"

"You mean the same black cocktail dress you wore to Jason's office Christmas party last year? The same black cocktail dress you wore to Yolanda Burton's engagement party? The same black cocktail dress—"

"Okay, I get it. I need something new."

"Something *not* black. The party starts at five and it's summer. Go light. Do you need me to come shopping with you?"

"Thanks, but I think I can handle this myself." I hang up and try to get back to work but Kimberly's call reminds me that I haven't been completely honest with Ben about the Trip Monroe interview. As my boss, Ben needs to know about my collaboration with the Yeager Agency. So before I leave for the day, I head over to talk to him. The door to his office is open but I still knock. Ben looks up from his computer screen.

"Do you have a few minutes?" I ask.

"Sure, come on in."

I sit on the sofa. "It's about the Trip Monroe article."

"How's that going?"

"Good, actually. At least I think so. You see"—I laugh nervously—"I've had a little trouble connecting with Trip. When I said Trip and I are like this"—I intertwine my index and middle finger the same way I did at the meeting two weeks ago—"that was kind of a . . . white lie."

"I know."

"You do? *How?*"

"Frazier, you've got to be the worst liar ever."

I'm not sure how to take this. I know I have the kind of face that gives everything away, but I had no idea it was this bad. If Ben could see through my Trip Monroe lie so easily, what else can he see? I really don't want to think about it.

"So you're not mad?"

"No, I'm not mad. I know how you are when you're working on an article. If you were Native American, your name would be Dog with a Bone. I figured you were working it out somehow."

"Oh."

"So where are you with this?"

I fill him in on everything I've done and triumphantly finish with the news of the celebrity charity event and how the Yeager Agency is paying my way. "Everyone wins here. I get a ticket to the cocktail party and my friend Kimberly gets an introduction to Trip Monroe."

"Good work," says Ben.

I start to leave when Ben says he wants to talk to me about something too.

"T.K. called a few minutes ago. He just saw the final mock-ups for the September issue. He loves the manatee article. Told me to tell you you're doing a fine job."

"Really? He said 'love'? Or did he say *like*? Because there's a difference, you know. What part did he like? Did he say anything about the Susie and Sam—"

"Why do you always do that?"

"Do what?"

"Second-guess everything until you beat it to death?"

Now, this stings. Ben has never been annoyed with me before.

He shoves a hand through his dark brown hair. "Sorry. I don't mean to be an ass. He said he loved it, okay?" Most of the sting is gone, but there is still a tiny bit that lingers. "This probably isn't the best time to ask, but I need a favor. You know I'm leaving for Vegas next Wednesday?"

Ben's best friend, Adam, who rowed crew with him at Columbia, is getting married in August in one of those fancy destination weddings in the Caribbean and Ben is the best man. Adam, Ben, and the rest of the male members of the bridal party, along with a good number of their buddies, are going to Las Vegas for a five-day four-night bachelor party. Four nights of drinking, gambling, and who knows what else (although I can imagine). Poor Amy. I almost feel sorry for her, but I don't.

"Do you need someone to go by your place and feed Lucky? I don't mind. I kind of like cats." Okay, this is a lie. Like Ben, I'm not a feline fan, but I am so glad he saved that poor sad cat from Richard and the hit squad at Animal Control.

"Lucky? Yeah, actually, Lisa has the cat now." He shrugs. "I was hardly ever home and he needed more attention than I could give him, so she volunteered to take him in."

"Oh . . . that's great."

"So, the thing is, I have about a week to catch up on what's essentially a month's worth of work and I was hoping you might be able to help me with some of it."

"Help like what?"

He waves his hand around the piles of papers on his desk. "Help edit some of these articles. Maybe read my latest 'Letter from the Editor' and tell me what you think of it. That kind of stuff."

"Tonight?"

"Yeah, I really need to start clearing off this desk."

Ben has asked for my help with this sort of thing before. Some people might think he's taking advantage of me by trying to get me to do his work for him, but this is not the case. I've told you that Ben is a genius, and that wasn't just because I thought I was in love with him. He really is the smartest person I know, and anything he can teach me, I want to learn. Normally, I have no problem working late. But tonight is different.

"I kind of promised Nick I'd Skype him this evening." I most *definitely* promised Nick I'd Skype him. At eight p.m., to be exact. "But . . . we didn't exactly specify a time," I lie. "So yeah, I can help."

"Are you sure?"

"Positive. This is work and work comes first, so show me the way, O Captain! My Captain!"

The instant I say this, my face turns hot. It is without doubt the geekiest thing I have ever said to Ben. I am usually a bit more guarded around him. But it's just like the day I asked him what his favorite word was. Before I knew it, the question was coming out of my mouth and I couldn't stop myself, and look where that got me.

But as I wait for the strange (as in, isn't this girl strange?) look to come over Ben's face, it doesn't. Instead he shakes his head and laughs. "Frazier, you are the only person I know who looks happy at the prospect of more work."

He prints out some papers and hands them to me. It's an article Richard wrote about a retired circus star from Ringling Brothers who has formed an amateur senior-citizen acrobatic troupe in The Villages, which is a huge retirement community not too far from here. Ben asks me to edit it.

I'm about to leave with the article when Ben says, "Stay." He motions to his couch. "We'll get more done if you're not constantly coming back into the office to ask me questions."

"Who says I was going to pester you with questions?" But Ben doesn't have to ask twice. I've already kicked off my shoes and made myself comfortable on the couch. This is way better than working in my cramped cubicle. I text Nick and ask if we can Skype later, like around ten. He texts back and says no problem.

"Everything okay?" Ben asks.

"Perfect," I say.

"I appreciate you staying late tonight." He picks up his cell. "You like Thai?"

Thai food is sometimes too spicy for my taste but I don't want to seem like a culinary wimp. "I love Thai food."

Ben orders us dinner then hands me his monthly "Letter from the Editor" and asks me to take a look at it. The letter is for the September issue, which will feature my big manatee piece. Ben's letters are always sharp and witty. But as I read this, I'm not sure what to think.

Let me start by telling you that Ben is the first editor of *Florida!* magazine who is not a native Floridian, so there are some things that he just does not get.

Take this conversation, for example:

Ben had been at *Florida!* about a month when he asked me what I thought about a certain businessman who had once run for mayor of Tampa.

"He's a nice guy," I responded. "A real cracker."

Ben blinked. "He's a bigot?"

"*What?* No, of course not. You're thinking of it all wrong. When I say he's a Florida cracker, I mean his family has lived here for generations."

Ben just shook his head and mumbled something about the heat. Try as I might, I never could get him to understand that *cracker* was actually an affectionate term among native Floridians.

Remembering that conversation, I try to think of the best way to word this without stepping on his toes. "This is . . . good."

"But?"

"But it's off."

"Go on."

"You see, what makes your letters stand out is that you're like this foreigner looking in from the outside. You see Florida from a nonnative point of view and that's good because you see things we don't. Like when you wrote about your first encounter with love bugs."

Ben cringes. "Nasty little crappers."

"Exactly. We're so used to them that, honestly? I don't even notice them, but you actually made them kind of funny."

"Glad I could provide a laugh."

"Remember when you were telling me stories about your rowing days at Columbia and about the time you rowed crew down here in Florida for a college regatta? And how your oar went out of sync . . . what's that called again?"

"Catching a crab," Ben says.

"Yeah! You caught a crab and got thrown in the river and this giant manatee came up to you and you started screaming?"

"Screaming like a girl, you mean?" I nod and Ben makes a face. "You want me to write about *that*?"

"How many other close encounters with manatees have you had?"

He reluctantly plucks the paper from my hand and goes back to his computer and I begin to edit Richard's circus piece. I was expecting a *Water for Elephants* kind of story, but instead, Richard's piece makes this guy's life sound idyllic. It's like the story was written from a five-year-old's point of view, only the five-year-old has an excellent command of the English language and is both witty and charming. It should be corny, but it's not, and I have to admit, I'm impressed. I begin to jot down a few notes, when Ben asks me to read the new version of his letter.

I go to his desk and read from his screen. The letter is all about how he ended up in the river with this humongous manatee and he started yelling, and the guys in his skull thought it was hysterical and they rowed off without him. Within minutes, Ben discovered that manatees are among the gentlest creatures on the planet. Besides being funny and real, the piece is also oddly sweet. Probably more so because it's written from a man's perspective.

"This is great," I say. "It's completely relevant to the issue and it's a personal story that only you can tell. The readers are going to love it."

"How on earth did you remember that story, anyway?"

"I don't know. I just did."

Ben looks at me funny and I feel myself get flustered. I think Ben would be seriously creeped out if I told him that I remember just about everything he's ever said to me. Luckily, I'm saved from saying anything else because our food arrives. Ben hands me a carton of noodles along with a pair of chopsticks and we take a break from work to eat dinner. He sits on the couch next to me. Just a couple of feet away.

"So tell me about this Vegas trip," I ask, before taking a tentative bite of my noodles.

"Fifteen guys, four hotel suites, lots of booze."

I swallow the noodles and am hit with a burst of red-hot flavor. I blink to keep my eyes from watering. "Are you going to see any shows?"

Ben eyes me over the top of his carton of food. "Not the kind you're probably thinking of."

"I think I'm thinking the same kind you are."

"For your information, Frazier, those kinds of shows are obligatory for a bachelor party. Not that I'm going to enjoy myself or anything."

I put my food down to cup my hands in the air a few inches over my breasts and make a jiggling motion. "You know none of those are real, right?"

"Right."

"But it doesn't matter, does it?"

"Nope."

"What is it with men and big breasts?"

"They don't have to be big." Ben is discreet, so I barely catch it, but there is no doubt he just snuck a peek at my chest.

It feels as if we're flirting with each other and I can't help but think it's because now that we're both seeing someone there is a freedom to flirt without being taken seriously that was not there before.

"So this guy you're seeing," Ben says, breaking through my thoughts. "Sounds pretty serious."

"Oh, well . . . not serious. I mean, we just started dating, but I've known him since high school, and you know—"

"A word of advice, Frazier? Don't overanalyze it. Just go with your instincts."

Then Ben does something unexpected. He plucks the carton of Thai food from my hands and exchanges it with the carton he's been eating from.

"You'll like this better," he says.

I take a bite of Ben's basil fried rice. He's right. This is less spicy and more to my liking. We resume eating interspersed with some occasional conversation about the magazine, and that is the end of that.

chapter eleven

·····

I leave work early Friday afternoon to go to the mall, where I hit Zara for something new to wear to the charity event. Kimberly is right. My black cocktail dress is old news. I rummage through the racks and quickly narrow my selection down to two choices: a black-and-white rayon polka-dot dress with three-quarter sleeves that surprisingly does not make me look like a whale, and a sleeveless lime-green-and-white print dress with a gathered skirt and narrow black belt.

The polka-dot dress is more conservative and I could probably wear it to work. I know Kimberly warned me off wearing black, but since it's got white polka dots, technically I don't think this counts as the stereotypical little black dress (which in my case would be the stereotypical, slightly-larger-than-average black dress). The lime-and-white print dress is . . . well, I'm not quite sure what to make of it, so I try it on and ask the salesgirl what she thinks.

"It looks fantastic," she gushes.

"You don't think it's too . . ."

"Sexy?"

I nod.

"What's the occasion?"

"A cocktail party, but it's a work-related function."

"It's perfect," she says. "You're right, it's sexy, but it still covers everything up. Plus, you've got terrific arms. Show them off!"

I'm still not convinced, but each dress is under a hundred dollars and I don't shop that often, so I buy them both.

I'm on my way out of the mall when I pass by Victoria's Secret. When I told you it had been an embarrassingly long time since I'd had sex, I wasn't exaggerating. Hence it's been a long time since I've splurged on lingerie. All my undies look like they've each spent a month on a *Survivor* castaway.

I buy four bras and twenty pairs of underwear and almost have a heart attack when I sign the credit-card slip. Is it strange that I just spent more money on my underwear than on two dresses? I kind of think it is, but then I imagine what Sophie Marceau or Audrey Tautou might do in this situation. They are both French and beautiful and sexy. I think they would have bought the underwear without even blinking. As a matter of fact, I think if forced to make a choice between the underwear and the dresses, they would both pick the underwear hands down.

I also think they would have stopped by the coffee shop on their way out of the mall and bought the croissant I am now at this very moment nibbling on. I forgo my usual café latte and order a bottled water. After all, I am practicing moderation.

I arrive in Catfish Cove around seven. My moms are both excited to see me. Being women of great intelligence, they can see that my dating Nick brings the added advantage that I will now be visiting home more often. Because I've only been dating Nick two weeks and because I respect my moms, I am not planning to sleep over at Nick's place. I'm sure they expect that Nick and

I will eventually have sex, but I really don't want them knowing that I've already fallen so easily.

Nick is picking me up at eight. I shower, wash my hair, and put on some makeup. All this takes about forty-five minutes, so I have a little bit of time to kill before he arrives. I decide to ask my moms' opinion on which dress to wear to the cocktail party.

I start with the polka-dot one, which I have now nicknamed the "unsexy" dress.

Mama J looks at it with a critical eye. Of my two moms, I secretly think she has the better taste for this kind of thing. "It looks very nice," she says.

"That's an awful lot of dots," counters Mom.

"Is that your subtle way of saying my butt looks too big?"

This is a mistake on my part because now I have to listen to a lecture on how society places too much emphasis on women's looks and not enough on their accomplishments. Mom ends with saying, "I just think there are too many dots, that's all."

I'm about to change out of the dress when Nick arrives and Mom asks what he thinks. I stand there while Nick's dark eyes roam over me. For some reason this makes me more nervous than the thought of Nick seeing me naked, which is silly, because he already has.

"Nice dress," says Nick.

"Try on the other one," says Mama J. "That way we can compare."

I change into the "sexy" dress and walk back into the living room, ready for the big reaction.

"That one!" says Mom.

Mama J nods in agreement.

Nick smiles. "That one looks nice too."

Nice? I have to admit, I'm disappointed by Nick's response.

He *has* to like this dress better. Doesn't he? I mean, this dress is stilettos and the polka-dot one is penny loafers, and everyone knows that given the choice, men prefer stilettos to penny loafers. Maybe he's just trying to be polite in front of my moms. It occurs to me that although I've known Nick for years, there's still a lot I don't know about him.

I put both dresses away and quickly change for our date. We go to dinner at Louie's, the restaurant next door to Mama J's bookstore. Louie's serves good old-fashioned Italian food and brick-oven-baked pizza and is owned by Nick's uncle Vinnie (why the restaurant is named Louie's, I'm not sure). Once we sit down to eat, I realize that taking me to Louie's is tantamount to Nick's announcing to his family that he has a girlfriend. Almost all of Nick's extended family who live in Catfish Cove work at the restaurant, as well as Nick's older sister, Anna, who acts as the hostess. A horde of Alfonsos come by our table to say hello and slap Nick on the back.

Anna does not seem surprised to see Nick and me together, so I can only assume that Nick has already told his family about us. She kisses me on the cheek and tells me she's so happy her brother has finally found a "nice girl" (there's that word again).

This makes me wonder what sort of girl Nick has been dating since his divorce from Shannon. I'd be lying if I said I wasn't a tad bit jealous. I want to make a joke about it, but I don't want to say anything that might bring up the subject of his failed marriage or Shannon or Ed because I can tell it makes Nick uncomfortable.

After dinner, we go back to Nick's place, where we basically tear each other's clothes off. I'm happy to say that Nick seems much more impressed by my new underwear than he was by my dresses. I think Nick's ancestors must have come from the part of Italy that borders France.

Three hours later we're both dressed and standing on my doorstep. Nick doesn't give me a hard time about not staying over at his place and this scores him a few extra brownie points.

The next morning I get up early and accompany Mama J and Walt to Carpe Diem.

Let me tell you about Mama J.

You already know her favorite poet is Walt Whitman, and if you haven't figured out by the name of her bookstore, her favorite movie of all time is *Dead Poets Society*. Like Mom, she's sixty-two, but she looks at least ten years younger. She's taller than my five foot six and thinner as well. Mama J used to be a runner and she's still in great shape. She has a master's degree in English literature and taught at one of the community colleges near Jacksonville before moving to Catfish Cove. I know she and Mom were introduced to each other by a mutual friend and that it was "love at third sight," as she likes to joke.

Apparently, Mom, who can be a bit intense, initially scared Mama J off. But besides being a little too serious at times, Mom is also one of the kindest, most generous people you'll ever meet. On their third date Mom gave Mama J a copy of *Leaves of Grass*. According to Mom, she had no clue at the time that Walt Whitman was Mama J's favorite poet. They stayed up all night talking and that's when they both knew they were going to spend the rest of their lives together. I think it's horribly romantic.

When Bill Clinton was caught doing the seminasty with Monica Lewinsky, Mom and Mama J weren't nearly as upset over his infidelity as they were when they read that he'd given Monica a copy of *Leaves of Grass,* something he'd also given Hillary when he was courting her.

"I'd leave him just for that," I remember Mama J saying.

Mom just clucked and shook her head.

Mama J's family belongs to one of those churches that think you are going to go to hell if you spit on the sidewalk, so you can imagine what they thought when she came out her sophomore year in college. I have never met any of Mama J's blood relatives, and personally, I don't think I ever want to.

Mom, on the other hand, had it easier. She didn't come out until the year I was born, and by that time, according to my aunt Susie (Mom's younger sister), everyone had already figured it out and it was no big deal. Aunt Susie and my uncle Jack live in Pensacola and we see them as often as most people see their relatives. I have two cousins, Marta and Tom. Tom works for a software company in California and Marta lives in Atlanta and is newly married. I wish I had more family nearby, but I don't.

Mama J unlocks the front door to the store. The smell of books assails my nostrils. I inhale deeply as the aroma reaches through to permeate the cells of my body.

What do books smell like exactly?

I think the answer to this is different for everyone. For me, who has always equated books with Mama J's store, it's simple. Books smell like her. Crisp and clean, slightly inky, laced with love and a whiff of peppermint tea.

I have a shameful confession to make.

Last year I bought an e-reader. The temptation to give in to one was just too great. I think I was secretly hoping I would hate the thing. But I don't. I love it. It's instant gratification. Books when I want them, whenever I want them. The thing is, though, while my e-reader is awesome, it doesn't quench my thirst to flip a page, or run a finger down smooth paper, or stick my nose in a book's spine and inhale. I read somewhere that one of those famous perfume designers has created a new fragrance that smells like books. His reasoning? To satisfy the public's craving for the smell of paper in this digital age. Go figure.

I flip on the lights and Walt immediately finds his place behind the counter. I fill his dish with water and he settles in, ready to greet customers who are used to seeing him in the store.

When I was a teenager I used to work here after school and on Saturdays. Once upon a time, before she got it into her head that I should become a lawyer, Mom used to hold out the hope that one day I'd follow in her and Grandpa George's footsteps and practice medicine. But the sight of blood makes me woozy. The sight of books makes me woozy too, but in the good way.

Mama J reaches under the counter and hands me a book of poetry. I stick the book in my tote and promise her I'll read it.

I spend the next couple of hours schmoozing with customers and catching up on the newest arrivals. Independent bookstores like Mama J's are almost extinct, but even in a little town like Catfish Cove, her store has managed to keep afloat. I think it's because she's such a keen businesswoman. She knows all her customers by name and remembers exactly what they like to read. She also allows her store to be used for private events.

For example, she has a small children's section at the back of the store filled with classic children's literature as well as a small assortment of toys and baby items. The walls in this section of the store are painted pastel green and there are comfy beanbag chairs and an oversize sofa for parents to sit on while they read to their kids. Mama J rents out this section to anyone who wants to host a birthday party or a baby shower and it's almost always booked for Saturday mornings. This, of course, brings more traffic into her store and results in more sales. Pretty smart, if you ask me.

This Saturday, Patrice "Tricia" Timmons Elby, whom I went

to high school with, has booked the store for a baby shower and the honoree is none other than her best friend of all time, Shannon Dukes Norris. The last time I saw Tricia was a couple of years ago when I ran into her at the Piggly Wiggly while I was on a visit home. She's married to Ed's "new" best friend, Casey, who's originally from Atlanta and settled in Catfish Cove after taking over Tricia's daddy's dental practice. Mama J is busy with customers, so I offer myself to Tricia, who is grateful for my help. She's also particularly chatty today. She reveals to me that Shannon had a difficult time getting pregnant and that she conceived with the help of the fertility drug Clomid. I also discover that this is Shannon's fourth baby shower. According to her seven sonograms, the baby is a boy and his name is Edward Louis Norris Jr.

The shower is being catered by Tricia's sister-in-law, who owns a local company called Fresh Impressions. There are two servers dressed in crisp white cotton shirts and black pants who have set up a table covered with a linen cloth. They will be serving virgin mimosas (in deference to Shannon's gestational abstinence from alcohol), fresh fruit, bite-size quiches, and caramelized onion tarts. For dessert, there are designer cupcakes, each one frosted in white and decorated with the initials *ELN* in blue icing. All very Junior League–ish, and chic for Catfish Cove, if you ask me.

I place a stack of presents on top of an end table. The baby shower's theme is "enlightening the mind," which means that baby Edward's library is going to be well stocked. Along with the standard *Goodnight Moon* and Beatrix Potter, there are plenty of newer children's works, like *On the Night You Were Born* and *Guess How Much I Love You* (a book I've fantasized about reading to my own baby one day). Little Edward would be one lucky kid, except that there is no Dr. Seuss in the pile. How can little Edward's literary education be complete without works from the greatest children's writer ever?

I'm pondering this in my head when Tricia turns and says, "I just can't believe you and Nick are dating now."

"Really, why?"

"Oh, you know. It's just so weird!" Tricia shakes her head and laughs.

Cognitively, I know what she's said. But my brain interprets it as *Oh, you know, because he's so hot and you're so not.*

"What's so weird about it?"

"It's just funny that after all these years the two of you would hook up. Kind of like fate, or karma or something."

I freeze. Tricia doesn't have to spell it out for me. I know she's thinking about the Dixie Deb Ball. That's the night Nick and I first danced together. I already told you that the day I won the senior poetry contest was the best day of my teenage life. Well, the Dixie Deb Ball was, without doubt, the worst.

I study her face and come to the conclusion that Tricia doesn't mean anything negative by her remark. She puts the finishing touches on the present table and looks up to see the door to the store open. It's Shannon, arriving for her shower. Other than the fact that she looks like she's about to tip over, she looks very elegant and cool in her sleeveless baby-blue maternity dress.

Tricia places her hand on my elbow and lowers her voice. "Be good to Nick, okay, Emma?" Then she puts on a bright face and goes to greet Shannon.

At first, this strikes me as a strange thing for Tricia to say. I suppose as Shannon's closest friend, she knows how much Shannon's infidelity hurt Nick. But Tricia has nothing to worry about. I am no Shannon. I could never cheat on Nick. The idea of it almost makes me laugh.

chapter twelve

· · · · ·

Later, I help Mama J clean up. I toss the two designer cupcakes that Shannon insisted I take home with me into the trash. "One for you and one for Nick," she'd said with a completely straight face that makes me believe Shannon is either the cruelest person on the planet or a complete twit. I'm betting on the latter.

"Some shindig, huh?" Mama J says.

"Do you ever wish you had a baby?" I ask her.

"Oh!" Her soft brown eyes go wide.

"Sorry, I don't mean to pry."

"Don't be silly. You have every right to ask that question." She straightens the cushions on the sofa. "I tried a few times, when you were around seven. But it didn't take and your mom and I thought it was for the best. She thought about having another baby too, but her practice was so busy and . . . well, we had you and that was more than enough." She turns around and smiles at me. "Are you thinking of having children?"

"I need a husband first."

Mama J raises her brow at me and we both laugh because I'm pretty sure we're both thinking the same thing.

"Well, I could go *that* route, but I don't think it's for me."

She places her warm palm against my cheek. "No, that's not for you, baby. You're the traditional sort."

The door to the store opens and we both turn around. It's Julie, the nice lady who was house-sitting for Frank Monroe. I'd meant to ask my moms about her but so much has been going on lately, I forgot. I grab the sleeve to Mama J's blouse and whisper in her ear, "Do I know her?"

"That's Julie Williams. She's the vice principal at the high school. Why?"

"She was at Frank Monroe's place. She seemed to know me, but I know I've never met her before."

Mama J looks startled. "When did you go to Frank Monroe's place?"

I shrug. "Last time I was in town. I thought he'd be a good way to get to Trip, but he was on vacation."

Julie approaches the counter. "Well, hello there!" She and Mama J exchange a few pleasantries and I find out the reason I don't remember Julie is that she only moved to Catfish Cove a few years ago.

"Did you hear from Frank?" Julie asks me.

"Yeah, I did." I hesitate, wondering just how much I should tell her. Julie seems genuinely interested, so I decide to be honest. "He kind of shot me down. Told me not to call him again."

"You talked to Frank Monroe?" Mama J asks me.

"Not really. I left him a voice mail asking him to get in touch with me. He left me a message basically telling me not to call him again."

Julie frowns. "That doesn't sound like Frank."

This is practically the same exact thing Nick said to me.

"It's no biggie," I say. "I'm going to see Trip at a charity event in a couple of weeks, so it all worked out."

Julie looks like she's on the verge of saying something more when Mama J interrupts by telling her she has a book that just came in that she's certain Julie will like and the two of them take off down the aisles in search of it.

I head to the Piggly Wiggly to pick up groceries then drive to Nick's place. Frank Monroe's house is on the way, so I can't help but drive by. There's an SUV in the open garage that wasn't there on our previous trip to his home, which leads me to believe that Frank must be back from his big fishing trip. I consider stopping to knock on his door. Maybe meeting me in person will change his opinion about nosy reporters.

But just as I pull up behind the SUV, I see a man walk out the side door of the house. Although he looks slightly older than the pictures in the auto repair shop, I immediately recognize him as Frank Monroe. He glances my way curiously.

You know how people describe that funny sensation they get in their stomach as butterflies? I always think of it as crawling worms. Yeah, I know. Pretty yucky. I feel like a long skinny two-foot worm is trying to wiggle its way out my belly button right now. I panic and stick my head out the car window. "Sorry, wrong house!" He gives me a friendly wave and I back out of his driveway as fast as I can and drive to Nick's.

Nick is in his front yard, pulling weeds. He looks sweaty and hot and utterly delicious. I have the makings of dinner and plan to cook for us, but before I can put the groceries away, Nick grabs me and pulls me into the shower with him.

Let me tell you about Nick.

He is sexually more adventurous than any guy I've dated, which is probably not saying a whole lot, but still. He is a perfect combination of rough and gentle. He doesn't push me to do something that doesn't feel right. And just as important, he doesn't think that because I was raised by two lesbians, I am some sort of sexual wild woman. I've dated a few guys who were sorely disappointed by their own ignorant assumptions about me.

Before Nick, I thought sex was like the cherry on top of the whipped cream of a good relationship. Now I'm beginning to think it's more like the ice cream. I cannot be very French about sex right now and practice moderation. Excess is what it's all about. Nick makes me feel sexy. And I haven't felt that for the longest time. I think Nick is like a drug. If I could bottle him, I'd be a millionaire.

Nick and I are in bed, naked.

I prop my chin on the heel of my hand and look down into his face. His eyes are shut like he's sleeping. Unlike most people, I find it hard to sleep after sex. I know it's supposed to relax you but it has the opposite effect on me. It winds me up. I think about what Tricia said to me at the store and this time I can't help but smile. I think Nick would agree that I've been pretty darn good to him today.

I also remember what his sister, Anna, said about me last night at the restaurant.

"So your sister thinks I'm a nice girl?" I ask, pretending not to notice that Nick is trying to sleep.

"You are a nice girl," Nick murmurs.

"Is that why you like me? Because I'm nice?"

Nick cracks open an eyelid. "Are we seriously going to have this conversation?"

Ben's advice pops into my head. *Don't overanalyze.*

So I say, "Okay, change of subject. I almost stopped at Frank Monroe's place this evening."

"Yeah?"

I tell Nick about my near encounter with Trip's uncle.

"Why didn't you talk to him?"

"I don't know. It just . . . didn't feel right."

"I think I have a pretty good idea why you want to speak to me and the answer is no. Please don't call again."

I've been a journalist long enough to be able to read people pretty well. I've been going over that message in my head, wondering what it is that's bothered me, and I've finally figured it out. I wasn't just some reporter trying to get to Trip. Nor was I some random girl from his hometown. There was something personal in Frank Monroe's tone of voice. But for the life of me I can't imagine what Frank Monroe would have against me. In all my years growing up in Catfish Cove, I can't remember ever even speaking to him.

Just thinking all this begins to agitate me, so I change the subject again.

I playfully punch Nick in the shoulder. "Hey, last night when I tried on those dresses, you had to have had an opinion. Tell me the truth, which one did you like best?"

"Does it matter? You're going to wear the one you want to anyway, right?"

"Of course, but I still want to know what you think."

"Okay," he says cautiously. He is fully awake now. "If you really want to know, I like the polka-dot one."

"Yeah?"

"Yeah. It looks more like . . . you."

This surprises me. I thought for sure Nick would go for the sexy dress. And what does he mean when he says the polka-dot dress looks more like "me?" That I'm not sexy? Clearly, he must find me somewhat sexy. I'm in bed with him, aren't I? A part of me wants to quiz him on all this, but I'm still thinking of Ben's warning not to overanalyze and I clamp my mouth shut before I can say anything.

Nick seems pleased that I have dropped the subject. He pulls me closer and I relax against him. Ben is right. For once in my life I'm going to refrain from dissecting what is clearly "a moment."

How strange is it that I'm taking relationship advice from Ben Gallagher?

chapter thirteen

· · · · ·

It's another Monday morning and I'm feeling pretty fine. For once, everything in my life is perfect. I'm dating the sweetest, nicest, sexiest guy on the planet and my work life is going pretty well too. In less than three weeks I'm finally going to connect with Trip Monroe, and once Trip sees me and I tell him that I really need an interview, I can't imagine why he wouldn't give me one.

I pick up the donuts and for the third week in a row Ben is already in the conference room. We only have a few seconds before everyone else arrives and Jackie announces that the Death Star is finally complete. They are closing on Friday and moving in this weekend and everyone is invited to a big housewarming party next month.

She passes around invitations and I notice everyone's envelope says "and guest" behind their name. Lisa has been dating the same guy for the last year, so I assume she'll bring her boyfriend, Tony. Richard changes girlfriends the way most men change the channel, so I imagine he'll bring the flavor of the hour. I wonder if Ben will bring Amy. I'm thinking this is a good opportunity for everyone at work to meet Nick.

That evening I call him.

"A housewarming party? Sure, sounds great."

We discuss the specifics and then Nick breaks the news that he will not be able to drive down to Tampa this weekend to see me.

"Sorry, babe, I have to pull a double on Saturday. You know how it is, small-town police department. We all have to cover for one another."

"I could drive up there," I offer.

"I'd love that, but it's hardly worth the trip. You'd see me two hours, tops." For one nanosecond I wonder if Nick is brushing me off, but then he adds, "You're a cop's girlfriend, might as well get used to the bad hours."

Despite the fact we've been spending all our free time together and each has the other listed as their Facebook relationship, this is the first time Nick has actually called me his girlfriend. I like the way it sounds when he says it.

The next couple of days go by without anything exciting happening. Ben leaves early Wednesday afternoon for his Vegas trip, and on Thursday Richard calls in sick. I don't ever remember Richard calling in sick other than his usual fourth Friday, which is not tomorrow, so he is completely out of sync here.

Richard's sick call puts Lisa in a complete panic. Although Lisa and Tony seem kind of serious, I'm pretty sure she has a crush on Richard. She hangs out by his cubicle more than she needs to, laughs way too long at his jokes (which, I admit, can sometimes be pretty funny), and always remembers the exact way he likes his turkey sandwich when we order takeout from the deli next door (white bread, lettuce, tomato, Italian dressing, provolone cheese, pickles, no mayo). Everyone else in the office has to write their order down and even then half the time Lisa still gets it wrong.

"Do you think I should go by his place and make sure he's okay?" Lisa asks. "I could bring him chicken soup."

I consider this for a moment, then remember the tan Richard got the last time he called in "sick."

"Nah, I'm sure he's fine."

With Richard absent today, I can turn the radio to any station I want, which puts me in a fantastic mood. The cocktail charity event is now only fifteen days away and I decide it's time to do some extra-intensive research on Trip.

Trip was born and raised in Catfish Cove, attended public schools, and worked at his uncle Frank's auto repair shop. He's an only child and his daddy died when Trip was sixteen (all this I already knew from firsthand knowledge). After high school graduation he continued working for his uncle but he also started a side business fixing up old race cars. He entered his first race when he was nineteen and placed third. After that, he began winning races on a steady basis and was able to quit his day job and concentrate on the racing circuit. At the age of twenty-four, he suffered a near-fatal injury at the Talladega Superspeedway. He came back to racing the next year as a born-again Christian and has stayed at the top of his game. He has never married, although he's been linked to several famous personalities. He's been described as "elusive" but "friendly enough." He also still fixes his own cars.

All this research is what I call the "bones." It's the structure on which I'll base my questions. But I'm still lacking the "muscle." This is the hook or the angle behind the article. I told Ben I planned to do a "Zero to Hero" story. Poor boy makes good. That kind of thing, and I'm still thinking it's the best way to go. I won't know for sure until I do more research. The final touch to the article will be the "fat," but I'll only discover that after I actually spend some one-on-one time with Trip.

I read every article, every word I can find in print, trying to discover the muscle, but I don't get the "aha!" moment I'm searching for. I need to look at this from another angle and that's when it occurs to me that I should look into the one person (besides his mama) who has had the most influence on Trip, and that's his uncle Frank.

I think about the Trip Monroe photo shrine that Uncle Frank has going on at his shop. It doesn't take a genius to figure out that after Trip's daddy died, Uncle Frank took over as Trip's father figure. Since another personal phone call to Frank Monroe is out of the question, I decide to call Mom and see what she knows about him.

"Hey, Mom," I say, "did you go to high school with Frank Monroe?"

"Emma, I'm in the middle of trying to get a peanut out of a four-year-old's nose. What's this about?"

"Oops. Sorry. I didn't mean for you to be paged stat or anything. It's research for my Trip Monroe article." Pause. "Soft-boiled or regular?"

"Soft-boiled, of course."

"So sorry! I'll call back later."

"It's all right," Mom says. "They've untied the ropes to let him up to go tee-tee. But make it fast." Sometimes Mom's attempts at humor are a little unsettling.

"So, did you go to high school with Frank Monroe?"

"As a matter of fact I did. He was a year older than me."

"Great. Okay, so what can you tell me about him?"

For a long time Mom doesn't say anything. "Mom, are you still there?"

"I'm here. Let's see . . . Frank Monroe, well, he was a very nice boy."

"That's it?"

"I went to prom with him."

I can't help but laugh. "You went to *prom* with Frank Monroe?"

"What's so funny about that, missy?"

"Nothing," I say quickly. "Okay, so this is good. What's he like? Any skeletons in the closet?"

"How exactly does this fit into your Trip Monroe article?"

"It's background information."

Mom sighs. "Honestly, Emma, there's nothing much to say. He was a nice boy who grew up into a nice man but I haven't talked to him in years. He doesn't even work at his own auto repair shop anymore. Whenever I take in the Volvo, there's always some teenager with acne behind the counter."

"Is there any reason Frank Monroe would have to dislike me?"

"Dislike you? What on earth are you talking about? Why would he dislike you? Did Frank Monroe say something to upset you?"

"No, of course not. I've never even spoken to him. I don't know. I thought maybe he had a previous bad experience with a reporter?" I omit the fact that I think it's personal because it makes no sense.

"Now you're being dramatic."

For once I agree. "Okay, well, that's what I thought."

I promise my mom to drive safely (something she makes me say at the end of each phone call) and we hang up. Two minutes later my phone rings. It's Jason.

"Want to grab a bite to eat?" he asks.

"Sure. Where do you want to go? Torie likes that new place on Kennedy."

"I was thinking it would just be you and me."

We make plans to meet at a restaurant near my office. I've never had lunch with just Jason before, and I have to admit, I'm curious. The waitress takes our order and Jason gets right down to it.

"I want to get back with Torie."

"All right," I say cautiously.

"You're her best friend. Has she ever said she feels the same way?"

Jason looks so eager that I can't help but try to give him some hope. "Not exactly, but she's never said anything against it either."

"I guess that's a start, huh?"

"Definitely!" Then I add, "Just go slow. Be natural. Don't overwhelm her."

I try my best to steer the conversation away from Torie, but Jason keeps veering it back. We end lunch with my once again cautioning him to take things one day at a time, and Jason promises to do just that.

I go back to the office, slightly depressed.

I really don't think Jason has a shot.

I work till both Lisa and Jackie leave, then lock up the office and head for my car. Despite the fact that I'm still miffed at Richard for his part in the "Facebook fiasco," I break down and call his cell.

"What?" he says, his voice rough and scratchy.

"Oh my God, you're really sick."

A nasty gurgling sound comes from his end of the receiver.

"Don't talk. I'll be there in ten minutes. No, make that twenty."

I show up at Richard's doorstep with a grocery bag filled with Gatorade, cough medicine, Kleenex, and a carton of take-out chicken soup from the deli at Publix.

He opens his door wearing a Tampa Bay Rays T-shirt, boxer shorts, and a pair of mismatched socks. His hair is sticking up and his eyes are bloodshot.

"You're thirty minutes late," he croaks.

I brush past him and head to the kitchen to put away the supplies. "Aw, Richard, were you counting down the minutes till I got here? That's so sweet." I open up the grocery bag and lay the contents on the counter.

He grabs the chicken soup and opens the lid. "You brought me soup?"

"It was Lisa's idea. She's been frantic all day, worrying about you." Pause. "I kind of thought you were faking it, so I talked her out of bringing it to you earlier. Sorry." I place my palm against his forehead. "You don't feel hot, so I guess that's good."

"I took some Tylenol this afternoon."

"Good boy."

I reheat the soup and hand it to Richard, who immediately starts chowing down.

"Glad to see this hasn't affected your appetite."

He grunts.

"Do you think Lisa is . . . into you?" I blurt. Considering my Ben crush, this is like the pot calling the kettle black.

Richard freezes, his spoon halfway to his mouth. "Lisa knows exactly how I feel about her."

He does not elaborate, and since it's really none of my business, I don't feel as if I should push it. Although . . . what does that mean? Exactly how does he feel about her?

I pick up the bottle of cough medicine and make a big show of reading the label. "So, if you take this right now—"

"I told Lisa she was a great girl but that I thought of her as a friend. End of story."

My head snaps up to meet his gaze. "When was this?"

"A few months ago."

"Oh. Okay." I try to act nonchalant but I have to admit, I am greatly relieved. I think it's because I like Lisa, and I don't want her to waste her time crushing on Richard if he's not crushing on her back. I've been there and done that myself with Ben and I know how much it hurts.

"So when did you start editing my articles?" he asks.

"Your—oh, the circus piece? I did that to help Ben clear his desk. You know, before he left for Vegas."

"That was awful nice of you."

"Sarcasm on top of sick isn't pretty."

"Sorry, let me try again. Gee, Emma, that was really nice of you to do Gallagher's work so he could fly off to Vegas with his buddies for a four-day bender."

I open my mouth to respond with something equally snarky then stop myself. It never occurred to me that Richard might be envious of my professional relationship with Ben, but clearly, he is. I decide to take the high road. "It's a great article," I say truthfully.

"Yeah?"

"I think it's one of the best things you've ever written."

"I must be hallucinating. What did you put in the chicken soup?"

I laugh, but I'm a little rattled by his response. Have I never complimented Richard's writing before?

I decide to keep him company in his misery. He slurps his soup down while we watch a zombie movie (I let him pick since he's sick), and after a while he falls asleep on the sofa. I find a blanket, tuck it over his shoulders, and lock the door on my way out.

chapter fourteen

· · · · ·

Before I know it, it's Friday night and time for another happy hour at Captain Pete's. I haven't been back here since the night of the Ben-Amy hookup. I force myself to walk through the same door by which Ben laid one on Amy, and plaster a smile on my face.

Tonight is completely different from any other night that I have previously been to Captain Pete's. For the first time in aeons, I am no longer one of many available girls looking for love in all the wrong places. I am a happy, confident woman involved in a relationship with a man who appreciates me for who I am.

> *How many loved your moments of glad grace,*
> *And loved your beauty with love false or true,*
> *But one man loved the pilgrim soul in you,*
> *And loved the sorrows of your changing face.*

While I haven't exactly had scores of men lining up to admire my "beauty," I can still find something in those famous lines by Yeats to draw an analogy to Nick's *I like you just the way you are*. I think Nick is drawn to my pilgrim soul. I'm not sure exactly what a pilgrim soul is, but I've always found the expression beautiful.

Torie and Kimberly are already at the bar, drinks in hand. So is Amy. I was really hoping she wouldn't be here tonight. She's wearing a tight, but not too slutty, leather miniskirt and the most outrageous heels I've ever seen. Her honey-blond hair hangs down her back, shiny and perfect. I really can't blame Ben for shnogging her.

"Emma! I'm so glad you made it." Amy gives me her standard we're-long-lost-friends hug. She then steps back to give me a thorough inspection. "You look awesome! Have you lost weight?"

I grit my teeth. This particular "compliment" has always struck me as disingenuous, particularly in light of the fact that despite practicing moderation these past weeks, I have gained two pounds. My pilgrim soul might be a thing of beauty, but my pilgrim ass is feeling a little jiggly tonight. I am not, however, going to let Amy know that. "Thanks! I feel terrific."

Torie catches the tail end of our conversation. "Doesn't Emma look *great*?"

"She sure does," says Jason, popping up behind me.

I turn around and give Jason a tight hug. I've been worried about him ever since our lunch yesterday. I thought briefly about talking to Torie. Warning her, really, that Jason was going to make a play to get them back together. But I don't trust Torie's acting abilities. If I speak to her about Jason, she won't be able to hide it around him and I don't want to break Jason's trust. Which means all this puts me in a really bad spot.

"Emma's-got-a-love-glow," Torie singsongs, winking at me.

"Where's your guy?" Jason asks, searching for Nick.

"Back home, serving and protecting the fine folks of Catfish Cove."

"Emma!" Amy narrows her eyes at me. "Are you *seeing* someone?"

Kimberly now steps into the action. She whips out her phone and shows Amy a picture she took of Nick and me at dinner. Kimberly spends more than a few minutes extolling Nick's virtues. I'm impressed by how many details she remembers about him. I know what my friends are doing. They're trying to show Amy that despite my "ugly friend" status, I have managed to nab this really great guy. My throat starts to feel lumpy. I am so lucky to have such loyal friends.

"Wow." Amy studies Nick's picture like he's a legal document she needs to memorize in order to win a case. "He's . . . *hot*!"

Torie gives me a smug smile that says, *So take that, Amy!*

"The guy's a riot," says Jason. "Too bad he's not here."

"I can't wait to meet him," Amy says.

Hah. Over my dead body.

"So how are things with you and Ben?" I ask.

For a second Amy looks blank. Then she gives me a shaky smile. "You know, Emma, that boss of yours is pretty terrific."

"I'm glad you think so."

"Enough about me! I want to hear more about this Nick. He's a cop? Back in your hometown of . . . Catfish?"

"Catfish Cove," I clarify. Amy is a native Floridian, but she's from south Florida and is not so familiar with the many tiny towns of the vast Panhandle.

"It must be tough having a long-distance relationship," Amy says.

"We're managing."

Jason interrupts to ask us what we want to drink. Amy is drinking beer tonight. I'm not in the mood for anything sweet, so I order a beer as well and Jason goes off to fetch our drinks, which isn't necessary, but again, Jason is a great guy. Although it doesn't start with a *p, nice* is really the best word to describe him. Kimberly tags along after him and Torie is . . . *uh-oh*. She's suddenly deep in conversation with a tall, well-dressed guy who reminds me of a young Pierce Brosnan.

This is bad on two scores. First off, I can tell by the way Torie is acting that she's into this guy, which is a bad sign for Jason. Plus, Torie's desertion effectively leaves me alone with Amy.

"So, back to you and this Nick. Long-distance relationships are all about putting in the effort," Amy says.

I have to bite my tongue to keep from making a nasty comment. "Sounds like you have some experience with that," I say instead.

Amy puts on her serious face. "Relationships have to be watered and nurtured."

"Don't forget the occasional dose of fertilizer," I joke.

Amy places her hand over my arm. "I'm serious, Emma, I don't want to see you hurt." She lowers her voice, which makes me lean in closer to hear her because it's so loud in the bar. "When I first moved down here, I was still involved with this guy back in Boston. But it was hard trying to make it work without the daily interaction."

"Thank God for unlimited cell-phone plans," I say in a chirpy voice.

"I found out Pete—that's his name—was seeing this girl behind my back."

"And Skype. Let's not forget about Skype!"

As if she isn't hearing me, Amy goes on. "She was a paralegal who worked at his new firm. Pete swore it didn't mean anything . . . and even though I was crazy over the moon about him, I still broke it off. I could never trust him after that."

If I didn't know any better, I'd swear Amy's eyes are tearing up.

Honestly. I'm just speechless. Does Amy really think she is being helpful?

Jason comes back with our drinks, which is Amy's cue to ignore me. She begins flirting outrageously with Jason, demanding to know why podiatrists are so "anti-heel." As if Jason were blind or hadn't noticed before, she points out her sexy shoes by lifting one foot in the air and giving a saucy twist of her ankle.

Jason laughs and tells Amy that he personally is not against women wearing heels, but as a health care professional who specializes in feet, he's very concerned about her arches. He catches my eye and winks as if to tell me that Amy is full of shit and he can see straight through her. Jason is looking very nice tonight. He's wearing jeans and a white oxford shirt. He also looks like he's been working out. I know I told you he's not superhandsome, but in my mind's eye I can't help but see him as having a certain appeal.

Torie interrupts our conversation to lead me away to introduce me to the guy she's been talking to. His name is Kurt and he's a medical sales rep.

"Emma, keep Kurt company while I slip off to the restroom," she says, giving me the check-this-guy-out-and-tell-me-what-you-think look.

Kurt and I make the most of our time alone with some perfunctory small talk. He must sense that in talking to me he's undergoing some sort of test because I can tell he's trying hard to make me like him. I feel like Torie's gatekeeper. How Torie can get a guy she's just met all worked up like this . . . well, all I can say is that I'm glad I don't have this effect on men. It just seems like too much responsibility.

After Kurt and I have exhausted every possible topic we can think of in under fifteen minutes, Torie comes back and I give her a discreet shrug. I know she's waiting for some other kind of sign from me but I honestly don't know what to tell her. I glance around the bar and see Jason staring at us. Or rather, staring at Torie and Kurt. He is smiling at something Amy says but his eyes look sad. Poor Jason.

Kurt offers to buy Torie a drink. He offers to buy me one too, but I politely decline.

"So what do you think?" Torie asks the second Kurt leaves to go to the bar.

"He's okay, I guess."

"Just okay? Emma, he's gorgeous!"

"It sounds like you've already made up your mind, so what do you care what I think?"

Torie looks stung. "You're my best friend. Of course I care what you think."

"He's too good-looking."

"That's impossible. You can never be too good-looking."

"What do you want, Torie? A trophy boyfriend or a guy who's in it for the long haul? Because, you know, we're not getting any younger."

"Talk about trophy boyfriends! I'm not the one who's dating Mr. Tall, Dark, and Handcuffs."

"I thought you liked Nick."

"I do like him." Her shoulders sag. "So, what are we arguing about?"

Torie is right. I have no business giving her a hard time. Just because I think Jason is the perfect guy for her doesn't mean she should feel the same way.

"Nothing," I say. "I'm sorry."

"So be happy for me!"

"I *am* happy for you." I give her a hug to show her I mean it. If this is what Torie wants, then I'm going to have to put my own feelings aside and support her. Because that's what friends do. Right?

Kurt comes back with Torie's drink and I leave them alone to be happy with each other. Kimberly says good-bye to everyone and makes a hasty exit. One of her clients is hosting a 5K marathon fund-raiser tomorrow morning and Kimberly is working the event bright and early. Kimberly puts in even more hours at work than Torie does, which is saying a lot. At this rate, she's going to take over the Yeager Agency.

Torie is now in full-frontal flirtation attack with Kurt and I am left to do . . . nothing.

Relationships have to be watered and nurtured.

Amy's advice is almost laughable. Except she has a point. If a girl who looks like Amy can get cheated on, then what can a girl who looks like me expect?

I try to block that thought from my head. Nick is not the type of guy who would cheat on his girlfriend. I know this because he's so sensitive about the whole cheating issue. Still, what am I doing here at Captain Pete's? What is the use of having a boyfriend if I'm not spending my free time with him?

I squeeze Torie's arm and tell her I'll call her tomorrow.

"You okay?" she asks.

"I'm perfect."

At least I will be in exactly three and a half hours because that's how long it will take me to drive to Catfish Cove.

This is crazy. It's almost one o'clock in the morning and I have no overnight bag, no toothbrush, and no plan. Unless you call jumping into the car with the clothes on my back to make a two-hundred-plus-mile booty call a plan.

Nick's house is dark and quiet. He keeps a spare key under the backdoor mat. I use the key and turn on the kitchen light. An empty Louie's pizza box sits on the counter. *Nick ate an entire pizza by himself?* I guess that's possible, but not likely. Nick is too health-conscious. He works out daily and watches his carbs the way I probably should, but don't.

I tiptoe down the hall and open the door to Nick's bedroom. My vision adjusts to the darkness. The only noise in the room is the whirl of the ceiling fan and Nick's lone steady breathing.

I feel like a stalker.

What am I doing?

I am *not* checking up on Nick. I am *not* the suspicious type. I am *not*—

Nick sits straight up in bed. "What the . . ." He flips on his nightstand light. *"Emma?"* He runs a palm down his face trying to wake himself up. "Is everything okay? What are you doing here?"

I am suddenly overcome with a myriad of emotions. Shame, for thinking that Nick might have been cheating on me (because let's face it, ever since Amy brought up that little nugget, it's been sitting in my brain refusing to vacate). Relief, because he isn't. Anger, for letting Amy get to me. And a horrible wave of shyness because I have absolutely no idea what to do or say right now.

"I . . . I just wanted to see you tonight. So I drove up." Does this sound as pathetic to Nick as it does to me?

Apparently not, because Nick's face slowly splits into a smile. "Come here," he says, his voice still husky with sleep. He turns back the covers and pats what I have now come to consider "my side" of the bed. I slip off my shoes and slide in next to him and he wraps me up in his arms.

"What's wrong, babe?" he asks softly.

"I missed you," I squeak. "Is this okay? I mean, I don't want to invade your privacy or anything."

"My privacy?" Nick laughs. "Yeah, this is okay."

A few hours later I wake up, covered in sweat. The ceiling fan is on but it's unbearably hot. I slip into one of Nick's T-shirts and check the thermostat.

"I think your air is busted," I tell him.

"Crappy old house," Nick says with affection. He gets out of bed and we raid the refrigerator. Between us, we eat a pint of vanilla ice cream and the rest of the Louie's pizza, which Nick had wrapped up in aluminum foil and stored in the fridge, to save for later (I told you he would have never eaten an entire pizza by himself). Afterward, he takes my hand and leads me onto the dock.

"What are we doing?" I ask.

"I know a surefire way to cool off." Nick yanks down his boxers.

"You're kidding."

"Nope," he says, right before slipping into the lake. Nick splashes water onto the dock and it hits my calves. It's hot and muggy, typical weather for late June in Florida, but the water is cool.

"Come on, Emma, it feels good in here."

I glance around. The house to the right is dark, but there are a few scattered lights along the shoreline and I'm nervous that someone will hear us, or worse—

"No one's going to see us," Nick says, reading my mind. "It's too dark."

"Are there snakes in there?"

Nick laughs. "Just one. But you don't have to be afraid of it."

I really don't want to get into the lake when I can't see what's swimming around me, but Nick seems so playful and I don't want to ruin what has turned out to be a terrific night, so I try not to act self-conscious when I strip out of my T-shirt and ease myself into the water.

I'll be honest. I've never skinny-dipped before. But Nick is right. It does feel good. The water is only waist-high, so Nick takes me out to where it's deeper, reaching to the tops of his shoulders. But I can't touch the bottom without my nose going under, so I hold on to him to keep my head above water and he starts to kiss me.

I already told you that Nick is an excellent kisser, so within a very short while I'm panting. I wrap my legs around his waist and it feels completely natural when he slides inside me. Until I realize that we're out here in the middle of the lake without a condom.

I immediately start to pull away.

"Don't," Nick says. His hands are on my bottom, urging me back.

"But—"

"Emma, baby . . . you have no idea how much I want you."

This is as close to my fantasy of having a guy tell me he's dying to sleep with me as I'm ever going to get.

"It'll be all right," says Nick. "I promise."

He sounds as if he's in pain. I'm in pain too, but my mind is working faster than my body and it's telling me this is probably not a smart thing to do. First off, making love in a lake is unhygienic, not to mention—

"You're just so pretty, Emma," Nick whispers in my ear.

My first thought is that despite the fact we just had sex a few hours ago, Nick must be pretty darn horny to come up with a whopper like that just to get laid. But as he's gazing into my eyes I can tell he really means this and this is what pushes me over the edge.

Nick could not have said anything else that would have convinced me to take a chance like this. His words are like a balm to my still-wounded female pride. How is it that I can't get Amy's ugly friend remark out of my head? I don't think any guy has ever made me feel so wanted, so desirable. I tighten my legs around his waist and Nick makes me forget everything except the two of us.

chapter fifteen

· · · · ·

For the first time in three years I don't bring in the Krispy Kremes.

"What happened?" Lisa wails.

"Sorry, I forgot."

"Forgot?" says Richard. *"What are you, pregnant?"*

In reality, Richard did not say that last part. What he really said was: "Forgot? How could you forget?" I'd like to remind Richard that he has conveniently *forgotten* how I saved his life last week by bringing him chicken soup and cold medicine. The ingrate.

Jackie eyes me like a wolf seeing her first lamb of the spring. I definitely think she's back on diet pills. She told me last week she wants to look "smashing" in her bathing suit for her house-warming party, which is also a pool party.

Great. Me and my extra-two-pound butt can't wait for that.

The truth is I forgot to buy the donuts because I have a lot on my mind. Namely what I am now calling "The Otis Lake Incident."

This is the text message I got this morning from Nick:

I know you're still worried about Friday night. STOP IT.

Saturday morning before I left Catfish Cove (or rather, *snuck* out of Catfish Cove so that my moms wouldn't know I was in town) Nick and I had a long talk. I told him we could absolutely positively never ever have sex again without a condom until I'm safely on the pill, and he agreed. I stayed up last night searching the Internet for articles on fertility, starting with a Google search for, "What are the chances of getting pregnant if you don't use a condom." Boy. What a mistake that was. It led to all sorts of articles about STDs, which led to more articles about other stuff I don't even want to think about.

I know all this worrying is probably for nothing, but I cannot help myself. I've been this way ever since the first time I had sex.

Let me tell you about that.

I was twenty-one years old and the oldest virgin left on the U of F campus (no lie). Alex and I had been dating for six months and I was crazy about him. He was a math geek. I was into stuff like poetry and literature, but despite the fact we didn't speak each other's "language," we totally got each other. He could quote old movies and wasn't into the party scene. He also wore his hair kind of long at a time when shaggy hair wasn't in and I loved that about him.

Before our "big" night, I got on the pill for a two-month cycle, even though I was supposedly safe after just one month (because you never know). I also used a diaphragm (terribly messy and uncomfortable), plus I made Alex wear a condom. He was a virgin too and the whole thing from start to finish took less time than it took for me to get my diaphragm in correctly. Eventually I relaxed enough to not put in the diaphragm. But I always made him wear the condom because the double protection made me feel better (plus we discovered that it made Alex last longer and that was an added bonus).

I looked up Alex the other day on Facebook and requested to be his friend. He's married and lives on Sanibel Island, where he retired last year after making it big in the stock market (who makes it big in the stock market nowadays?). Anyway, I'm really happy for him. I really hope he doesn't have to wear a condom anymore.

My cell phone pings. I have another text from Nick.

Babe, everything is going to work out the way it's supposed to.

The way it's supposed to?

What does that mean?

Nick is always so confident. Why couldn't he have said something more reassuring, like:

Relax. There's not a snowball's chance in hell that you could have gotten pregnant from one time. Trust me on this. I am a cop and we know these things.

Or:

Emma, I probably should have told you this when we started dating, but the doctors have told me my sperm count is nonexistent.

Not that I want that for Nick, but I need strong, confident, nothing-is-going-to-happen Nick. Not wishy-washy-Hare-Krishna-tambourine-thumping Nick.

It's like he's almost *hoping* something will happen. Is it any wonder that donuts are the last thing on my mind?

Everyone is still grumbling about the lack of donuts when Ben walks in. I haven't seen him since Wednesday, before he left for Vegas. He's gotten a haircut. He's also wearing a suit again.

"Let's get down to the nitty-gritty. How was the bachelor party?" asks Richard.

I really hope this is not man code for *did you get laid?*

Not surprisingly, Ben is mum on the Vegas specifics, but after some more grilling from Richard we all discover that he won a thousand bucks playing blackjack.

"No way," says Richard. "How did you do it?"

Ben says that it's more skill than luck and tries to explain his method to Richard, which sounds a little complicated but at the same time logical. After a couple of minutes of repeating the same thing over and over and Richard asking him to repeat it yet again, Ben gives up and starts the meeting. He does not bring up the missing donuts and for this I am grateful.

The meeting breaks up and Ben asks to speak to me. "I'm driving over to Dunhill headquarters this morning to see T.K. Want to come along?"

"*Me?*"

"Yeah, you. Unless there's another Emma Frazier who works for *Florida!* magazine."

I've told you before that Dunhill Publications owns *Florida!* but this hasn't always been the case. The first issues of *Florida!* were printed by a small independent publisher based out of Ybor City. It wasn't until fifteen years ago that Dunhill Publications swooped in and bought the magazine because it was financially successful. Slowly, over the years all production has moved to the Orlando office, but we've kept our editorial presence close to the heart of the magazine's birthplace. I've only been to Dunhill Publications headquarters a few times in the six years I've worked for the company. I wish I'd worn something a little dressier to work this morning.

"Don't worry, you look fine," says Ben.

This is so irritating.

"Am I really that easy to read?"

"Yes . . . and no."

I'm not sure what he means by this but I have no time to figure it out. Jackie and Richard are green with envy when they discover I'm going to Orlando with Ben.

"Why didn't he ask me?" Richard says, stuffing a donut into his mouth. Immediately after the meeting broke up, Richard dashed out the door and returned thirty minutes later with a dozen Krispy Kremes. I guess this is his way of telling me that I can easily be replaced as the office donut pusher.

Jackie eyes the donuts with a fierceness that borders on the scary. "Well la-di-da," she says to me. "Make sure you order the most expensive thing on the menu." At the look on my face, she clarifies: "I'm sure T.K. will take you to lunch at the Citrus Club."

How Jackie knows this, I'm not sure. I've never set foot in the Citrus Club, but I've always wanted to eat there.

I have to admit, at first the idea of visiting Dunhill headquarters with Ben seemed like a great way to spend a Monday (especially this Monday, when all I can think about is the Otis Lake Incident), but now I'm a little nervous. T.K. is nice enough but he can also be intimidating.

"Don't look so worried," Ben says. He pulls out of the office parking lot and merges his Prius onto northbound 275 traffic without looking in his rearview mirror.

I tighten my seat belt. "Just get us there in one piece, okay?"

He's wearing his aviator sunglasses and I can see myself reflected in them when he turns to look at me. "What happened this morning? With the Krispy Kremes?"

"I was running late," I lie. "So how was Vegas?"

"Vegas was good."

"I thought Richard was going to bust a vessel trying to figure out your blackjack system."

Ben grins.

"I saw Amy at Captain Pete's Friday night." Why I say this I have no idea.

Ben loses his grin. "I've been meaning to talk to you about that. She's a nice girl and all, but that's not going to work out."

I still. "What do you mean?"

"I know she's your friend and you probably thought we had a lot in common . . ." Ben shrugs. "Sorry."

I'm momentarily speechless.

"Did . . . did you think I was trying to set you up with *Amy*?"

"Weren't you?"

He's looking straight at me now. And still driving way too fast for comfort.

"Eyes on the road, please! Does everyone drive this crazy in Massachusetts?"

"Yes," Ben says, like he's talking to a little old lady he's trying to placate, but I notice he slows down. "So you weren't trying to fix me up with her?"

"Not really."

"Oh. Well, in that case, no harm no foul."

I know Ben is my boss and there is a professional boundary I shouldn't cross. I know the question is indelicate. Tacky even. But I *have* to know. *Did you sleep with her?*

But I can't ask it, so instead I say, "What about that kiss?"

"What kiss?"

"I'm pretty sure I saw you kiss Amy at Captain Pete's. Not that I was spying on you or anything."

Ben seems initially confused and then a light of recognition crosses his face. "Oh, that."

Yeah, that.

"We were playing darts and she was so drunk she couldn't

even hit the dartboard, let alone stand up. You looked like you were a having a good time, so I offered to drive her home but she refused to walk out the door until I kissed her. So I did. Then I took her home, where she promptly passed out, but not before chucking up a few times in the toilet."

My jaw drops.

"I made sure she was okay before I left and the next day she called to thank me and insisted on repaying me with dinner. Her treat. So I think, 'Hey, why not?' She's a cute girl. Maybe she was just having an off night, and if Frazier thinks we'll hit it off, maybe we will. But the truth is, she's more obnoxious sober than she is drunk. So end of story."

Ben and Amy did not sleep together.

Ben thinks Amy is obnoxious.

It takes every ounce of willpower I have not to scream *"yes!"*

I wasted a perfectly good bottle of Absolut, not to mention an entire week of my life wallowing in abject misery.

Then I come back down to earth.

If Ben thought I was trying to fix him up with Amy, then he must never have thought my friends were trying to fix him up with *me*.

The whole time at Captain Pete's when I thought we were hitting it off, Ben was just being his normal, friendly self. He sees me as someone who works for him and a potential friend.

I suppose I should be happy with that.

Correction. I *am* happy with that.

I'm with Nick now. And Nick is terrific. I have every expectation that our relationship will continue to blossom and that I'll fall in love with him. Deeply, madly, passionately in love. Heck, even now I could be pregnant with Nick's baby.

Oh God. I didn't just think that.

I send up a prayer like Mama J taught me. *Please, God, don't let me be pregnant with Nick's baby. Not that I might not want that eventually, sometime down the road. Way way way down the road. Just not now.*

"What's wrong?" Ben asks. "You look like you're about to be sick."

"No, I'm great," I say, smiling big to convince him.

We arrive at Dunhill Publications and Ben starts to act weird on me. Not weird in a bad way, but weird in a goofy way, and this makes me both suspicious and nervous. It's like the moment before you enter a room and you realize on the other side of the door are fifty of your best friends ready to scream "Surprise!" Only it's not my birthday.

T.K. rushes to greet us and this is when the weird feeling turns into a feeling that I can't describe except to say that at this moment I wish the only complication in my life was that I *was* pregnant with Nick's baby.

"Here's the girl of the hour!" T.K. gushes.

Before I can ask what this is about, he leads me into a conference room. The entire sales team is present, and when they see me walk through the door, they all stand and give me a round of applause. I smile at the reception, but I'm sure it's the same kind of smile the duck gives right before the hunters commence firing. Only the bullets are questions and the sales team starts shooting them off mercilessly.

"How's the article going?"

"Is Monroe as tall as he seems on TV?"

"Did he spill all his dirty secrets to you?"

T.K. laughs and tells them all to calm down. Everyone will

have a chance to read the article in due time. I am then shown a "pre-mock-up" of what is now being called "Zero to Hero, the Trip Monroe" issue. Ad space will go for double and some slots triple what they normally sell for.

A woman stands in the doorway and motions to T.K. He rises from his chair and goes over to speak to her in private. She glances at Ben and smiles.

Ben leans over to whisper, "That's Abby, T.K.'s assistant. Very competent. T.K. can't do anything without her." Ben has mentioned Abby a few times before. For some reason I pictured her as an attractive but older Moneypenny kind of character. Abby is attractive all right, but she's probably only about twenty-five.

I continue to stare at the "pre-mock-up" issue. After a few minutes alone with T.K., Abby enters the room, picks up a remote control, and turns on a flat-screen TV. T.K.'s eyes bulge with excitement. Two talk-show hosts from ESPN appear on the screen. They are doing that sort of loud guy sports chitchat in which one guy constantly interrupts the other one (think of it as the male version of *The View*). Apparently, something big has occurred in the world of sports and these two guys are excited about it and they want to get the audience excited about it too. A still photo of Trip flashes across the screen. My breath catches.

This is when we learn that a spokesperson for Trip Monroe has just announced that Trip will be pulling out of all his races this season due to "personal circumstances."

The entire conference room at Dunhill Publications goes silent.

Back on-screen, the guy in the red tie turns to the other guy and says, "What does this mean for NASCAR?"

"Well, Mike, I think this means there's an open field right now."

"Do we know anything more about these personal circumstances?" Red Tie guy asks.

"Nothing. His people are completely mum on the whole thing."

The two of them go on to talk some more, except I can't hear what they are saying because the conference room has erupted in chaos. The sales team is ecstatic. Trip Monroe is now the story of the hour.

T.K. says something about how it's too late to make the August issue but maybe we should dump the manatee story and replace it with the Trip Monroe article.

"But isn't our September issue always focused on marine life?" someone asks.

"Screw the marine life, we can sell ad space for four times its normal value!"

Everyone starts to congratulate me all over again. After a little speech of encouragement from T.K. urging the sales team to "divide and conquer," T.K. takes us to lunch at the Citrus Club. Abby joins us (which I think is kind of odd) but apparently T.K. really can't do anything without her, including order his own food.

I ignore Jackie's advice and order the cheapest thing on the menu, because I have absolutely no appetite whatsoever. Despite my inability to focus on anything other than the Trip Monroe interview, I can't help but pick up the not-so-discreet looks that Abby gives Ben, who seems not to notice.

He does, however, notice how quiet I am on the drive back to Tampa. "Everything okay?"

"They aren't serious about pulling my manatee article? I worked really hard on that piece."

"Nah," Ben says. "That was just the excitement of the moment."

I don't say anything.

"Relax, Frazier, no one's going to mess with the sacred 'Life Beneath the Water' issue. But I have to admit, I had no idea how popular this NASCAR guy was until I did some research on him. And now that he's dropped out for the season? We couldn't have timed this interview any better."

"Yeah . . . fantastic."

Ben gives me a hard stare. "You're sure you're going to connect with this guy?"

"Of course I'm sure," I say, trying to sound deeply offended that he would ever doubt me.

Ben relaxes and starts to talk about which photographer we should use for the piece and all I can do is nod like some dazed marionette. It's not that I haven't worked under pressure before, but this Trip Monroe thing has clearly become the biggest story of my career. I cannot blow it. I also cannot wait for the next few weeks to be over with.

chapter sixteen

· · · · ·

It's been exactly two weeks since the Otis Lake Incident and I am now officially "late." I should have had my period yesterday. Last night I dreamed I had Nick's baby. Dark curls, chubby cheeks, and the brightest brown eyes you could imagine. In my dream, Nick was changing the baby's diaper and I was in the kitchen (not the kitchen in Nick's house but in some random kitchen I've never been in before). What that means, I'm not sure, but there is probably some Freudian theme there.

The idea of Nick and me ending up together is something I've been thinking about a lot lately. Last weekend Nick drove down to Tampa for the Fourth of July holiday. We spent three whole days fused at the hip. We went to the beach, grilled steaks on my tiny patio, had drinks with Torie and Kimberly and Jason and Kurt (talk about awkward), shopped for some artwork for Nick's house, and spent the rest of the time in bed. There was one day when I was almost certain Nick was going to drop the L-word but he didn't. I think he's getting pretty close to it, though. A part of me thinks it's too soon, but on the other hand, we're not kids anymore.

Would I be happy being a small-town cop's wife? I never

thought I might one day end up back in Catfish Cove, but there is always that possibility. I can see it now. Nick and me fixing up the house by the lake, painting the walls in the bedroom downstairs a bright and sunny yellow for our baby with the chubby cheeks. Me, working at Mama J's bookstore and writing the great American novel while Nick helps to keep Catfish Cove safe from crime.

The idea of it both excites and terrifies me.

I crawl out of bed and try to put my inconveniently late period out of my head in order to face myself in the mirror. Today is the big day.

I have to admit I'm a little nervous seeing Trip again after all these years. It's like going to your high school reunion, but you're only facing one person and that one person has become ultrafamous and desired by women everywhere.

I *have* to look good today.

The cocktail party begins promptly at five. Kimberly is going to pick me up at the office at four so we can ride to the hotel together, which I think will help calm my nerves. I wear something easy to get out of and bring both cocktail dresses to change into later. I've pretty much decided to wear the sleeveless lime-green-and-white print dress with the gathered skirt. It's the one I like best and I think I look pretty decent in it. But I bring the black-and-white polka-dot one along too, for backup. Nick liked it best and I can't help wondering if I'm overlooking something here.

I spend my lunch hour at the Estée Lauder counter at the Nordstrom in the International Mall, where I'd already arranged for one of the consultants to do my makeup. I tell her I'm going for casual chic (not to be confused with the decorating term *shabby chic*). I take off my glasses and pop in my contact lenses.

The consultant spends what seems like forever applying at least a couple dozen products on my face. Surprisingly, the end result looks very natural, except that my eyes look huge, my skin looks flawless, and my lips look like I've just had collagen injections. I buy everything she's used on me and force myself not to look at the total on the credit-card slip.

At 3:45 p.m. I go the bathroom and change. Everyone at work is excited for me and for what this interview could mean for the magazine. I decide to go with the lime-green dress.

"Love it!" says Jackie.

"Wow!" says Lisa.

"You look very nice," says Ben, in the same tone he'd probably use to compliment a younger sister.

"Yeah, you look . . . nice," says Richard, in the same tone he'd probably use to compliment a streetwalker.

Kimberly arrives fifteen minutes later. "Awesome!"

Just in case, I bring out the black-and-white polka-dot dress to get a second opinion, but no one likes it. I guess Nick just has different taste.

Now that everyone is done fussing over me, we all turn our attention to Kimberly, who is absolutely rocking it today with an ultrasleek white linen shift. Not many women can get away with wearing solid white, but Kimberly is one of them. She's also wearing red stilettos and the combination is deadly.

Jackie immediately wants to know where she can get the same dress, and Kimberly generously tells her. She slips off her red stilettos so that Lisa can try them on, and offers to loan them to her anytime. Richard then makes a crack about also wanting to borrow the red stilettos and you'd think it was the funniest thing ever, Kimberly laughs so hard. Ben is all friendly smiles but Kimberly is coolly aloof with him.

I've been so worried about the pregnancy thing that I forgot to tell Kimberly that we don't hate Ben anymore. I also haven't told Torie or Kimberly about the Otis Lake Incident. Right now the two of them are on a need-to-know basis (and they don't need to know how stupid I was having sex without a condom).

Once we get in the car, I fill her in on the Amy and Ben story.

"So he didn't sleep with her?" Kimberly asks as we cross the bridge over to St. Pete.

"Nope. He drove her home, where she threw up." (I can't help but smile here). "They went out to dinner, there was no chemistry, end of story."

Kimberly mulls this over a bit. "So what are you going to do?"

"What do you mean, what am I going to do?"

"*Emma,*" Kimberly says, "how do you feel about the fact that Ben is still available?"

"I feel absolutely nothing. I'm with Nick now and I'm really happy. I'm totally over Ben Gallagher."

This seems to convince Kimberly because we don't talk about either Ben or Nick the rest of the drive and I'm glad. I need to focus on Trip and getting this interview.

The cocktail party is being held at the Don Cesar, a hotel resort located on the beach. I've never been inside but I've always wanted to. It was built in the 1920s and resembles a pink castle. No kidding. Very cool. Kimberly opts for the valet parking, which is great because it's grossly humid today and arriving all hot and sweaty to the cocktail party is not in my visual game plan.

Today's event is being hosted by a local woman's civic group both to raise money for children's cancer research and to honor the celebrities who have already donated lots of bucks to the cause. Besides Trip, this includes another NASCAR driver whom

I've never heard of, a couple of big-time golf pros, a tennis star, and some Tampa Bay Rays baseball players.

Kimberly and I enter the hotel lobby and make our way to the banquet room, where a guy wearing a tux asks to see our invitations. We show him our invites and he asks us if we have cameras. Both of us say no. He tells us that if we are "caught" taking pictures of the celebrities with our cell phones, we will immediately be escorted off the premises. I've never been to a thousand-dollar-a-ticket cocktail party, so I'm not sure if this is usual or not.

The banquet room is elegant with chandeliers and wooden floors and lots of beautiful people milling about. Over 50 percent of the women are wearing some variation of black. The rest have on a rainbow of summer colors but only Kimberly is wearing solid white and she stands out in the very best way, and this is awesome for me. Simply because I am with Kimberly I already have a drink in my hand, thanks to the lovely waiter who practically tripped over himself to serve us first (although no one around us had a drink). Wherever we go people step aside to let us through and most stop to make small talk. Even though I'm used to this from the many times I've been out with Kimberly, it still amazes me how much a pretty face and a fabulous figure can do for a woman.

I glance around the room, hoping to see some sign of Trip. I don't see any of the celebrities and I imagine that's because they will probably make some kind of grand entrance. Kimberly introduces me to the other two members of the Yeager Agency who are present this evening. They are both male, in their midthirties, and work in advertising. They also seem to know all about the Trip Monroe angle. Apparently, everyone at the agency is salivating at the prospect of nabbing him as a client.

I finish my drink and a waiter immediately appears to ask if

I'd like a refill, which I'd love, but I politely decline. I need to stay sharp tonight. Plus, there is that tiny percent chance that I could be pregnant and I don't want to have to get angsty over all the stuff I'll probably find on the Internet if I Google "what kind of harm can I do to my fetus if I drink in the first trimester."

I head to the hors d'oeuvre table when a sudden increase in the noise level makes me turn to stare at a young woman who has just made an appearance. She looks like she's fifteen and in no way old enough for this cocktail party.

"That's Bonita Harris," Kimberly whispers. "She's the number-three-seeded woman's tennis player in the world."

I'd heard of Bonita Harris and I've seen pictures of her but she looks different in a cocktail dress and heels. It's been fourteen years since I've laid eyes on Trip. I wonder if I'll have trouble recognizing him.

Within the next hour a few more celebrities join the party and a man goes up to a mike to welcome us all to the Don Cesar. On behalf of the resort, he sincerely hopes that we are all having a great time and if we desire "anything" we are to flag down one of the many waitstaff who are eager to serve us. He then introduces a woman named Esther Finnegan, who is the chairwoman for the group hosting the party. She singles out each of the celebs by name, giving a brief bio and heartfelt thanks for their charitable contributions. Everyone claps and cheers loudly.

I wait for her to introduce Trip but she doesn't. She goes into a spiel about children's cancer research, and while it's all very noble and heartwarming, I have trouble concentrating. Where is Trip? What if he canceled on the party? All my planning and scheming will have been for naught.

Just when I think Esther is done with her speech, she says, "And last but not least, I'd like to take this opportunity to thank one of our most generous supporters, NASCAR superstar Trip Monroe!"

The cheers are louder for Trip than for any of the other celebrities. I crane my neck to try to get a glimpse of him. Everyone else in the crowd does too.

"Unfortunately, Trip could not be here tonight. It seems he's come down with a little stomach bug—" Esther gives the Don Cesar guy a wide-eyed apologetic look before saying, "Of course, not from anything he's eaten here at this wonderful resort!" The crowd laughs politely. "I know you'll join me in a round of applause for his generous contributions."

The crowd claps again and everyone returns to their previous conversations. I don't know if I'm more stunned, disappointed, or worried. It never occurred to me that Trip would be a no-show.

I think about all the advertising space T.K. hopes to sell in the "Trip Monroe" issue and try not to panic. Is this unexpected illness of Trip's related to his dropping out of the racing circuit? What if Trip is *really* sick? Maybe he's contracted some horrible disease and doesn't want the public to know. Maybe that's the reason Frank Monroe was so abrupt with me in his phone message.

The rest of the cocktail party goes by in a blur. The other two members of the Yeager Agency ignore Kimberly and me and I find this strange, so I ask Kimberly what's up. She shrugs and says "nothing," only I can see something is bothering her.

After the party Kimberly grabs my hand and leads me straight to the hotel lounge, where she orders us shots from the tequila bar. "Here's to our jobs," she says, and downs her tequila.

"You might want to slow down. You're driving, remember?"

"How much do you think it would cost to take a cab back to Tampa?"

"Cheaper than getting a room here for the night, that's for

sure." We both cringe because neither of us wants to think about how much a room at the Don Cesar might cost.

"Then you drive," she says, handing me her keys. "I've noticed you haven't been drinking." Kimberly flags down a waitress and orders another tequila. I slide my untouched drink her way. I think she needs it more than I do. I've never seen Kimberly so morose.

"I'm not giving up on Trip Monroe," I say. "This is just a setback."

"What if you can't reach him? What if you do, but he shoots you down?"

"That's not going to happen." *At least I hope that's not going to happen.*

"How do you do that?"

"Do what?"

"Be so sure of yourself. I wish I had one-tenth of your confidence."

"You're kidding, right? Because I'm pretty sure you were there that night at Captain Pete's when Amy outed me as the ugly friend."

"I can't believe you're still harping on that. You have everything. A great job, friends, a fantastic boyfriend who's crazy about you."

This is how Kimberly sees me? As someone who has *everything*?

"You have those things too," I say. "Maybe not the fantastic boyfriend, but you *could* have one. All you have to do is snap your fingers and a dozen guys run to your side."

Kimberly makes a face. "There are two kinds of guys who are interested in me. The ones who want to take me out because they think it makes them look good and the ones who want to say they've dated Jake Lemoyne's ex. How do you think I got my job at the Yeager Agency? It wasn't because my PR skills are so damn fucktastic, it's because of who I know because I was married to Jake."

"That's called networking. Lots of people get jobs that way."

"You don't get it, do you? Emma, I'm an office *joke*. Nothing I do is good enough. Half the place thinks I'm sleeping with Murray and the other half thinks I'm still sleeping with Jake."

This takes me aback. Kimberly is smart, hardworking. The fact that she's beautiful should be a boon. But according to her, it *isn't*?

"Please tell me you're not sleeping with Murray," I say, trying to make her laugh. Not that Murray is horribly unattractive or anything but he's losing his hair, and instead of just going with it or shaving his head like most guys do now, he's taken to doing a comb-over à la Donald Trump, which is just plain unacceptable.

Kimberly's face breaks into a sloppy grin. "Hell no; not that he hasn't tried."

I play around with the edge of my napkin. Remember I told you before that Kimberly is a really private person? After graduating first in her class at Catfish Cove High, she went to Florida State, where she majored in communications. Her first job was as an events planner at one of those ritzy golf and tennis resorts. This is where she met Jake. Their marriage lasted less than two years and Kimberly got a decent settlement, but she's not rich (she had to sign a prenup). Shortly after her divorce, she went to work for the Yeager Agency, a move that brought her to Tampa, and this is when we reconnected. She's never told either Torie or me much about her marriage, and I've gotten the feeling it's because it's still too painful for her to talk about. Kimberly rarely dates and it's just occurred to me that maybe this is because she's still holding on to feelings for Jake.

"You aren't still sleeping with Jake . . . are you?"

Kimberly shudders. "I barely slept with him when we were married."

"*What?*"

"The truth is we spent more time in counseling than we did in bed." Kimberly takes another shot of tequila and continues: "Jake didn't want a wife. Well, he did, but he didn't want the kind of wife I wanted to be. He didn't want kids or to make a real home. He was embarrassed by the way I talked and the way I used to dress. Did you know right after we got married Jake sent me to a stylist? I was dazed by his looks and his money and everything that came with it. We both jumped into marriage way too soon."

Kimberly might look sophisticated, but on the inside she's still a Catfish Cove girl. Once, Torie and I discussed Kimberly's marriage and we concluded that her divorce was probably the result of her and Jake being from such different backgrounds. Now that I know our theory was right, I can't help but feel sad for her.

Kimberly burps, then lets out a tiny giggle. This is the first sign that she's getting drunk. Maybe I should let her keep drinking. She's always so calm and in control. It might be good for her to tide one over and let everything out. I already have the keys to her car and I've only had the one drink during the cocktail party, which was so watered down I could barely taste the liquor, so I can easily drive us home.

I reach out and squeeze her hand. "Kimmy, I'm so sorry."

She smiles at the old nickname. "I was really hoping to score Trip Monroe as a client. He was someone I could bring to the agency without being connected to Jake. Now I'm going to have to explain how I basically wasted two thousand dollars on nothing." I try not to show any reaction to this, but as usual, I obviously can't hide my feelings because Kimberly immediately says, "I didn't mean that the way it sounded. It's not your fault Trip didn't show. I took a gamble and lost. Totally my screwup."

I feel horrible for involving Kimberly in this Trip Monroe deal. I used our friendship to score a ticket for this event and it never once occurred to me that she could end up with egg on her face. I *have* to make this up to her.

The waitress comes by and asks if we want a refill. Kimberly is in the process of ordering when out of the corner of my eye, I spy a man who looks familiar. The lobby is crowded and I have to stand and crane my neck to get a better view, but I'm right. He *is* familiar. It's Frank Monroe.

chapter seventeen

.....

"That's Trip's uncle!" I say, pointing to Frank.

Kimberly snaps to attention. "Where?"

"The tall guy with the glasses."

"Are you sure?"

"Positive."

Something Esther Finnegan said in her speech comes back to me. She said Trip did not get sick eating the food at the Don Cesar. I know it was a joke, but it's also telling. Could Trip be staying here at the resort? It would make sense that if he was coming for the cocktail party, he would book a room. More than likely all the celebrities have a complimentary room for the night. My heart begins to race. Trip Monroe is right here under my nose, puking into an expensive toilet, and I'm *not* leaving the Don Cesar until I talk to him. I toss some money down and pull Kimberly from the table.

"What are you doing?" she protests as I lead her toward the lobby. "I'm not finished with my tequila."

"I think Trip is staying here at the hotel. And if he is, Frank Monroe is going to lead us right to him."

"Oh. Good idea." Kimberly flattens an imaginary wrinkle out of her dress. "Okay, so what do we do now?"

"We're going to follow him."

Kimberly frowns. "Why don't we just go up and ask him where Trip is?"

"Because Frank Monroe has a thing against reporters. If he wouldn't help me connect with Trip before, he sure as hell isn't going to do it now with Trip lying up there sick. I don't think he knows me by sight, but we can't take any chances, so you'll have to do it."

"*Me?*"

"You have as much to gain from this as I do."

Kimberly ponders this for a quick second and nods. "Okay. Wait right here."

"Stay close by, but don't let him see you," I whisper, but I'm not sure if she hears me because she's already taken off.

I watch Kimberly weave her way through the throng of people toward the check-in desk, where Frank Monroe is having a conversation with a hotel clerk. Kimberly is usually a pro in her four-inch heels, but even across the lobby I can see she is wobbling. Two shots of tequila in a row are catching up to the drinks she downed during the cocktail party. She stands very close behind Frank Monroe, then turns around and searches the crowd until she spots me. She places her hands in the air and makes a great big crisscross waving motion as if to say, *Here I am!*

I guess she thinks I need a signal or something.

Kimberly is drunk. Or at the least, very tipsy. Thank God Frank Monroe can't see what she's doing because she's attracting a whole lot of attention. Partially because she is doing this strange waving thing, and partially because, well, she's Kimberly and she's gorgeous and she's always going to draw attention. I should have thought of that before I sent her out on this covert operation. She is totally going to blow it before it even gets started.

Frank turns around and luckily Kimberly has enough presence of mind to drop her arms and act inconspicuous. He walks over to the elevators and Kimberly follows him into the car as if she knows exactly where she's going, and the elevator doors close. There is nothing I can do now except wait and hope she doesn't do something crazy.

After what seems like forever, but in reality is less than five minutes, Kimberly emerges from the elevator. Her cheeks are flushed and her blue eyes are shining with either excitement or drunken glee, or both.

"I feel like Harriet the Spy!"

"Did Frank Monroe see you follow him?"

"No way. Didn't you see how crafty I was?"

"Yeah. Good job. So what did you find out?"

She tells me she got off at Frank Monroe's floor and "discreetly" watched him go into a room. She gives me the room number, and I have to say, I'm really pleased at how well Kimberly has done considering how drunk she seems. "You're sure you have the right room number?"

She frowns at me. "I'm not a dummy, Emma."

"Of course you're not," I say, humoring her.

We go back to the lobby bar and start to strategize. If I go up to the room now and Frank Monroe answers the door, chances are he'll shut it in my face. I could always call the room number and ask to speak to Trip, but he's probably in bed, and chances are again that Frank will answer the phone. I really don't want to bother Trip while he's sick. I just want to leave my card with him and ask him to get in touch with me when he feels better. Maybe I could slide my card under the door. Or better yet, leave it in an envelope marked *Confidential for Trip Monroe only*.

Which sounds very amateurish even to Kimberly, whose mind is not working 100 percent right now, so I guess that option is out.

I'm at the end of my ideas when I see Frank Monroe again. This time he's walking away from the elevator to the hotel entrance. His hands are jammed inside his pants pockets and he looks angry. Maybe this is his normal, everyday expression. Maybe he's going out to get Trip medicine, I don't know. Everyone is always telling me what a nice guy he is, but I've yet to see any evidence of it. The only thing I know is that this is my chance to get to Trip and I'm going to take it.

"Wish me luck," I say to Kimberly.

"Do you want me to go with you?"

"Thanks, but I'm going to make this quick." Pause. "Are you sure you're going to be okay down here all by yourself?"

"Of course I am. Shoo!" she says, waving me off. "Good luck!"

"Thanks. And Harriet? No more tequila, okay?"

I'm standing outside Trip's door trying my hardest to slow my heart down. Its beating so loudly I can't hear myself think. I also have to use the bathroom and this is a fine time for my bladder to make itself known. I could go back downstairs and use the bathroom in the lobby, but I'm afraid if I leave now, Uncle Frank might come back and I don't want that happening.

I knock on the door and immediately come face-to-face with a middle-aged guy who is definitely not Trip. "Yeah?"

My spirits take a nosedive. Kimberly must have gotten the room number wrong.

The guy takes in my appearance and frowns, but then he

opens the door all the way and ushers me inside. "You here to see Trip?"

Well, that was easy. This guy must be part of Trip's entourage. As difficult as it's been to connect with Trip, I guess I expected more of a challenge. I raise my chin in confidence. "Yes, as a matter of fact, I am. I'm an old friend of his."

I've been in some nice hotel rooms before but nothing like this. The suite looks bigger than my town house and has a killer view of the bay.

"I'm Chuck," says the guy. "Want a drink?" He goes over to what looks like a well-stocked bar and pours himself a glass of liquor.

"Um, no, thanks."

He motions to the sofa in the living area. "Have a seat. I'll get Trip."

I sit on the sofa and wait, and this is good because it helps to calm my nerves as I process the situation the way it stands. Trip is sick with some kind of stomach flu but he's obviously not so sick that he can't come out to see a friend who presents herself at his door, which is awful nice of him.

Chuck returns and takes a seat across from me. He stares at me for a few long seconds. "You're not what we expected," he says.

"Um, what were you expecting?"

He shrugs. "You know, the usual."

I'm about to ask the *usual what,* but something tells me to keep my mouth shut. I fumble through my purse and pull out my business card. "Do you have a pen?" In case Trip is too sick to remember details, I want to jot some information on the back of my card.

"What's that?" Chuck asks, pointing to the card in my hand.

"My business card."

Chuck laughs rudely. Which is odd. Why would he find me having a business card funny?

I can hold my bladder no longer. "Can I use the restroom?"

Chuck takes a sip of his drink and watches me the way a lioness would eye a wounded zebra. "Down the hallway," he says.

Does he know I'm a reporter after a story? He seemed friendly enough at first, but from the way he's acting now, I conclude that he must know, and he obviously does not have a high opinion of those in my profession. He's probably sorry he let me in the door. I should be ready to be kicked out on my keester any second now.

I slip inside the bathroom. I can barely pee I'm so nervous. I'm washing my hands when I hear the door open and close. I whip around to find Trip just a couple of feet away. If I hadn't seen recent pictures of him, I would never have recognized him as the boy I went to high school with. He looks exactly like he does in his pictures from all the magazines—tall and tanned with his blond hair cropped short. He's the epitome of the all-American boy, except his blue eyes are slightly bloodshot and it looks like he hasn't shaved in at least three days. He's also not wearing anything except a pair of faded jeans. I can't wait to tell Richard that Trip's six-pack abs are not a product of trick photography. For some reason I can't look Trip in the eye (or anywhere else), so I stare down at his big bare feet.

"Oh, hi!" I say. "I guess I didn't lock the door? Listen, Trip, I'm so sorry to come barging in here. I can see that you're not feeling well and—"

"I thought Frank said you were a blonde." My gaze shoots up to meet his eyes. He shrugs. "No matter."

A blonde? At the mention of Frank's name my mouth goes

dry. Why would Uncle Frank tell Trip that I'm a blonde? Then it occurs to me that maybe he noticed Kimberly following him. But why would he remark on it to Trip? Unless maybe he thought Kimberly was a groupie? None of this is making much sense at the moment.

"Trip, don't you remember me? I'm Emma Frazier."

"Of course I remember you."

Relief! I sag against the counter behind me. "You have no idea how hard it is to get ahold of you, you big celebrity you," I tease.

Trip grins.

"I know this is a terrible time, what with you being sick and all, but I was hoping we could talk."

"Talk? Sure, you can talk . . . I actually kind of like that."

I notice Trip is slurring his words. It's probably from the medication he's on. I really hope this is just a tiny cold or a flu and that Trip is not seriously ill.

"Are you okay? Do you need to lie down?"

"Nah. We can do this standing up."

"Here? In your bathroom? Wouldn't you prefer the living room couch?"

He comes in close and this is when I smell the alcohol on his breath.

"With Chuck lookin' on?" Trip chuckles. "I'm not really into being watched. I just like the dirty talk."

Dirty talk?

He's looking down at me with glazed eyes. Trip is not sick. He's skunk-ass drunk!

"Look, I guess this isn't the best time. Maybe I can leave my card and you can call me?"

Trip looks momentarily confused.

"Trip Monroe, you really have no idea who I am, do you?"

"You're . . . Emily?"

"I'm Emma Frazier from Catfish Cove. We went to school together. Don't you remember senior year I won the poetry contest? My poem was about my moms and how I was conceived with the help of a sperm donor? You wrote in my yearbook that you liked it."

"You need a sperm donor? Sorry, baby, I don't do that kinda thing."

All these weeks of scheming on how to get an interview. Involving Kimberly and the Yeager Agency. The money I spent on my new dress, the makeup session at the Estée Lauder counter. All of it just to get this one moment with Trip and he's so drunk he can't even remember where he went to high school. I want to scream with frustration. Instead, I take a deep breath.

"All right, obviously you're in no condition to think rationally. I'm just going to leave my card with your friend Chuck and you can call me later. Or I can call you. Whichever you prefer." I try to squeeze past him but he blocks me.

"Ah, c'mon, honey, don't be mad. Stay awhile."

"No, thanks," I say firmly. "Trip, listen up. You're going to move away so I can leave and then you'll call me later. Right?"

He smiles and looks so goofy I almost laugh. "Sure I'll call you again."

I set my palm against his chest and try to shove him out of the way but it's like moving an iron column. He grabs my hand and lays it over his crotch, holding it firmly in place.

My face goes up in flames. "Give me my hand back. *Now*."

"But it feels so good where it is." He places his mouth against my neck and starts laying a series of slobbery kisses on me.

I try to shove him away again but it's useless. He's not listening to me. Trip must be at least six foot three and a good two-hundred-plus pounds of solid muscle. There is no choice. If I want to get away from him, I'm going to have to go for the big guns. I muster up all my strength and knee him in the balls.

He lets out a howl of pain and doubles over. "What the hell! What's wrong with you?" he asks, wild-eyed.

"What's wrong with *me*? What's wrong with *you*? Besides being a drunken asshole, that is!"

"I don't understand. Are we gonna fuck or not?"

"The answer to that is *not*."

Trip looks more confused than ever.

I make a motion to shove him aside. This time he practically jumps out of my way. I open the bathroom door and scurry out as fast as I can, tossing my business card to a stunned-looking Chuck on my way out.

chapter eighteen

· · · · ·

On the drive home I tell Kimberly my story, down to the last dirty detail.

"What are you going to do?" she asks.

"Pray that Trip calls me?"

"So he can what? Apologize? Emma, he thought you were a *prostitute*." Kimberly is almost back to her old self again. Her ability to metabolize alcohol is nothing short of amazing.

I sigh dramatically. "Maybe he would have taken me more seriously if I'd worn the polka-dot dress."

We both laugh, and this lightens our mood a bit.

I've been dissecting what went down with Trip. I wonder who came up with the stomach-flu story. I really don't think Esther Finnegan has a clue. The whole world thinks Trip is this great guy. And maybe he is. But he's got another side to him that he's managed to keep out of the press. I read once that Jackie Kennedy used to smoke cigarettes but the powers that be didn't want it known. Photographers knew that if they published a photo of her with a ciggy to her lips, they'd be blackballed from the White House. I don't think Trip has that kind of power, but I find it hard to believe that something negative hasn't been written about him before. Is he an alcoholic? Or just a party boy who doesn't care about his responsibilities? Either way, it looks like I'm not going to score the interview of a lifetime.

I had hoped to spend the weekend writing up my interview, which, of course, isn't going to happen now. Nick has plans to fish with some buddies in Destin, so driving up to Catfish Cove is moot. I call him and tell him about my run-in with Trip.

"I don't care who he is, I'm going to kick this guy's ass."

"Can you say that again? I'm getting all hot and bothered."

"I'm serious, Emma. You could have been assaulted. Hell, you were!"

"Not really," I say, thinking back over the incident. "Well, almost, maybe. I honestly think he was so drunk he didn't know what he was doing."

"Don't make excuses for him. You should expose this guy for the asshole he is."

Nick isn't suggesting anything I haven't thought of already, but *Florida!* isn't that kind of magazine. Plus, I don't really know what went down in that hotel room. Was it a onetime, isolated incident? A nightly occurrence? Has Trip been tested for every STD under the sun? These are the questions that have me spinning. As a journalist—

"Did you get your period?" Nick asks.

"Um, not yet."

"Shouldn't you do one of those home pregnancy tests? I think you can tell almost right away now."

"Maybe in a few days," I say.

■ ■ ■

Thankfully, Ben has gone to Orlando for some mysterious workshop, so we skip the Monday-morning staff meeting. I really don't think I could have taken all the questions about the Trip Monroe "interview." I know I have to tell Ben what happened but I'm relieved I've gotten a reprieve. Despite the fact there is no meeting I still bring in donuts, because I certainly don't want to cause a riot or anything.

I'm sitting at my cubicle, trying my hardest to act productive. Richard leans over and places his hand on the back of my chair like he does whenever he wants my attention. "So, how'd the cocktail party go? You and Trip hook up?"

I know Richard does not mean "hook up" in the popular sense, but I still find his choice of words ironic. This is also the first time Richard has gone out of his way to talk about the Trip Monroe story to me. It's like he knows the whole thing was a disaster and now he wants to gloat.

"I'd tell you, but then I'd have to kill you."

"Guess I'll just have to read about it with the rest of the schmucks."

"Those schmucks are our loyal readers."

"Yeah, whatever."

Richard goes back to playing with his cell phone. I wish I could escape into something mundane but all I can think about is all the advertising T.K. planned to sell that isn't going to happen now. I am, without doubt, the biggest loser ever. Can I get fired over this?

"Richard," I say impulsively, "what would you do if you didn't work for *Florida!* anymore?"

He immediately stops Twittering. His eyes meet mine and I

suddenly feel like a jerk. It's no secret Richard's dream job would have been playing professional baseball. He covers almost every kind of sports story under the sun, *except* baseball. He only does that when forced. Even though he never talks about it, the Dr. Phil in me thinks it's because it's all too painful for him. Or maybe I'm just giving Richard too much emotional credit.

"Have you ever thought about writing for *Sports Illustrated*?" I ask him.

He shrugs. "Those who can, do. Those who can't, write about it."

"But there must be something you feel passionate about."

Richard studies my face a second. "You seriously want to know?"

I nod.

He places his hand on the back of my chair again and leans in until he's only a couple of inches away from me. Once, a few years ago, I think Richard hugged me at Stuart's New Year's Eve Party. We were both slightly drunk at the time but I'm pretty sure I hugged everyone that night. Other than that, however, I think this is the closest physically I've ever been to him. Even though it's not yet noon, his jaw is shadowed with his five o'clock beard. I catch a whiff of his cologne, which is subtly pleasant. I try to scoot my chair back but he holds it firmly in place with the back of his arm and lowers his voice to a rough whisper. "If I didn't have this gig to go to every day, I'd have time to finish revising my novel."

This is the last thing I expected Richard to say. I'll admit, for a second there . . . well, let's just say Richard is not my type but I understand why Lisa finds him appealing.

"You're writing a novel?"

"Not just a novel, I'm writing *the* novel. The one that's going to make Steve Danger a household name."

Richard's last name is Sutter. "Who's Steve Danger?"

Disappointment flashes through his eyes. But only for a second, because then he grins at me and says, "That's my pen name. You don't think I'd publish my novel under my real name. Do you? I've got a lot of hot sex scenes in there and I've got a professional reputation to worry about."

Although I've known Richard forever, I sometimes have trouble figuring out whether he is pulling my leg and this is one of those times.

"What's the novel about?" I ask cautiously. "It's not . . . erotica, is it?"

"It's about corruption and loneliness and greed and love and betrayal. It's about the American dream and how fighting to achieve that dream takes its toll on your soul."

"Wow."

"Yeah, and it's got horny vampires and werewolves in it too. Think *The Great Gatsby* meets *Twilight*."

"Wow," I say again, even more stunned than before (which I would have thought impossible).

"Want to read it? I have a rockin' first draft but I can always use some professional input."

"Um, sure, okay."

Richard's eyes light up. "Honest?"

"Sure I'll read it."

Richard rolls his chair back to his desk and starts tapping away at his keyboard. A few seconds later his head pops back around the cubicle wall. "I just sent it to you. It's kind of on the long side but I'm really anxious to hear what you think."

"Just how long is it?"

"About a hundred and eighty thousand words. But, I know that needs cutting," he quickly adds.

A hundred and eighty thousand words? How did I get myself into this mess?

"So how'd the interview go?" he asks again. Before I can respond, Richard says, "Let me guess. Trip Monroe spilled all his deepest darkest secrets to you, making you the reporter of the hour. Shit. Forget that, making you the reporter of the year, and you're now writing up the article that's gonna score you even more points with *Ben*."

The way Richard says Ben's name makes me blink. I was right. Richard is jealous of my professional relationship with Ben.

"That's not exactly how it went down," I say.

I wasn't going to tell anyone else what happened at the Don Cesar, but since it's all I can think about, I decide, why not confide in Richard? At the very least, I'll make his day. I roll my chair over to his cubicle and spill my guts to him. I tell him all about how Trip was a no-show at the charity event and how he was drunk in his hotel room and almost accosted me.

"I hope you kicked his ass." Richard sounds angry. I'm both surprised and a little touched at his concern.

"Actually, I kneed him in the balls."

"Good girl. And remind me never to make a pass at you."

"I think we both know it would be a cold day in hell before *that* ever happened."

I expect Richard to make a joke but he doesn't. "So what did your boyfriend the cop say when you told him?"

"He said he wanted to kick Trip's ass, as opposed to, you know, your suggestion that I do it myself."

"Hey, that just shows how much confidence I have in you." Richard places his hand on my shoulder and gives a gentle squeeze. "Listen, don't sweat the interview. You did the best you could. Gallagher and T.K. are just going to have to get over it."

"Thanks." As strange as it sounds, I actually feel better now. If it was anyone else but Richard consoling me, I'd reach out and give him a hug. But this is Richard, and it would be too weird.

"So are you bringing the cop to Jackie's big party?"

"Yep, Nick will be there."

"I look forward to meeting him," he says sincerely.

"Are you bringing anyone?"

"Yeah, I'm just not sure who exactly. I'm kind of dating two girls at the same time, you know?"

No, I don't know, but I'm not surprised.

Richard leans back in his chair and watches me closely as he says, "I hear the boss is bringing an old girlfriend. Someone he was actually engaged to at some point."

"You mean . . . *Ben*? Ben was engaged? When?"

"A couple of years ago when he was working in New York. He and this chick made it two weeks away from walking down the aisle. Then he called it off." Richard frowns. "Or she called it off. Not sure who blew who off. She's here in town for a few weeks."

"How do you know all this?"

"Ben told me the other night when we were at McDintons."

"You and Ben went out?"

"Sure. We go out every once in a while and kick back a few beers, go catch a Rays game, you know, guy stuff." He pauses. "Don't look so shocked. Some people actually enjoy my company."

I flush. I suppose it makes sense that Ben and Richard have socialized outside the office They are both guys, both single, both work at the same place. But I would have never guessed that Ben would confide something as personal as a broken engagement to

Richard. I can't think of two people who are more different than those two men. Ben is an intellectual and Richard is . . . well, he's smart, but earthy. If Richard was born in Catfish Cove, he'd be what the locals call "a good ol' boy."

"So what's she like?" I ask.

"I haven't met her, but she's apparently some hotshot cancer doctor. I think she's here doing research at Moffett. Some big presentation or symposium or something."

Ben was engaged to a research oncologist? I can picture her now. Tall, elegant, sophisticated. No wonder Amy and her Harvard law degree weren't so impressive. It's pretty hard to top someone out there trying to cure cancer.

"That's great. Can't wait to meet her. Do you think they're getting back together?"

"Who knows? Who cares? When do you think you'll get back to me?"

"On what?"

"My manuscript."

"Oh, well, give me a couple of weeks at least."

"Are you really going to read it?"

"Of course I am. I said I would, right?"

My cell phone buzzes. I glance at my screen but I don't recognize the number. "Hello," I say.

"Is this Emma Frazier?" asks a deep male voice that I instantly recognize. My heart begins to pound. I whisk my chair back to the privacy of my cubicle.

"Yes, this is she."

"Miss Frazier, this is Chuck Miller, Trip Monroe's manager. Can we talk?"

chapter nineteen

. . . . .

I meet Chuck for lunch at Jackson's on Harbor Island and we get a table by the water. I'm sweating, but Chuck looks cool as a mint julep. Here is how our conversation went down:

"How did you find me?" I ask.

"Your card, remember? Trip is extremely embarrassed that you witnessed his unfortunate reaction to the cold medication he's taking. It's my fault, really. I should have been monitoring him closer." Chuck gives me a smile that I'm sure has won over many a female.

I, however, am not just any female. I am a serious journalist and Chuck needs to know this right off the top. "Trip was *drunk* and he thought I was a hooker. And so did you. That's why you laughed when I showed you my card."

Chuck feigns a shocked expression. "I called you a hooker?"

"Not exactly."

"Miss Frazier, if I said or did anything that you interpreted as disrespectful, then I apologize. As for Trip, the cough syrup made him temporarily act out of character. You'd think the FDA would regulate the alcohol levels in that stuff better."

The Catfish Cove Community Theatre would probably love

to get their hands on Chuck. Good male leads are hard to come by.

"Let's say I buy all this. Am I getting an interview?"

"Of course you're getting an interview."

I try my hardest to keep a poker face but it's all I can do not to pump my fist in the air in triumph. I'm getting an interview! I'm not going to be fired. Everything is going to be all right, after all.

The waiter brings us our food and Chuck waits till he's gone to speak again. "You're getting an *exclusive* interview. Trip hasn't done one of those in a long time," he says (as if I didn't already know this).

"So, Trip remembers me? From high school?"

"Trip couldn't stop talking about you. Said you were great friends and all."

I can't help but be disappointed by this little white lie. "Uh-huh. I guess that's why he practically accosted me."

Chuck ignores my sarcasm. He pulls out his smart phone and starts scrolling. "Let's say a week from Wednesday? We can do the interview at Trip's beach house in Naples. We'll have a driver pick you up."

"Why not do the interview today?"

"Trip is on his way to California for a little R and R." Chuck reaches into a thin leather satchel and hands me what appears to be a legal document. "You'll have to sign this. Standard operating procedure and all that."

I stare down at the papers in my hand. "I've never signed a contract before an interview."

"I suppose most manatees aren't too fussy about the sort of exposure they're going to get, are they?"

"How do you know about my manatee article? That issue won't be available until the second week of August."

"Miss Frazier, it's my job to look out for Trip's best interests. You don't think we would offer you this opportunity without making sure you were legit, do you?"

"And here I thought you were offering it to me because Trip and I were such great pals in high school."

Chuck does not rise to the bait, but continues to smile at me blandly.

I'm a little creeped out by the fact Chuck had me investigated, but he's right. I've never done this kind of piece before. Maybe this *is* standard operating procedure in the world of big celebrity interviews.

I tuck the document into my tote bag. "I'll have to get my lawyer to read it first."

"Of course," Chuck says.

The rest of the lunch goes by uneventfully. Chuck tells me that once I sign on the dotted line, he'll set me up with the limo driver and we can make a mutually agreeable arrangement for the drive to Naples. He pays for lunch and shakes my hand good-bye. I wait one full minute before I reach inside my bag and snatch out the papers. I begin to read the contract, but after the first page I give up and head to Torie's office.

"This is pretty restrictive," Torie tells me, glancing through the contract. "You can't ask him about his love life or anything about his parents or even anything about the people who work for him."

"The theme of the article is Zero to Hero. How am I going to show Trip's rise to fame if I don't mention his parents?"

Torie reads the next section aloud. "You can make absolutely no reference to the incident that occurred in the suite at the Don Cesar on July 11 of this year." She glances up from the contract. "What incident is he talking about?"

I tell her everything.

"Why the hell didn't you tell me this sooner?" Torie demands.

"I tried calling you all day Saturday but your cell kept going to voice mail."

Torie looks part embarrassed, part ecstatic. "I was with Kurt. We went down to Perdido Key for the weekend."

"You just met him two weeks ago."

"Yeah, and like you said, I'm not getting any younger. I'm fast-tracking him."

"Good thing you're not rushing into anything." I know this is hypocritical of me considering how fast my relationship with Nick has developed, but that is totally different.

Torie ignores my barb and turns her attention back to the contract. "You can make no references to alcohol, drugs, or any other substances which might be construed as mind-altering. There is also to be no discussion whatsoever of the reasons behind Mr. Monroe's decision to cut the rest of this year's racing schedule. And here's the kicker: Mr. Monroe will have final editing privileges."

I let out a muffled scream of frustration. "That is completely unheard of."

"He's got you by the balls, Em. If you want an interview, you're going to have to play by his rules."

"No way am I going to sign that. There's nothing left to ask him!"

"No signature, no interview."

"What's to stop me from writing what I know on my own?"

I say, more to myself than to Torie. But before Torie can answer, I slump back in my chair. "Forget it."

First off, *Florida!* is not a scandal rag. It would never print inflammatory material about a celebrity, or anyone else, for that matter. The magazine's focus is Florida lifestyles and the beauty and grace of the natural environment and how man fits into that environment, blah, blah, blah. Second off, even though Trip practically assaulted me in his hotel room, I still kind of like the guy. At least I like the seventeen-year-old Trip. The one who was shy and had acne. I'd like to think that the teenage Trip is still alive somewhere, dormant, waiting for something or someone to wake him up. I want to tap into that part of Trip that existed before he became the Sexiest Man Alive and had money and women falling into his lap. But I can't do it if I don't get some one-on-one time with him.

"You can always ask him what his favorite color is," says Torie. I know this is her attempt to make me laugh, but all I can see is that this is going to be the worst article ever.

I take the contract from Torie's outstretched hand and place it back in my tote. "Okay, so back to you and Kurt. You really like him, huh?"

"Oh, *yeah*. Hey! The four of us need to get together for drinks. I know Kurt and Nick are going to get along great."

I think about how Nick and Jason got along great and can't help but feel some nostalgic sadness. Deep down I always knew Torie and Jason would never get back together but this seems to cement it. Still, I have to try.

"What about Jason?"

"I don't think Jason and Kurt have much in common."

"Other than the fact that they're both into you." Torie doesn't deny this, so I decide to plunge headfirst, for Jason's sake. "Jason still loves you, Torie. He wants to get back together with you."

"He told you that?"

"Well . . . not in so many words." Of course, he did tell me this in so many words, but I have to allow Jason a bit of dignity here. "I can just sense it."

"Jason is great but we had our shot," Torie says dismissively. "C'mon, let me walk you to the elevator. I have a three o'clock I can't keep waiting."

I thank Torie for looking at my contract and take the elevator down to the ground floor, where I run into Amy.

I've never seen Amy in her work clothes before. She's wearing a conservative-looking skirt with matching jacket and no hint of cleavage. Her heels are a moderate three inches and her hair is pulled back in a low sleek ponytail. Even her makeup is understated.

"Emma! What are you doing here?"

"I came to see Torie and get a little free legal advice."

"Everything okay?" she asks, looking concerned. Amy is another possible recruit for the Catfish Cove Community Theatre.

"Sure, everything's fine."

"Good, I'm glad." She fidgets with a legal folder in her hand.

"Well, it's good seeing you," I say, ready to bolt.

"Emma, wait. I was wondering . . . do you think we can get a drink sometime?"

"Sure. I'll be at Captain Pete's on Friday." This is a flat-out lie because I have plans to drive home this weekend.

"I mean just you and me. I've wanted to talk to you about something for a while now."

"Oh yeah, like what?" I tap my foot impatiently.

Amy's face goes pink. "I know this sounds incredibly trite and all, but I've wanted to apologize for my behavior at Captain Pete's that night."

Just like *that* night, I feign ignorance. "I'm not sure what night you're talking about."

"I think you do, Emma. I called you . . . well, I said something to Torie while we were in the bathroom that I'm pretty sure you overheard."

I'm surprised Amy wants to bring this up now. Is she really sorry? Or is it just an act? And if it's an act, what does she hope to gain by it?

"Okay, Amy, you got me. Let's call a spade a spade. You called me the ugly friend, and yeah, I heard it. But I didn't run out and jump off a building, so don't worry about it. Your conscience is clear."

"That's just it. My conscience isn't clear. I've felt really bad ever since that night, and I want to make it up to you."

Like you did when you oh so subtly suggested that Nick might be cheating on me? But I don't say that. Instead I say, "Really, Amy, it's not necessary."

Amy looks defeated. "Okay, well, I'd hoped we could maybe be friends, but at the least I wanted you to know I'm really sorry." She looks away. "I don't have a lot of friends, Emma. Not real friends anyway. I guess I'm socially retarded. At least, that's what Pete used to call me. Looks like he was right."

Amy is pulling out the big guilt guns here. How can I ignore this?

"All right, here's the deal. I'm pretty sure I'm heading up to Catfish Cove this weekend, but maybe we can catch a drink some other time. Okay?"

"Perfect! How about next Friday? Or Saturday? You name the date, the place, and the time. I'll be there."

"Why don't I just give you a call?"

Amy's face falls. "You're not really going to call me, are you?"

"Sure I am."

"Really? Because there's something important I need to speak to you about. It's kind of urgent, but it will only take a few minutes."

I have to admit, my curiosity is now piqued. "I have a couple of minutes right now."

"It's guy advice," Amy says. "And since you know the guy really well, I thought . . ." Her face actually goes red.

I'm flabbergasted. If this doesn't take the cake, then I don't know what does. Amy wants advice on how to get Ben back? *From me?* I'm beginning to think her ex is right. Amy is probably one of those people with a genius IQ (I mean, she did get into Harvard Law) who are somehow missing a social awareness gene.

Despite the fact that I don't like her, I can't help but feel sorry for her. I think about what Richard told me this morning about Ben's ex-fiancée. I'm pretty sure that brilliant cancer-fighting-doctor-ex-fiancée trumps self-absorbed-clueless-money-grubbing-attorney.

"Amy, I think Ben has an ex in the wings that—"

"Ben? Oh, no, I wasn't talking about Ben. I mean, he's a great guy, but that didn't work out. I was thinking about Jason."

"*Jason?* You mean, Torie's Jason?"

"I kind of got the impression that they've been broken up for a long time. Plus, she's seeing this new guy. The one she met at Captain Pete's the other weekend?"

Under normal circumstances I would never encourage Amy toward Jason. I hate to be a snob but she simply isn't good enough for him.

On the other hand, Jason is a big boy and he finds Amy attractive. Jason is about to get his heart sliced and diced (if it hasn't been already). Maybe Amy is just what he needs to get over Torie.

"I'll be honest, I think Jason is still into Torie, but you're right, she's moved on. So all I can say is proceed with caution. But if you really want him, then go for it."

"Really?"

"Sure."

She reaches out and gives me one of her insincere hugs, only this time I think she might really mean it. "Thanks, Emma! You're a doll."

chapter twenty

· · · · ·

That evening I call Ben on his cell phone and tell him I need to see him asap.

"Can it wait till tomorrow?" He sounds tired and I'd love to put this conversation off but I can't.

I tell him it's about the Trip Monroe story and we make plans to meet at an Irish pub near the office. Ben is obviously a regular because he greets all the servers by name.

"Nice upgrade from your usual mate," our waiter says to Ben.

I wait till he's gone to say, "Your usual mate?"

Ben shrugs. "Richard and I have eaten here a few times."

I can't help but still find that friendship kind of strange. It's like there is a whole other side of Ben and Richard that I never knew about.

We both order a beer and the corned beef and cabbage. I show Ben the contract Chuck wants me to sign and give him Torie's recap.

Ben scans the document and point-blank asks me what "the incident that occurred in the suite at the Don Cesar on July 11 of this year" refers to. I try to scramble my way out of telling him but he doesn't buy it. He gives me one of his hard stares and I come clean with the whole story. How Trip was a no-show at the charity cocktail party and how Kimberly played Harriet the Spy and we got Trip's hotel room number and how he was drunk and almost accosted me in the bathroom. By the time I finish, Ben's face is red. "This guy deserves to have his ass kicked."

"That's exactly what Nick said. Richard, on the other hand, said *I* should have kicked Trip's ass, which—"

"You told your boyfriend but you didn't tell me that you were nearly raped while on the job? I'm your *boss*."

For some reason, Ben's "concern" annoys me.

"Of course I was going to tell you. Isn't that what I'm doing now? And I wasn't nearly raped. I know it sounds bad, but I don't think it would have gotten that far. Trip was confused. It was the alcohol."

"You sound like you belong on one of those pathetic daytime help shows."

I wish I had a clever retort to this, but unfortunately, Ben is right.

"You're not doing the interview," Ben announces. And then he does something totally unexpected. He rips the contract in two.

"What did you do that for!"

"Screw the interview. You need to press charges against this guy, not go off in some limo to meet him at his beach house. I thought you were smarter than this. What the hell are you thinking, Frazier?"

"What am I *thinking*? I'm thinking that maybe Trip Monroe is a lot more complicated than meets the eye. I'm thinking that maybe even despite this damn contract, maybe I have the upper hand here. That maybe once I can talk to him, there'll be a tiny speck of the boy who grew up in Catfish Cove and that I can score the interview of the decade."

Ben opens his mouth to say something, but I cut him off.

"So even if all Trip says is yes and no, an interview with Trip Monroe is an interview that's going to sell magazines and that's what T.K. would want because that's what's best for Dunhill Publications, and ultimately for me and my career. *That's* what I'm thinking!"

Our waiter clears his throat. I'd almost forgotten we were out in public. He lays our plates on the table and takes off. Everyone in the restaurant is staring at us. A part of me wants to tell Ben that this is all his fault. That if he hadn't wanted something "sexier" I would have never come up with the brilliant idea to interview Trip Monroe, but that's ridiculous. I take a deep breath and the atmosphere in the room returns to normal. Although it wasn't exactly professional of me to raise my voice to my boss, I have to admit, it felt good.

Ben looks at me as if he's never seen me before. "Okay," he says slowly. "You're right. But you're not going on this interview alone."

"What? Like I need a chaperone?"

"Exactly."

"I don't know if Trip will be able to let loose if there's a third wheel in the room."

"Tough. It's either that or there's no interview."

"All right."

"That's it? You're giving in?"

"Yes, I'm giving in," I say. "Unless I have a choice?"

"No."

"Okay, then."

I can tell Ben is suspicious of my easy capitulation, but after a few seconds he begins to dig into his corned beef and cabbage. I pick up my fork and play around with my food. I feel unsettled.

Ben and I have never argued before. It feels both strange and strangely intimate.

"So how was your workshop?" I ask, trying to lighten the mood.

"I didn't go to a workshop."

I put down my fork. "I thought Richard said you were—"

"I was in Orlando to meet with T.K. to discuss closing the Tampa office."

"What?"

"Frazier, you're a smart girl. In this economy it makes no sense financially to keep the office open when we can do everything from Orlando."

"But *Florida!* has been based in Tampa for over forty years. It's a tradition." I can tell by the look on Ben's face that he isn't impressed by tradition. "So what does this mean? For all of us? For Richard and me and Jackie?"

"Nothing, really," says Ben. "Actually, it might be a good move. You can work out of your home. The only time you'd have to come to Orlando would be for the weekly staff meeting, and even then we could use Skype. Everything else can be done by Internet or phone."

I think Richard and Jackie are going to love this. But me? Probably not so much.

"What about Lisa?"

"Lisa will be offered a job in the Orlando office. I hope she takes it, but . . ." He shrugs, like he already knows the answer to this. Lisa has lots of family here in Tampa as well as her boyfriend, so even though Orlando is close by, I don't see her wanting to make the move.

"I guess you'll be moving to Orlando too?" I ask.

Ben hesitates. "T.K. is retiring next year."

Why Ben is telling me all this, I'm not sure. Then it hits me. "And you're taking over? As publisher?"

"I'm thinking of it. I have a few other . . . options, as well."

What other options? I want to find out what he means by this, but since Ben isn't volunteering any more information, I figure it's not my place to ask.

Is Ben reluctant to take the job because of his cancer-fighting-doctor-ex-fiancée? Are they getting back together? Is Ben moving back to New York? I'm dizzy with all the questions that are whirling through my head. I push my plate to the side.

"I'd appreciate it if you keep all this to yourself until I make an official announcement about the move."

Now that Ben has had a little time to digest what happened at the Don Cesar, he reverts to editor mode. "Don't sweat it. You're right. This Trip Monroe interview will all work out," he says, mistaking my lack of appetite for worry over the article. "You can spin straw into gold. Just take whatever crap Monroe dishes out, write it up your usual way, and the readers will eat it up. We'll sell all the advertising T.K. wants and everyone will be happy."

Great. Ben is expecting another miracle like the one I pulled off with the manatee article. No pressure there. I don't think I can stand talking about this Trip Monroe thing one more second.

"Richard says you're bringing your ex-fiancée to Jackie's party," I blurt.

Ben clears his throat. "He told you that?"

"He said she was a research oncologist. Sounds pretty impressive." I really do mean this, but I have an ulterior motive for bringing up the ex-fiancée. Call it curiosity (or rubbing salt in the wound) but I want to know what sort of woman Ben would marry.

"Elise is in town doing research for a few weeks. She's a good friend and I thought she'd get a kick out of meeting the people I work with. I also didn't want to be the only one to show up without a date."

"I hear Richard has two lined up. You could always take his leftovers."

Ben laughs.

I play around with my food and neither of us says anything for a second. Then, out of the blue, Ben says, "Elise and I were supposed to go to dinner tonight but I was a little wound up after my meeting with T.K., so I canceled."

"I guess you have a lot to think about, huh?"

He meets my gaze and slowly nods. "Yeah. I do."

I excuse myself to go to the ladies' room and this is when I discover that I'm not pregnant with Nick's baby. Later that night I call Nick to tell him the big news. He tries to hide it, but I can tell by his tone that he's disappointed. I wish I could say the same, but I can't. Besides discovering that the Trip Monroe interview is now on, this is the best thing that has happened to me all day.

I have Chuck e-mail me a copy of the contract with the flimsy excuse that I ruined the first one. I print it out, sign it, and mail it to the address Chuck provided. He's "thrilled" that I'm going to interview Trip. I feel like calling the Yellow Rose of Texas and saying "told you so!" However, I have a feeling this interview is going to be about as bland as reading one of Trip's PR packets. At least I'll get a chance to tell him about Kimberly and the Yeager Agency. Maybe he'll feel guilty about the incident at the Don Cesar and make it up to me by hiring Kimberly. I know this is a long stretch in the wishful thinking department but I'd really like to see something good come out of this.

Plus, I haven't been able to get Kimberly's confession out of my mind. Despite that Kimberly is so private, I really thought I knew her pretty well. The fact that I had no idea her marriage to Jake Lemoyne was a complete fiasco rattles me, and I wonder what else she is squirreling away in that gorgeous head of hers. The thought that Kimberly—beautiful, smart, funny Kimberly—has had no luck in the men department seems completely unfair to me. What is the point of being drop-dead gorgeous if your life isn't perfect?

chapter twenty-one

· · · · ·

Friday rolls around and I drive up to Catfish Cove for "Parents' Weekend." Tonight, Nick and I are having dinner with my moms, and tomorrow, it's the Alfonsos' turn. I think it's a little premature, but Nick insists it's time we get to know each other's family better. Although technically I have known the Alfonsos all my life, I have never had a real conversation with either of Nick's parents, let alone spent an entire evening in their company.

"Don't worry," Nick says, "my mom is going to love you."

"How do you know that?"

"How could she not? Just watch out for her X-ray eyes."

"Her *what*?"

"My mom is part Gypsy. One look in your eyes and she can read your soul."

I laugh, but I do not happen to find this funny in the least. I'd like to keep my soul all to myself, thank you.

Mama J makes spinach lasagna, and it's not half bad. Mom makes a pineapple upside-down cake and the pineapples end up everywhere but where they are supposed to be. I think Mom took the "upside" down part literally. After dinner, the four of us sit outside on the deck, sipping wine and inhaling the sweet smell of hibiscus flowers.

We talk about Nick's job, and before I know it, I announce that Dunhill Publications is shutting down our office in Tampa.

Everyone talks at once.

"If you can work from home, then you can work from anywhere. Right?" Nick says.

"I guess so."

"You could move right back here to Catfish Cove," says Mama J.

Nick and Mom nod encouragingly and even Walt gets into the act by barking and thumping his tail.

I never thought of that. Why didn't I think of it before I opened my big fat mouth? Do I want to move back to Catfish Cove? As much as I love my moms and love visiting home, I'm pretty certain I'm happy with things the way they stand. I've thought a lot about that dream I had. You know, the one where I gave birth to Nick's baby and we were redecorating his house? Once I found out I wasn't pregnant, I began having another dream. In the new dream I'm typing away on my laptop, drinking a cup of coffee and laughing at something Nick is saying to me. At least I think it's Nick. I can't see his face but I definitely know that I'm in the living room in my town house. I also know that I'm happy. I think this is a sign that for now at least, I'm meant to stay right where I am.

Maybe it's because I've lived in the "big city" for so long that I've gotten used to all its amenities. Sure, the traffic sucks, but I love living in Tampa. The weather is brutally hot and muggy in the summer, but we have the nicest winters in the world. I love the old-world feel of Ybor City, the great restaurants and concerts, the clear blue water of the Gulf, which is just a bridge and a thirty-minute drive away. I love wearing my pirate hat to the Bucs games and tailgating with Kimberly and Torie and Jason and watching the Gasparilla Day Parade while wearing my party beads and drinking cold beer.

I love my town house, which I bought two years ago (completely on my own, even though my moms offered to help with the down payment). I love my tiny yard that I've been meaning to landscape myself whenever I get the time. I even love the potted fern on my porch that I always forget to water. Honestly? The only reason I'd have to move back home would be if Nick and I ended up together . . . and he could just as easily move to Tampa. Couldn't he?

Later I go to Nick's to spend the night. I told my moms I'd be staying there from now on and they both seemed to accept this as a given. As a matter of fact, they both looked downright happy about it. I promised Nick I'd help him paint the inside of his house. Tomorrow morning we're starting with his living room, which is currently littered with boxes from his old place that he hasn't bothered to unpack. I begin to haul boxes off to the spare bedroom, which Nick thinks is a waste of time.

"Why don't we just shove all the boxes to the middle of the room?" he says.

"Because we're going to be painting the ceiling and they'll be in the way. If we're going to do this, then we're going to do this right."

Obviously this has not occurred to Nick because he glances up at the ceiling with a frown. He seems so distraught at the idea of how much work moving the boxes will entail that I start to laugh. He laughs too, but our good mood is cut short when I discover a box that belongs to Shannon.

"I guess she forgot this when she moved out of the old place." Nick picks up the box and I follow him as he takes it through the kitchen and tosses it out the back door.

"What are you doing?" I ask.

"I'll drop this off at the Dumpster tomorrow."

"You can't do that. It belongs to Shannon."

"Watch me."

"But what if it contains something valuable?"

"She hasn't missed it these past five years, so I doubt it's anything she wants."

"Nick, you can't know that."

"Fine," he says, "you take it to her."

"All right, I will."

Nick stomps off to the bedroom. "You coming?" he asks over his shoulder.

If this is not some sort of red flag, then I don't know what is. I decide not to make a big deal of it. I'm tired and obviously so is Nick. We brush our teeth and collapse in the bed, and for the first time since we've been together, we do not have sex.

Sometime in the middle of the night Nick nudges me awake. "I'll drop the box off at Shannon's first thing in the morning."

I nod in acknowledgment and roll over.

"Hey," he whispers in my ear. "Sorry I was such an asshole earlier."

"It's all right." I want to say something more but I don't. This has become a disturbing pattern in our relationship. I want to talk about Shannon and their marriage, but Nick seems to think there is nothing to talk about, so I don't ever mention it.

"Can I make it up to you?"

Without waiting for an answer, Nick proceeds to make it up to me in the very best way possible. Afterward, he falls asleep almost instantly but I'm wired (I already told you, good sex has this effect on me). I go to the kitchen and pour myself a glass of water. I open the back door and bring Shannon's box inside and place it on top of the kitchen table. I tell myself the reason I'm doing this is because I don't want the box to get wet in case it should rain tonight, and this being Florida and the middle of summer, there is every possibility it will do just that.

But in reality, I'm curious. Shannon is such an enigma. Yes, I grew up with her, but we were never friends. I just don't see what Nick *saw* in her. Maybe a pretty face and a great body is enough for most guys, but I'd like to think Nick is better than that.

I know I shouldn't do it, but it's impossible not to. I get a kitchen knife and tear through the masking tape to open the box. It's full of high school memorabilia. Shannon's yearbook sits on top, and I'm going to burn in hell, but I still open it and begin to read. Most of the inscriptions are like the ones from my own yearbook—lots of "We'll be best friends forever" stuff or "Remember that day we went to the lake . . ."

I honestly can't remember if I signed Shannon's yearbook, but if I did, I would get a big kick out of seeing what I wrote. I scan through all the pages and don't find any evidence of me, but I do find what Nick wrote. I wouldn't read it, except it's so short that I can't help it.

Shannon,
I'll always love you.
Nick

I know I shouldn't give any credence to this. Nick was seventeen years old at the time and I'm sure he believed with all his heart and soul that he and Shannon would be together forever. Heck, he married her just a few years after he wrote this, and although I didn't attend the service, I'm sure they both promised to love each other forever. Still, it shakes me up. It's my own fault, though. I should never have snooped through Shannon's yearbook.

I go to place the yearbook back in the box when a pink velvet photo album catches my eye. I have the same exact photo album. Or at least I did, before I tossed it in the trash. It's the album the Dixie Debutante committee gives to all its teen debs as a remembrance of the night they were presented.

I already told you that the Dixie Deb Ball was the worst night of my teenage life.

Let me tell you why.

Being a Dixie Debutante is just about the highest honor to which any teenage girl in Catfish Cove can aspire. Dixie Debutantes are "presented" to the community at the Gulf Bay Community Club during a black-tie ball. A ticket to this grandiose event is hard to come by but even harder to obtain is an invitation to become a Dixie Deb yourself. There is only one way a girl can become a Dixie Deb: She must be a legacy. In other words, if your mother and your grandmother and your great-grandmother weren't debs, you can hang it up.

Lucky me. It just so happened Sheila Frazier was a Dixie Debutante. This is something I knew my whole life because my grandparents had a portrait of both my mom and my aunt Susie dressed in their white debutante ball gowns hanging in the living room. Whenever I went to their house I'd stare at Mom's picture and dream of the day I'd become a Dixie Deb too. But honestly, I never thought my mom, with all her feminist ideals, would go for an outdated custom that basically reduced young women into presenting themselves as social cream puffs.

I was wrong.

When I turned seventeen and my invitation arrived in the mail, my moms were ecstatic. If you didn't know any better, you'd have thought I'd hit the Publishers Clearing House jackpot. Looking back, I think their excitement was due to the fact that I wanted it so much and they wanted me to be happy. I didn't have the greatest teenage life (let's face it, who does?). I was "pleasingly plump," as my grandmother used to say, always had my nose in a book, and was shy around boys. Plus, there is the fact that I've always been different. And by that, I mean the whole "my mothers are lesbians" different. I already told you that only the dumb rednecks ever hassled my moms, but there were always lots of tiny little snubs that I never really "got" until I was old enough to figure them out. My moms ignored them and tried to teach me to ignore them too, but when you're seventeen and want nothing more than to be just like everyone else, that's easier said than done.

After I received my invitation, my moms took me to Atlanta to buy the perfect white dress. For the first time ever all the girls in school were envious of me. There were only seven debs that year, including Shannon and her best pal, Tricia.

As a deb, you had to provide your own escort. A few of the girls had steady boyfriends (like Shannon) but the rest chose to honor their fathers with that privilege. I didn't have either a boyfriend or a father, so Mom lassoed a friend's son (who was in the tenth grade) to be my escort. This was a humiliation I was willing to overlook because the highlight of the Dixie Deb Ball was the presentation waltz, in which all the Debs switched up partners, which meant I'd get to dance with Nick Alfonso.

I already told you that I had a huge crush on Nick in high school, so I was looking forward to that presentation waltz like you wouldn't believe. I even got Mama J to drive me to Tallahassee to take dance lessons from a lady who specialized in teaching young people "manners." I starved myself for days so that I would look good in my white chiffon gown and slathered my face every night in Clearasil to scare the pimples away.

Then two days before the ball, I got the news. Mrs. Atwater, the head of the Dixie Deb committee, called to speak to me about a problem with my biography (this is the pumped-up three- or four-sentence introduction they read about you as you're being presented), so I went by her house after school to meet with her in person, as requested.

This is what happened:

Mrs. Atwater looked at me with her pinchy gray eyes. "Emma, I'm afraid you'll have to redo your bio."

"Is there a problem?" I asked innocently (boy, was I a gullible Nellie back then).

She showed me the index card and pointed to the top line, scrawled in my overly neat type A high school handwriting with the curlicues.

Emma Louise Frazier is the daughter of Dr. Sheila Frazier and Jennifer Brewster.

"Darlin', you know you can't list Jenny as your mother."

"Why not?"

Mrs. Atwater tsked and shook her head. "Because she's not."

I can still remember the way my face went hot. I'm ashamed to say it wasn't all in anger either. A part of me was angry but I was also embarrassed. Why couldn't anything ever be simple for me? At that moment I would have given a leg to trade places with

Shannon. She had everything—looks, popularity, Nick, a regular mother, and a regular father.

"But Mama J helped raised me. Doesn't that make me her daughter?"

"How about we just put your real mama's name here. I'm sure Jenny will understand. She's a sensible woman and so is your mother."

"I don't think that would be right," I said, trying hard not to panic.

"It's such a *little* thing, Emma, there's really no need to make a production out of it. Is there?"

"If it's such a little thing, then why does it matter?" By now I couldn't help myself. The tears were running down my cheeks.

Mrs. Atwater put on her most sympathetic face. "I'm sorry, Emma, but I've discussed this with the rest of the committee. Either you fix your bio or we'll have to ask you to withdraw from the ceremony."

Looking back at this conversation as an adult, I can see how wrong it was for her to confront me on this without one of my moms present. But as a seventeen-year-old girl, all I could think of was my white dress and how I was going to dance with Nick and if I dropped out now how everyone at school would know I had to abdicate my Dixie Deb status all because of my mothers' sexual orientation. The whole thing was just so *unfair*. I'd been dreaming about the Dixie Deb Ball since I was a little girl. It was my moment to shine. To wear a beautiful dress and have people smile at me.

I wish I could tell you that I stood up and told Mrs. Atwater that she and the rest of the Dixie Deb committee could go straight to hell.

But I didn't.

Instead, I changed the bio on my card to read:

Emma Louise Frazier is the daughter of Dr. Sheila Frazier.

I was the last deb to be presented that night. The seven of us stood in a line, each holding her escort's arm, awaiting our big moment in the sun. Shannon was first. They called her name and read her bio.

Shannon Marie Dukes is the daughter of Mr. and Mrs. William Dukes. Shannon is a senior at Catfish Cove High School and is captain of the cheerleading squad. She's a member of the pep squad committee, Future Homemakers of America, and Civitans, as well as treasurer of the Spanish club. Shannon designs all her own clothes and hopes to open her own dress shop one day.

It's weird how I still remember Shannon's bio, word for word. I think this is because I knew the bit about her designing all her own clothes was a big fat lie. Shannon used to brag that the 5-7-9 shop at the mall in Tallahassee didn't have clothes "small" enough to fit her, so she had to have her clothing specially ordered in size zero petite. I wore a junior size thirteen and would have given anything to be able to shop at 5-7-9.

As each girl was presented, I felt sicker to my stomach. Then it was my turn. I'll never forget the look on my moms' faces when they read my bio. They went from proud smiles to confusion to disappointment. It was the most miserable moment of my life. I danced the presentation waltz, but despite my lessons I kept messing up the steps.

And then it came time to switch partners.

My heart was beating so fast I couldn't hear the music. Nick was last. He didn't meet my eyes. His gaze kept wandering back to Shannon. I stepped on his foot and that's when he really looked at me. Only instead of the admiration I'd been longing to see, his gaze said, *Wow, are you clumsy or what?* Despite it being my mistake, though, he mumbled an apology and we switched back to our original partners. Even back then, Nick was a nice guy.

I didn't dance again the rest of the evening. After an hour I told my date I wasn't feeling well and I asked my moms if we could leave. The silence on the drive home threatened to make my ears explode. I walked through the front door and ran to my bedroom, tore my dress off, threw myself down on my bed, and cried myself to sleep. I had never felt more ugly in my life.

Sometime in the middle of the night, the door to my room creaked open. My moms crawled into my bed and cocooned me up in their arms. It was all I could do not to start bawling again.

"What kind of sandwich are you?" Mama J whispered.

My voice cracked as I answered. "Stinky bologna with rotten tomatoes."

"Yummy," said Mom, her voice cracking too as she pulled me tight. "That's my favorite."

chapter twenty-two

· · · · ·

In the morning I wake up first. I've already made the coffee by the time Nick comes into the kitchen. He spots Shannon's box on the table and his dark eyes immediately bore into me. "Did you open this?"

I was positive I taped the box identical to the way I found it. I guess I'm not as sneaky as I think I am. The truth is, I think I wanted to get caught. I want Nick and me to talk about this box. And more importantly, what it means. "Sorry, I couldn't help myself."

Nick shrugs and pours himself a cup of coffee. He doesn't ask me what's in the box. Isn't he curious? Unless . . . he already knows what's in it. Which would mean that he knew he had it all along and kept it on purpose. I really don't want to think about that scenario.

"I can take the box by Shannon's place later this afternoon," I tell him.

"I thought you were going to Carpe Diem after we finished painting."

"I can drop it off on the way there."

"Okay," he says, reaching for the newspaper.

We drink our coffee in silence. I know technically we "made

up" last night but I've decided enough is enough. If Nick and I are going to have a shot, then we need to talk about his past.

"Tell me what happened between you and Shannon," I say.

He puts down his paper. "I knew you were going to want to hash this out today."

"Guess what? You were right."

"I wish you wouldn't make a big deal out of it. We were married, she screwed around on me, and we got a divorce. End of story."

"Nick, I'm having dinner with your family tonight and that officially makes *us* a big deal. If our relationship is going to go any further, then I need to know what I'm dealing with here."

Nick's jaw tightens. Maybe I'm asking too much, but I don't think so.

"The box is full of albums. Her high school yearbook, that sort of stuff," I say in the hope that he's clueless about the contents. "Nick . . . do you remember the Dixie Deb Ball?"

He seems relieved that I've dropped the topic of Shannon. "Sure." He takes a sip of his coffee. "You were a deb, as I recall."

"You remember our dance?"

He half frowns, half smiles, like he doesn't remember but wishes he did. "We danced together?"

"Yeah. I stepped on your foot."

"Ouch." Nick winces playfully, then winks at me. "Guess what? You're forgiven."

He goes on to talk about painting the living room, but I don't say anything, and after a while he lets out a big sigh. He comes over to my side of the table and drops to his knees in front of me. "Emma," he says, reaching out to clasp my hands. "I don't know what you want me to tell you. I married Shannon because I was in love with her. I was happy and I thought she was happy. But she wasn't. She hated being a small-town cop's wife. She hated living in a rented duplex with crappy air-conditioning. I kept hoping she'd wait it out, till I got more seniority, better pay, but she didn't. She fucked around with Ed because he was a better life for her. End of story."

"I'm sorry," I say softly.

Nick stands up and I melt into his arms and into the kind of hug I've wanted to give him for what seems like forever.

"The good thing is, I have you now, and you're *nothing* like Shannon."

The vehemence in his voice is startling.

Something tells me this is the most honest thing Nick has ever said to me.

I glance at the slip of paper in my hand. I got Shannon and Ed's address from the phone book. They live five miles outside of Catfish Cove, right on the Gulf. The house looks like most new beach construction. Very chic and Mediterranean.

Ed answers the door. He looks surprised to see me.

"Hi, Ed. Is Shannon home? I've got this box that belongs to her."

It is now my turn to be surprised because Ed does something unexpected. He invites me inside. I really thought he'd just take the box and that would be that. He offers me some water and I take it. Partly because I'm thirsty, but mostly because it gives me something to do instead of fidgeting. I'll be honest, I'm a little nervous here.

After about five minutes Shannon comes down the stairs. She's wearing shorts and a T-shirt and for some reason doesn't look as hugely pregnant as the last time I saw her. She must notice that I'm staring at her stomach, because she smiles wearily and says, "I've dropped. The doctor says it should be any day now." She's not wearing any makeup and her face looks puffy. Her long blond hair is pulled back in a ponytail and there is an innocent girlishness about her I find unnerving.

I hand her the box. It takes her a full minute to realize what I've just given her. "Oh my God. Babe!" she says to Ed. "Look!"

Ed comes rushing to Shannon's side like an eager puppy. There is something here between them that I missed at cow-chip bingo. They seem more like a young couple in love than the horny evil schemers who ruined Nick's life.

"I've searched everywhere for this box," she says. "And . . . and Nick has had this all along?"

"He had no idea. It was mixed up with a bunch of his stuff."

She and Ed exchange a look. "Thank you for bringing it to me." And then Shannon does something truly horrific. She gives me a great big hug, and proceeds to tell me all about her marriage to Nick.

After my two-hour visit (yes, you read that correctly) with Shannon and Ed, I swing by Carpe Diem. Mama J is closing up shop. I really did want to spend some time at the bookstore today but I couldn't abandon Shannon in the middle of her emotional meltdown. I'm supposed to meet Nick and his family at seven p.m. at Louie's Restaurant, so I have an hour to kill.

"Mama J, I need some advice."

"Let's take a trip to the park."

At the word *park* Walt turns into a maniac. Mama J settles him down long enough to clip on his leash. It rained earlier this afternoon, so it's not as hot as usual. We stroll through downtown with Walt pulling Mama J along by his leash, anxious to reach our destination. On the walk over, I tell her about the box and about Nick's inscription in Shannon's yearbook.

"It's a high school yearbook and they were sweethearts. What did you think Nick would write?"

"I'm just afraid that he'll never get over her." This is the first time I've voiced this thought out loud. It feels good to get it off my chest.

"Maybe he won't."

I stop walking. "What?"

"Sometimes it's hard to let go of the people we love. Even if they've betrayed us, or we think they have."

I hustle to catch up to her. "Do you think Nick is capable of falling in love again? Even if he's still harboring feelings for Shannon?"

Now it's Mama J's turn to stop in her tracks, which makes Walt a little crazy. He paces in a circle around us, tangling us both in his leash. "I don't know. The point is, are *you* in love with him?" She studies my face and seems to come to some sort of conclusion. She shakes her head sadly. "I told Sheila not to get her hopes up."

"What's that supposed to mean?"

"It means that your mom is one step away from booking the reception hall."

I knew Mom liked Nick, but knowing that she's practically got us engaged worries me. "I hope you've tried to bring her back to reality."

"So you don't think Nick is the one?"

"I don't know," I answer honestly.

We untangle ourselves from Walt's leash and reach the park. Saturdays from six to seven p.m. they rope off a grassy section in the middle of the square and you can let your dog run free. It's called Saturday Evening Dog Park and it's Walt's favorite thing in the whole wide world. Today there are two Labs, a Chihuahua, and a mutt of questionable heritage. Walt is in heaven. We find a bench where we can keep an eye on him and resume our little mother-daughter talk.

I find myself telling Mama J everything that Shannon laid on me. How Nick was working all the time and how she was lonely and found herself attracted to Ed, blah, blah, blah. I don't know what she hoped to accomplish by telling me all this. Absolution? I'm not the injured party, so I don't think so. The one thing I did get out of this afternoon's faux therapy session is that I truly believe Shannon and Ed love each other. It doesn't excuse what they did to Nick, but there it is. I also now feel the added burden that I've been fraternizing with the enemy. If Nick knew what went down, he'd be upset or angry or possibly both, so this is something else I'm going to have to refrain from talking over with him.

I also tell Mama J all about Ben.

"So that's why you were crying," she says, remembering that day not so long ago when I showed up on the kitchen doorstep in tears. "I told Sheila those were man tears." Mama J studies my face again. "Is this Ben the one?"

"I thought so . . . but no. He has this ex-fiancée and . . . no," I say again with more conviction. "Ben isn't the guy for me." At least, I'm pretty sure he's not.

She takes my hand. "Emma, you're a smart girl. You'll figure it all out."

"How? How do you know when you find the right one?" I know I sound like a little girl but I really need Mama J's advice.

Mama J gives me one of those wise smiles that mothers have

probably been giving their daughters for centuries. "All I know is that when you love someone, and I mean *really* love someone, there isn't anything you wouldn't do for them. Including moving out to the middle of nowhere because that's where they think they need to be. And if that's what makes them happy, then it makes you happy."

My breath hitches. Mama J is talking about herself, of course. I know when she and Mom got together Mama J tried to persuade Mom to move somewhere "more civilized." Somewhere where being themselves wouldn't be a daily struggle. I know this because I overheard them talking when they thought I was asleep. At the time I didn't understand the conversation. It wasn't until a few years later that I *got it*.

"There's no place that's completely easy, Jen," I remember Mom saying.

"Hell, Sheila, Catfish Cove, Florida? Really? You can practice medicine anywhere. Think of Emma."

"I *am* thinking of her. This is her home. It's *my* home. It's where my daddy practiced medicine and where I want to practice medicine. These people . . . they really aren't so bad. Change doesn't come easy, but it doesn't come at all if you don't try."

I think about that conversation and about what Mama J just said, about how we hold on to the people we love even if that love has hurt us. Although Shannon didn't outright accuse Nick of withholding the box from her, she didn't have to. I remember his reaction when I found it. He was more annoyed than surprised. I feel disloyal thinking it, but a part of me wonders if Nick hasn't known about that box all along. Maybe holding on to the box has been his revenge against Shannon. Or maybe it has nothing to do with revenge. Maybe holding on to the box was Nick's only way of holding on to *her*.

Either way the whole thing makes me want to cry.

We spend the hour watching Walt, and discussing poetry, just like we did when I worked back at the store. As difficult as those teenage years were, they were also some of the happiest times of my life.

At exactly five minutes to seven I stand and brush off my skirt, ready to head to Louie's and "meet" the Alfonso clan. I hope Nick's mama's X-ray eyes are off-kilter tonight, because I'm afraid this weekend has proved one thing to me. My soul is now officially confused.

chapter twenty-three

•••••

This promises to be a huge week for me. In exactly two days I'll be going down to Naples to meet Trip. I've expended so much energy on this interview that I feel like it's taken over my life. I honestly can't wait till the whole thing is over. Then Saturday is Jackie's housewarming party. I tried on my bathing suit yesterday and I've concluded that the French are not all they are cracked up to be. I am feeling very American right now, which means I'm starving myself in order to fit into the bathing suit that at the beginning of summer looked pretty decent on me. Why does Jackie's party have to involve water?

For the first time ever I consciously decide to skip the Krispy Kreme donuts. The temptation to bite into one would just be too much.

Lisa and Jackie look ready to kill when they see me come in the door to the conference room empty-handed. Richard arrives a couple of minutes later and plops a box of Krispy Kremes onto the table.

"Never fear, Richard is here with the backup dozen." He looks at me and shakes his head. "I had a strong feeling you'd let us down again."

"Please put those at the other end of the table," I say.

Lisa grabs a donut, and even Jackie, who hasn't eaten a donut on the past two Mondays, gingerly pulls one out of the box.

"Go ahead, Emma, they won't bite," Richard says.

"No thanks, I have a bathing suit to fit into this weekend." I glare at Jackie. This is all her fault. Why couldn't she have a housewarming party *inside* the house we are supposed to be ogling?

"The cop giving you a hard time about your weight?" asks Richard. "Personally, I like a little junk in the trunk." He then pretends to give my butt a very thorough examination.

"Stop," I say.

"You won't be saying that once I actually start."

Lisa giggles and Richard rewards her with a smile. I confess, I almost giggled myself. The lack of food must be skewing my sense of humor.

"Don't believe him, Emma. All men like their women to be fit," says Jackie.

I stare at the donuts and sigh.

Ben arrives and calls the meeting to order. We do the same thing we do every Monday morning at the editorial staff meeting—we brainstorm stories and Ben catches us up on anything newsworthy. I wait for him to make an announcement about the move to Orlando, but he doesn't mention it. Instead, he ends the meeting by telling everyone that I'm going to interview Trip on Wednesday in his private home in Naples.

Lisa and Jackie murmur their congratulations. Richard looks surprised. I give him an I'll-tell-you-later look and he nods. Weird. Richard and I are now communicating in secret code.

"When do you think you'll have the article written?" Ben asks me.

"Um, maybe sometime next week?"

"Do you think you can give me a rough draft by Monday? Just something I can show to T.K. and the sales team?"

"Sure."

Ben ends the meeting the same way he always does, by telling us to Facebook and Twitter, only he doesn't bother looking at me because he knows it's a waste of time.

I make arrangements with Paul, Trip's limo driver, to pick me up at eight a.m. Wednesday morning at the office. I'm to spend the day at Trip's mother's house in Naples, then Paul will drive me back to Tampa. Since Ben insisted on coming along for the interview, I call his cell phone, which goes instantly to voice mail, and I give him the details. But when I arrive at the office, instead of Ben, Richard is waiting for me.

"The boss says I'm not to let you out of my sight."

"Why isn't Ben here?"

"Sorry to disappoint you, but he's got business to take care of."

There's been a lingering tension between Ben and me ever since our dinner the other night, so I wasn't looking forward to spending what will essentially be six hours alone in a car with him. Now that I recall, I don't think Ben ever said he would be the one coming along, so given the choice between Ben and Richard I'm actually kind of relieved that it's Richard. My relief is short-lived, however, because all Richard wants to talk about is his novel.

"Have you even opened up the file?" he asks.

"I've just been so busy with this interview—"

"You're not going to read it, are you?"

"Of course I'm going to read it."

"That's what everyone says, but they never do."

"Who else did you give your novel to?"

He hesitates. "Jackie."

I give Richard the stinky eye.

"Okay, I tried to give it to Ben too but he wouldn't even let me send it to him."

"Am I the last person in the office you asked to read your novel?" Before Richard can answer, I add, "Besides Lisa?"

Richard shifts around in the seat.

"You asked *Lisa* to read your novel before you asked me?"

"I honestly thought you'd shoot me down."

Unbelievable. I was Richard's last choice. Should I be insulted? Oddly, I'm not. What I am is . . . hurt. "I promise, as soon as I get this interview written up, I'll start reading. But let me warn you, I'm going to be brutally honest."

Richard looks offended. "I never asked you to be anything else." He stretches his long legs out in front of him and settles into a nap.

The limo is stocked with bottled water and juice and is a lot roomier than my cramped cubicle at the office. Since there is no longer any reason to try to impress Trip, I have dressed for comfort—lightweight slacks, a sleeveless blouse, and flat sandals. I'm armed with my laptop, a legal pad, a small tape player, and my high school yearbook (for nostalgia's sake).

I open up my laptop to review the notes I've made regarding the interview and jot a few of them down on my legal pad. I know this sounds like extra work but I'm a visual person, and the more I see something in different formats, the more it sticks with me. Since Trip has pretty much eliminated anything that the public would be interested in knowing about him, I've had to come up with questions that will pass the "Trip Test." I'm working on these when I catch Richard peering at my computer screen.

"So you write notes before you do an interview?"

"Of course I write notes."

"You probably do research too, huh?"

"How do you know what questions to ask if you don't research the subject?"

"I do research. Sometimes. But sometimes I just go off my gut instinct." He eyes my legal pad. "So first you write notes in your computer, then you rewrite them all over again on that thing? Seems like a lot of wasted time to me." He reads my notes and frowns. "Don't tell me those are the questions you're going to ask this guy?"

I fill him in on my meeting with Chuck and the specifics outlined in the contract.

"And you *signed* it?"

"What choice did I have? I wasn't getting the interview without signing it."

"Does Gallagher know about this?"

"Of course he knows."

Richard shakes his head at me.

"And what would you suggest I have done?"

"You should have said thanks, but no-the-fuck thanks, Chuck. This is America and I'll write whatever the hell I want."

"Maybe that works for you, but it's not my style. Besides, Trip is an old high school friend. Sort of. I really think that once we sit down one-on-one, it'll all be fine."

"Uh-huh."

I put away my legal pad. "Okay, obviously we're not going to agree about this. So tell me, O Great One, what do your *instincts* tell you about Trip Monroe?"

"I won't know till I meet him. I'll be honest, this is the last place I thought I'd be today."

"Speaking of which, how did you get roped into babysitting me?"

"The boss called and said he had some last-minute meeting to go to in Orlando. So he asked me to do him this favor and I thought, 'Why not?' You, me, Trip Monroe. I've always wanted to try a ménage à trois, except I was hoping it would be me and two chicks. Still, it beats sitting in my cubicle all day."

I can't help it. I start laughing. "Are you for real?"

"Want to find out?"

Although this is the sort of banal flirtation Richard and I have come to excel at, something in his tone flusters me and all I can come up with is a weak, "Um, no, thanks."

He shrugs. "Your loss."

"So what's this last-minute meeting about? Do you know?"

"Probably something to do with the move to Orlando. Or about Ben taking over T.K.'s job when he retires."

I spin about in my seat. "*You* know about all that?"

"Did you think you were the only one Ben told?"

"Well . . ."

"He said he was meeting with T.K. to finalize something, so I assume it's about the big move. But the feminine side of my intuition tells me that poor Benjamin is conflicted about something. It sounded to me like he didn't want to be alone with you." Richard looks me directly in the eye and says, "What did you do? Confess your undying love for him?"

I almost choke on my bottled water. "Ben said he didn't want to be alone with me?"

"Of course not. But I'm good at picking up subtext."

"Honestly, I don't know—"

"Admit it, Emma. You have a crush on Ben."

And Ben calls *me* Dog with a Bone? It's obvious Richard isn't going to let this go, so I might as well make his day. "Okay, you win. I had a crush on Ben. As in *had*."

"I think you're getting your tenses mixed up."

"Think what you like." I stare out the window for about five seconds before I can't stand it any longer. I turn to face Richard again. "How long have you known?"

"Emma, we've worked together now, what? Six years? It's not like I haven't figured you out."

"Does Jackie know too?"

"And Lisa. Don't forget her."

I slump down into my seat. "I feel like a world-class idiot."

"Hey, it's not like he discouraged you."

This makes me sit straight back up again. "What do you mean?"

"I mean that he shouldn't have led you on. Gallagher could have nipped it in the bud anytime he wanted, but he didn't. Personally, I think he got off on it."

"You think Ben led me on?"

"Look, I like the guy, but he's a schmuck. He's a good boss and a good editor, but he's a *guy*, and guys like to have their egos stroked, and there you were every day, running at his beck and call, looking at him with those brown doe eyes of yours, laughing at everything he said—"

"I didn't run at his beck and call!"

Richard glares at me.

"Okay, maybe I did run. Just a little. But that's in the past."

"Whatever. But as a twenty-first-century kind of guy, I found the whole thing rather . . . disturbingly old-fashioned. Single, lonely spinster pining away for her boss. Very *Mad Men,* if you ask me. So when you found yourself a boyfriend, I thought maybe Don Draper deserved some payback."

"Payback?" I struggle to come up with whatever it is Richard is talking about. And then it hits me. "You mean the *Facebook fiasco*?"

"You don't think that skit was spontaneous, do you?" Richard suddenly looks pleased with himself. "I guess my acting skills are better than I thought."

"Let me get this straight. You *planned* that little show?"

"I came up with the original premise. Lisa and Jackie ad-libbed some of it. I thought they did a pretty good job."

I am completely speechless.

"Look," Richard says, "the minute I saw you'd hooked up with this other guy, I thought, why not rub it in Gallagher's nose? Let him know your days of oohing and aahing at everything he said were over. And it worked. You should have seen the look on his face. He was like a little kid who just lost his new toy truck."

I don't know whether Richard is a Machiavellian genius or my Knight in Shining Armor.

"Thanks, I guess."

"Hey, you're like a little sister to me, so it was my pleasure. Girls like you, Emma, you don't give yourselves enough credit. So you're no Jennifer Aniston. Who is? Lots of guys like your cop are smart enough to see that you've got a lot to offer. Don't sell yourself short."

chapter twenty-four

· · · · ·

We pull into the mansion. "We are definitely in the wrong business," says Richard, peering out the car window. "Get a load of that view."

Trip's mother's house is probably the largest house I've seen. It's also directly on the Gulf. I don't want to think how much Trip must pay in hurricane insurance coverage alone. It's probably more than I make in a year. Richard doesn't wait for the limo driver to open the door; he does it himself and offers me a hand. We're immediately greeted by Chuck, who ushers us inside the house. Chuck does not like the fact that Richard is here. When I explain that my boss insisted I be accompanied by another journalist, Chuck clamps his jaw and nods curtly. *No way am I going to be alone with you people,* my smile says to him. Not that I'm afraid of Trip. But Chuck? I don't trust him as far as I can throw him.

Chuck shows us a room where we can "freshen up." We learn that Trip's mama is away on a cruise with friends. The cook has fixed us a light brunch and we have until one p.m. to complete the interview. This gives us barely two hours. Chuck makes it clear he will be present the entire time.

Trip looks nothing like the way he did in his hotel room. This time he's wearing a shirt and shoes. He's bright-eyed and clean-shaven and looks decidedly sheepish as he shakes my hand. "Emma, it's good to see you."

I have to admit, I'm relieved that he seems so "normal." "It's good to see you too, Trip."

This seems to relax him and we make some perfunctory small talk about the weather, his beautiful house, etc. We're served a seafood quiche and a salad and mimosas. Trip demurs at the mimosas and opts for water instead. Richard breaks into the food with a gusto that makes me smile.

"We really missed you at the ten-year reunion," I say to Trip.

"Reunion? Oh, yeah. Sorry I couldn't make it."

"Busy racing?" I ask.

"I'm not sure why I didn't go." Trip frowns.

"So, Miss Frazier, what have you been up to these past years?" Chuck asks in a smooth voice. "I'm sure Trip would love to know."

Prompted by Chuck, I tell them all about my work at *Florida!*, emphasizing the really great stories we do on conservation and wildlife, in hopes that Trip will show some enthusiasm. I tell him that his interview will be the headliner in this October's "Famous Floridians" issue, which has featured some really awesome people in the past, like Jimmy Buffett and Carl Hiaasen. Trip smiles politely. I get the sinking feeling he's never even looked at a copy of *Florida!* magazine.

"So tell me, big guy, what do you like to shoot?" Richard asks Trip.

Richard calling Trip "big guy" is sort of funny. I bet Richard is just as tall as Trip.

"Anything that moves," Trip says.

"Except humans, of course," Chuck chimes in.

Richard laughs. "Too bad. There's a couple of those I wouldn't mind bagging."

All three of them laugh now.

Why don't I happen to find this funny? I clear my throat and start to open my mouth to comment, but immediately stop when I feel Richard's hand on my knee beneath the table. He squeezes firmly in warning. I feel my face go warm. Strangely, I feel a few other parts of me go warm too. *Yuck. This is Richard,* I tell my girl parts, since they appear to be confused.

When it's obvious I'm not going to interrupt him, Richard inconspicuously removes his hand. I know what he's trying to do. He's using his "instincts" to lead the conversation in order to draw Trip out. But this isn't going to be another one of *Florida!* magazine's stories on hunting and fishing that Richard loves so much. This is my story, damn it. Not his.

I am now subjected to listening to Trip's hunting antics for the rest of lunch. He promises to show Richard his fishing gear before we leave and Richard practically has an orgasm at the thought of seeing Trip's fishing poles. Finally, lunch is over and we move to a living area that faces a beautiful swimming pool. Chuck asks me if I want to "freshen up" again.

"No thanks, I'm ready to start." I glance at my watch. It's almost noon, which means I have exactly one hour to conduct the rest of this interview. I take my things out of my tote bag—the laptop, the tape recorder, the yellow legal pad, and my yearbook—and place them on the coffee table in front of us. Trip sits in a wingback chair, facing the sofa on which Richard and I are seated. Chuck stands behind us, in prison-guard stance. I feel like one wrong move and Richard and I will be cuffed and thrown back into the limo, never to be seen or heard from again.

I lean forward and turn on my tape player.

Chuck comes around to the table and turns it off. "Sorry, no taping allowed." At the look on my face, he adds, "It's in the contract."

Trip shrugs as if to say Chuck is in charge and knows what he's doing.

Before I can ask Trip my first question, Chuck hands me a folder. "I thought this might be a good starting place." I open the folder and find two slips of paper. One has a listing of all the charitable boards Trips belongs to, all the monies he's donated, things like that. The other paper contains a list of ten questions. I guess this is what I'm supposed to ask Trip.

"Before I start, I wanted to give you this." I hand Trip one of Kimberly's business cards. I give one to Chuck too, since it's obvious he's the decision maker.

"The Yeager Agency?" Chuck says. "I've heard of them, of course, but we're perfectly happy with our PR firm in Dallas."

"Yes, well, they're a friendly bunch, I'll give you that. But since Trip's home base is here in Florida, I thought a local agency might be convenient. The rep on the card is a Catfish Cove alumna."

Trip peers at the card.

"Kimberly Lemoyne," I say, addressing Trip specifically. "She graduated a few years after us. She's top-notch. A real sharp cookie."

"Thanks for the recommendation," says Chuck. "Now, can we get on with the interview?"

I'd love to clobber Chuck over the head just about now. I know if Trip could ever meet Kimberly she'd be able to persuade him to at least give her a shot at a real presentation. As frustrating as it is, I go back to the sheet Chuck gave me and read question number one aloud. "What got you interested in racing?"

Trip gives me what sounds like a stock answer, which I jot down on my legal pad. I go through all the questions and this takes about twenty minutes.

Chuck claps his hands and rubs them together, satisfied. Any second now I expect him to throw a bone my way as a reward for good behavior. "So it looks like we're done here." He looks at Richard. "Ready to see the fishing equipment?"

"I thought we had till one p.m.," I say.

"Yes, but I think we've covered just about everything, haven't we?"

"Not quite." I scroll through my legal pad and try to think of something (anything) that will prolong this interview. "So . . . what's your favorite color?" I ask Trip.

Richard stifles a choking sound.

"Red," says Trip.

"Favorite food?"

"Pizza?"

"Is that a definite? You sound uncertain."

Trip begins to look uncomfortable.

"Tell me about your uncle Frank's auto shop," I ask.

Chuck jumps into action. "I'm afraid any mention of Trip's relatives are out of the scope of the interview."

"I understand. I'm not asking about his uncle, I'm asking about his uncle's *shop*. I believe that was your first job?" I say, looking directly at Trip.

For a moment Trip looks confused, like he's not sure whether he should answer. "Yeah," he says finally. "I worked for Frank after school. You know, after my daddy died."

I nod sympathetically.

"I really loved that place," Trip says.

"I love all the pictures on the wall. Especially the one of you with the grease smudge on your forehead. You're standing next to Frank with your arm around him and the inscription reads, 'To Uncle Frank, love, Trip.' That one's my personal favorite."

"Yeah," Trip says, frowning.

"You haven't seen it?" I ask.

"I remember signing the picture, but I didn't know Frank had it displayed in his shop."

"Oh, there's *lots* of pictures of you at the shop. There's even one of you from high school playing basketball." I pump my fist high in the air. "Go Crusaders!"

Trip smiles weakly.

"I think that's enough questions for today," Chuck says. "Trip, you were going to show these fine folks your fishing gear before they left?" Chuck begins to usher us out the back door.

Sigh. I guess that's that. I start to scoop up my stuff.

"Let me get that for you," Richard says. He picks up the tape recorder and places it inside my tote. "You go ahead with Trip. I'll meet you in the boathouse after I hit the little boys' room."

"Sure, okay." I mean, what else can I say? Richard is obviously trying to give me some alone time with Trip and for that I'm grateful, but alone time with Trip also includes Chuck, so it's essentially worthless.

We're in the process of checking out Trip's fishing lures when Richard joins us in the boathouse. He hands me my tote bag and proceeds to act immensely interested in a bunch of fake worms tied together. Or maybe he truly is fascinated by the lures. Who knows? With Richard, it's hard to tell. One thing I've discovered about him in the past week is that he's more complex than I thought.

After the fishing show is over, Trip and Chuck escort us to

the front door, where Paul the limo driver is waiting. Chuck hands me his card. "I look forward to reading your article," he says to me.

"Can I have your card as well?" I ask Trip.

"That won't be necessary," Chuck says. "All Trip's business dealings go through me first."

"Okay, well, here's my card, just in case." I hand it to Trip personally. What's Chuck going to do? Rip it out of Trip's hands?

Trip takes my card but he doesn't say anything. I'd really hoped that our past relationship (as limited as it was) would have made a difference today, but apparently it hasn't. We get in the limo and drive off.

Richard waits a full five minutes before he starts to chuckle. "What's your favorite *color*?"

"Hey, I was desperate."

"I can see that." He shakes his head. "No worries. Just embellish it the way you did the manatee article and all will be well."

This is almost exactly what Ben said to me. "I didn't embellish the manatee article. Ninety-nine percent of it was based on fact. I simply added an extra twist to it."

"Yeah, well, you're going to need a lot of that extra twist to make any of that crap back there sell."

Richard isn't telling me anything I don't already know. I pull out my legal pad and start to look at Trip's answers, trying to think of how to work some of the "fat" into my article. The problem is there is no genuine fat here. It's all strictly lean, no flavor whatsoever. After about an hour of jotting down my impressions, I go to pull out my laptop, and that's when I notice my yearbook is missing.

Richard appears to be napping. I nudge him awake. "Richard, where's my yearbook?"

He keeps his eyes closed as he answers, "Whoops, I must have forgot it."

"Forgot it? Richard, that's my high school yearbook! I can't get another one of those." I pull out Chuck's card and start to dial his number. Richard comes fully awake. He yanks the phone from my hand and hits the end button. "What did you do that for?" I ask. "I was going to let Chuck know where to send my yearbook."

"You know what you need to learn? Patience. You'd suck at fishing."

"I happen to be an excellent fisher person," I say.

"In that case, let the yearbook sit on the table. Who knows? Maybe Trip will take the nibble."

"You forgot it on purpose?" I start to get excited. "You think if Trip looks at my yearbook it might help trigger some memories of us? Make him more open? Make him want to call me back?"

"It's a long shot, but it can't hurt, can it? You gave him your card, at least give him time to call you back personally before you ring up Chuck."

"That was really smart of you." I have to give Richard credit, in his own way he's actually been a plus on this trip. "So what was the secret signal at the table for?"

"What secret signal?"

"You know, when you squeezed my knee to get me to be quiet. What were you trying to get Trip to say then?"

"Nothing. I've just always wanted to squeeze your leg and it seemed like a good time to try." Richard closes his eyes and goes back to his nap with a grin on his face.

Once again, I have no rebuttal.

Richard, two.

Emma, zero.

chapter twenty-five

·····

"I've Been a Bad, Bad Boy."

This is the title of one of the Trip Monroe articles I've written. It begins with our "encounter" at the Don Cesar and pretty much relates verbatim all the events that follow. It costars Chuck as some sort of NASCAR Svengali who controls Trip's every word and thought. As a reward for being Chuck's meal ticket and puppet, Chuck supplies Trip with booze and women.

Of course, this is not the article I'm turning in. For one thing, it violates almost every clause of the contract Chuck forced me to sign before I could interview Trip. And second, it's not something *Florida!* would ever print. At least I don't think so. Still, writing it was almost cathartic.

The other article, the "real" article, is titled "I Just Want to Go Fishing," which is my lame attempt at a clever spin-off of Greta Garbo's famous "I just want to be alone" quote. It is almost two thousand words of pure vanilla using Chuck's "guidelines." I have tried to embellish and twist it into something worthy of *Florida!* standards, but it's no use. The thought that my name is going to be attached to this makes me want to stay in bed with a pillow over my head.

The good news (this is the optimist in me fighting to stay alive) is that this is Friday and I still have till Monday morning to give Ben my rough draft. Ben is in Miami today, meeting with advertisers. Or rather, schmoozing the advertisers. I really think Ben is going to take T.K.'s job. Which leads me to wonder who will take Ben's job. I would be lying if I said I haven't considered the possibility of T.K. offering it to me. But Richard has been with the magazine longer than I have and I'm not sure how much seniority will play into it.

Jackie is in Fort Myers on a fam trip at a resort spa, undergoing an "exciting" new exfoliation treatment that uses natural seashells. Basically, she's going to be wined, dined, sloughed, and moisturized, all in the hope that she will write a favorable review of the place. I'd give anything to trade places with her right now.

Lisa is out running errands, so Richard and I are the only ones in the office. I place both articles on his desk.

"Read these and tell me what you think? Pretty please?"

He looks up from his cell phone. "Have you read my manuscript yet?"

"I told you, I can't start reading until I get this Trip Monroe thing done. It's due to Ben by Monday and—"

"Yeah, yeah." Richard picks up the first article. "'I've Been a Bad, Bad Boy'?" He grins. "I like this already."

I wait patiently in my cubicle while he reads. After a while he leans over and places his hand on the back of my chair. I lean in closer. "So what do you think?"

"Trip likes to party. Big deal. He's not married, so only a few born-again Christians are gonna get their panties in a wad over this. Still, it makes good reading. I have a friend over at the *National Enquirer* who'd probably pay high five figures for this. Maybe even six, seeing as how you're the first to write anything negative on the guy."

"Do you know someone at *every* publication in the country?"

"Just about."

"So you think this is worthy of the *National Enquirer,* huh?"

"Oh yeah. I especially like the part where Trip mistakes you for a hooker."

Sigh. "Obviously, I can't submit that. Or the other one."

"Yeah, I figured it was best not to mention that other one."

"Richard, what am I going to do?"

Maybe it's lack of sleep that has my guard down, but I'm virtually at the point of tears. I don't think I've ever let Richard see me so vulnerable. I brace myself for a smorgasbord of sarcasm.

"You're going stop acting like a victim and start acting like a journalist. Grow a pair and go after the real story here."

"*Grow a pair?* God, you sound like my mother."

"Which one? The doctor or the bookseller?"

Although I've worked with Richard forever, I don't remember ever discussing my family in detail with him. "How do you know what my moms do for a living?"

"I pay attention."

"Oh. So how exactly do you propose I grow a pair?"

"Try it from a different angle."

"I've thought about that, but—"

"Think hard, Emma. If you don't get what you want the first time, do you just give up? Figure out another way to reach this guy. To get a real interview. *Without* Chuck the bulldog at his side. I guarantee you, if you don't go after the real story, someone else will. This guy's a time bomb. It's only a matter of the right leak to the right person before it all comes out."

I know what Richard says is true. But if I'm going to make this story work, then I'm going to need help from the one person I'd really hoped I wouldn't have to call again.

I glance at my watch. It's almost noon and tomorrow is Saturday, which is the night of Jackie's big party and I certainly can't miss that. First off, she would kill me, and second, I've waited almost two years to glimpse the Death Star and I'm not about to miss the big unveiling. All this means I have about twenty-eight hours to drive to Catfish Cove, convince Frank Monroe to help me, then drive back to Tampa and have enough time to look stunningly gorgeous in my bathing suit. Richard is right. I'm going to have to man up.

"Hey, Richard?"

"Yeah?"

"Thanks."

For the second time this summer I find myself sneaking into Catfish Cove. It's not that I don't want to see my moms or Nick. But I'm on a tight schedule here. If I let them know I'm in town, they're going to want me to visit and that will distract me from my mission.

I drive directly to Frank Monroe's house and knock on the door. I'm so nervous the sweat is running down the back of my legs.

Frank opens the door and smiles at me. "Yes?"

"Mr. Monroe, please hear me out," I say quickly, in case he plans to slam the door in my face. "My name is Emma Frazier. I left you a message back in June. Do you remember?"

I see the recognition cross his face. He opens the door all the way and steps to the side. "Now that you're here, you might as well c'mon in," he says.

I meekly enter his house. He takes a long look at me and shakes his head. "Damn, but you look just like your mama."

"So everyone tells me. She says the two of you went to prom together."

"Did she? Well, that was mighty nice of her to remember." His voice is thick with sarcasm.

"Um, yeah. She said you were a very nice man, and frankly, sir, I'm at the end of my rope. I really hope you can help me out here."

He looks like he doesn't know what to make of this but he invites me to take a chair in his living room and offers me an iced tea, which I gratefully accept. My attention is drawn to the kitchen, where I hear someone puttering around.

"That's my friend Julie," Frank says. "I believe the two of you have met."

"Yes, we have. Thanks." What I'm thanking him for I have no idea. I guess I'm just hoping that the right words will come to me. He goes into the kitchen and comes out alone with two glasses of tea, one for me and one for himself. I thank him again, this time for the tea. Julie does not make an appearance, for which I'm grateful because I think what I'm about to say is better said in private. I take a long, grateful sip of my drink. "This is delicious. Did Julie make it?"

"No, I did. It's my mama's special recipe."

I would ask him for it but something tells me he won't give it to me, so I don't bother. It's not that he's acting hostile, but he's not overly friendly either. More resigned than anything. I might as well get this over with.

"I know you're very protective of Trip, and I get that. We went to high school together and I remember how rough he had it after his daddy died."

"What do you want with Trip?" he asks suspiciously.

"Mr. Monroe, I'm a journalist for *Florida!* magazine. You've heard of it, haven't you?"

"'Course I have. I subscribe to it. Have for years."

I can't help it. I smile the same way I do whenever I hear someone praise the magazine. "So the thing is, I've been trying to get an interview with Trip—"

"Trip has a PR firm to deal with that kind of stuff."

"Yeah, I know. The one in Dallas."

I decide to gamble and reach inside my tote bag to produce the "I've Been a Bad, Bad Boy" article. I hand it to him. "You might want to see this."

Frank pulls a pair of glasses from his shirt pocket and starts reading. He doesn't even make it to page two before he slams the article across his knee. "Young lady, you have a lot of nerve showing up here at my house with this . . . this *crap*."

"Everything I wrote is true."

His face turns a weird shade of purple.

Uh-oh. The last thing I want to do is give Frank Monroe a heart attack. "But I'm not submitting it to my editor." Of course, technically, according to the contract I was tricked into signing (yes, that's how I'm choosing to remember it), I *can't* submit it, but Uncle Frank doesn't have to know this.

"Mr. Monroe, I want to write a real piece on Trip but I can't do that if he doesn't open up to me. I remember Trip from high school. He was a real nice boy. Shy, and kind of sweet. Maybe even a little sensitive. I want to write about that Trip and how he really feels about being *People* magazine's Sexiest Man Alive and why he's quitting the racing circuit this year. I know he's having problems.

"That story and everything else is going to leak out eventually.

Probably a lot sooner than you think. I want to write the story from Trip's point of view. I want to write it fairly, and sympathetically, because I like Trip. I don't think he's going to get that sort of break from any other journalist."

"What do you want from me?" Frank asks. The pain in his voice tells me everything I need to know about this man. It's obvious he loves his nephew. If I convince him to help me, I have to do what's right by him, as well as Trip.

"I want to interview Trip for real. Without Chuck Miller in the room."

Frank's jaw tightens. "That bastard ruined Trip."

"Do you think you can help me?"

"Trip doesn't listen to me anymore. I've tried getting him professional help. Getting him away from Miller, but it's no use."

"I know. I saw you visit him at the Don Cesar."

He looks surprised, so I tell him the whole story. How I spotted him at the hotel and how I got Trip's hotel room number by having Kimberly discreetly follow him.

"She a good-looking blonde?"

I nod.

"I remember her from the elevator. I thought—well, never mind what I thought."

"You thought she was a hooker." I put the pieces together and figure out that this is why Trip was expecting a blonde. Frank must have assumed she was on her way to meet Trip, and from the look on Frank's face when he got out of the elevator, my guess is that they argued about it.

He nods, maybe a little embarrassed. "If I help you, if I call Trip and ask him to speak to you, you promise me you'll write up a fair article. One that isn't going to shame his mama?"

"I promise, I won't write anything that will hurt any of Trip's family."

He takes a long minute to think this over.

"All right. I'll call him. But like I said, he doesn't listen to me so much anymore. I can't guarantee he'll call you back."

I hand Frank my business card. "He can call my cell phone twenty-four/seven." I have an urge to hug him but I don't think it would be appropriate. "I hate to bring this up, but a rough draft of the article is due on Monday, so if you could put a rush on this, that would be great."

Frank shakes his head and chuckles. "Pushy. Just like your mama."

"So the two of you were like, friends in high school, huh?"

"Friends? I'd say we were more than friends."

"Oh yeah?"

Frank looks at me strangely. The funny worm sensation in my stomach hits me again. I really hate worms. "That message you left me? The reason I told you never to call me back was . . . well, never mind."

"I have to admit, I thought your refusal to talk to me was a little over-the-top."

"I didn't know your message had anything at all to do with Trip."

"Then what did you think I was calling about?"

"You said it was urgent and I thought—aw, hell, I thought you were trying to figure out if I was your daddy."

I laugh. "Why on earth would I think that?"

"Because it's a fairly logical conclusion based on the fact your mama and I used to be married."

chapter twenty-six

·····

Five days of good old-fashioned American dieting has done the trick. I am now seven pounds lighter than I was last Monday and my bathing-suit bottom feels . . . well, it feels okay. I'll be honest, the reason I've been able to stick to my diet is that between the stress of Trip's interview, learning about Mom's secret marriage to Frank Monroe, and checking my cell phone every few seconds to see if Trip has called, I haven't had much of an appetite. I know if Mom knew about my reaction to finding out she was married, she would say I was being "dramatic." I know I should have immediately hashed it out with her, but instead I slipped out of town like I'd just written a bad check.

This is what Frank told me:

He and mom were high school sweethearts and dated all through college. They broke up while she was in med school, but got back together when she moved home and began working in Grandpa George's medical office. They secretly eloped (at mom's insistence) and Frank thought they were happy (how weird is it that Nick used this same expression to describe his marriage to Shannon. Are all men so out of touch with reality?). Then one week after the marriage, before they even announced the "good news" to their families, Mom blindsided Frank by telling him she wanted a divorce. They separated and Frank thought it was just a matter of time before he could talk her into coming back to him. He kept fighting the divorce, until finally six months after they separated, Mom went to see him, and surprise! She was pregnant with another man's baby. Frank didn't need more than that to propel him straight to a lawyer's office.

"She got herself a baby from a damn sperm donor," Frank said. "Sorry to talk about your, um . . . daddy that way."

"No worries," I said.

Mom wanted a divorce and she found a way to get it. I guess I was her "fuck you" to Frank Monroe. No wonder he didn't want to talk to me.

If I'd stayed in Catfish Cove last night and talked to Mom about all this, then the real drama would begin. I can't help it. My feelings are hurt. I know Mom loves me but how could she have had what basically amounts to a secret life and never told me about it? How could she have kept this from me my entire life? Does Mama J know? Of course she does. They tell each other everything. I feel like the third wheel in my own family. Plus, if I'd stayed in town, then Nick would have found out and I don't think it's fair to drag Nick into my family soap opera without first knowing the real story myself.

I can't deal with any of this until after Monday.

I check my cell phone for the hundredth time today. Trip has not called, texted, or tried to reach me in any way. I guess Frank was right when he said he didn't have much influence over Trip anymore.

I do however get a text message from Richard.

Have something important to tell you.

I call Richard but I get his voice mail. I'll see him tonight at Jackie's party, so I guess I'll find out what the big important something is then.

Nick arrives in Tampa by early afternoon. He's looking forward to Jackie's party and seems genuinely eager to meet my work friends.

"So what if I don't pass the test?" Nick asks.

"What test?"

"The boyfriend test."

"I have no idea what you're talking about."

Except that I think I do. Torie, Kimberly, and Jason have given Nick the gold seal of approval. My mothers love him. Now all he has to do is charm the people I work with and he's basically won the Triple Crown. In terms of meeting the significant people in each other's life, Nick has gotten off relatively easy. He's been allowed to gradually wade into the ocean. I, on the other hand, was forced overboard during a hurricane without a life jacket.

Remember I told you I was having dinner with Nick's parents last weekend? Well, it turned out to be Nick's parents, his uncle Vinnie and aunt Elaine, his sister Anna and her family, five of Nick's cousins, plus Nick's grandmother and a few assorted cops who work with Nick, including his best friend Jeff and his wife and kids. We took up the entire banquet room at Louie's that is normally used only for special occasions. Visualize the scene where John Corbett is introduced to Nia Vardalos's family in *My Big Fat Greek Wedding*. Instead of looking into my soul, I think Nick's mother concentrated more on my childbearing hips. Whatever she saw, she liked, because Nick said, "You passed with flying colors."

"What's the matter?" Nick asks. "You seem distracted."

"It's this article. I almost wish I could skip Jackie's party, except I really want to go and she'd kill me if I don't show."

Nick puts his arms around me. "Are you sure that's all it is?"

I think about telling Nick what Frank Monroe told me but it seems disloyal to talk about it with him before I discuss it with my moms.

"That's it," I say brightly.

I spend an incredible amount of time getting ready for tonight's party. I know my makeup will wilt in this July heat but I have to put forth an effort. I'm wearing the same yellow sundress over my bathing suit that I wore the night Nick and I met Jason and the girls for the first time. My hair is smooth and my eyes are overly bright (probably a wolfish gleam from lack of food). Nick gives me a smile of approval and we drive to Jackie's new house.

"Emma!" Jackie says, greeting me at the door with a hug. Jackie looks chic in a sleek one-piece black swimsuit with a fuchsia-colored wrap skirt tied around her hips and flat gold sandals. I've met Jackie's husband, Chris, before and he greets me warmly. I introduce Nick, who reaches into our towel bag to produce a bottle of wine with a red bow tied around the neck. I'm embarrassed to say I've been so preoccupied I didn't even think of a housewarming gift. Thank God for Nick and for his mama with the X-ray eyes who raised him right.

Jackie pulls me aside. "Emma, he's gorgeous!" she whispers in my ear.

I assume she's speaking of Nick and I smile knowingly. "Thanks, he's pretty nice too."

Jackie eyes my ensemble. "You look very sparkly," she says. I guess this is her way of saying that if I can't be thin, then I might as well shine in some other way.

A college-age woman wearing above-the-knee black linen shorts and a white oxford shirt hands me a drink that looks frothy and is sugary to the taste. She tries to hand Nick a drink as well, but he tells her he prefers beer and Chris leads him outside to the bar. This leaves Jackie and me alone.

"I've been dying for you to show up," she says. "You won't believe Richard's date. I told Chris to card her to make sure she's at least twenty-one."

"No!" I laugh.

Jackie lowers her voice. "And wait till you meet Ben's ex." She frowns. "Although if he brought her here, maybe she's not his ex anymore. Maybe she's his O." Jackie giggles at her own cleverness. I think she's had more than just a few of those frothy sugary drinks already. Combined with the fact that she probably hasn't eaten in days, it wouldn't take much to get her plastered.

"So what's she like? Ben's ex, I mean."

"You'll see," Jackie says in a singsong voice.

I'm about to interrogate her, when Lisa and her boyfriend, Tony, show up. Lisa is not here two seconds before she shows us her diamond engagement ring. Jackie and I both hug and congratulate her. Lisa says they plan to get married sometime in late winter or early spring when the weather will be cool enough (but not too cold) for a beach wedding. I think this pretty much cements Lisa's staying in Tampa.

Tony wanders outside to the bar and Jackie gives us a tour of the house. The Death Star is exactly the kind of house you would expect a successful plastic surgeon and his thin, glamorous wife to build. It's over six thousand square feet of stucco walls and red-tiled roof with a killer view of the bay. There are five bedrooms and six bathrooms. Jackie hired a well-known interior designer to decorate the home and it shows. I think Jackie will love working out of this house. I know I would. Has Ben told her about the move to Orlando? According to Richard, he probably has.

"The house is absolutely beautiful," I say, genuinely happy for her.

"Thanks!" says Jackie.

Lisa and I follow her outside to the pool area. Stringed white lights form a canopy roof, making the whole area feel like one giant party room. Citronella candles abound on the many tables. There must be at least a hundred people here. Besides all of us from *Florida!,* there are plenty of Chris's medical associates and all of Jackie and Chris's personal friends. There is an oversize pool with a gurgling waterfall but no one is swimming, and other than Jackie and Lisa and me, none of the other women seem to have on bathing-suit attire. It appears that I have starved myself for nothing. I make a mental note to eat something as soon as possible.

Nick is by the summer kitchen, where a bar is set up. He's got a longneck in his hand and is talking to Chris. Tony is wandering around looking like a lost puppy, and Lisa goes off to "save" him.

Nick is the best kind of boyfriend to take to a party. He mingles easily with other people and this is a great relief because I've had boyfriends who've had to be babysat, and this can be really inconvenient when you just want to kick back and have a good time. I down my sugary drink (which I discover is the caterer's version of a lemon drop). There is a food table near the edge of the waterfall and that is where I find Richard. He's wearing a Rays baseball cap and stuffing his face full of shrimp.

A girl with curly red hair à la Nicole Kidman in her heyday wearing a skimpy skirt and tank top appears at Richard's side. He introduces me to his "friend" Becky. This is the first time I've met one of Richard's girlfriends and I'm not disappointed. Becky is exactly the type of girl I've always envisioned Richard with— tall, thin, with great boobs and even better hair. Becky wanders back to the bar area. I grab the edge of Richard's Hawaiian shirt to pull him off to the side where no one can hear us.

"Richard, how old is your date?"

"Who? Becky?" He pops another shrimp into his mouth and shrugs. "I dunno know. Why?"

"Do you think she's over twenty-one?"

"God, I hope not. I don't like them *that* old."

I punch him in the arm. "I'm serious! She's over there drinking beer . . . Oh, God, now she's talking to Nick."

Richard checks Nick out. "So that's the boyfriend, huh? What is he, the alcohol police?"

"No, it's just . . . oh, never mind." It's not like Nick is going to demand to see Becky's driver's license (she probably has a fake one, anyway).

"Relax. Becky's twenty-three."

I raise my brows.

"I know this for a fact because I've known her since she was a baby. She's the kid sister of one of my old high school buddies."

"*Ew,* you're dating someone you knew as a baby?"

"It's only a ten-year difference," he says in mock indignation. "Besides, what do you care who I date?"

Richard is right. He could date the entire waitstaff at Hooters and it wouldn't matter to me one bit. I grab another lemon drop off the tray of a wandering server. I definitely need to chill.

"What's wrong with you? You're even more uptight than usual." Before I can respond, he says, "So how's the Trip Monroe thing going?"

This reminds me to check my cell phone. I whip it out to find no messages. "Dismal at best."

"You still have two days."

"Great. All I need is a couple of loaves and a few fish."

"So, did you get my text?"

"Yeah, what's so important?"

"I'm going to tell you something I shouldn't because I'm probably going to lose a friend over this, but screw it." I've never heard Richard so serious before. Although we're away from the crowd, he still lowers his voice. "Trip checked himself into Betty Ford last week. My buddy at *Sports Illustrated* got the tip last night and he's not the sharpest blade in the kitchen, *capisce*? So if he knows, at least half a dozen other bloodhounds are on the same trail. I predict within the next few weeks we're going to be seeing a lot of interesting stories on your friend."

"But . . . how could Trip have checked himself into Betty Ford and been in Naples just a couple of days ago for my interview?"

"Time off for good behavior and a fast jet at his disposal?"

I wish I could dismiss this as a rumor, but unfortunately, Richard's story makes perfect sense. "A little R and R in California, my *ass*!" I down the rest of my lemon drop.

"You might want to go easy on those," Richard warns.

I ignore him and find a waiter to refill my drink.

"So while every other magazine in the country is free to print whatever they want about Trip, thanks to that contract I signed, I'm stuck with my 'I Just Want to Go Fishing' story. God, we're going to look like morons."

"Pretty much."

I can't believe how gullible I was, falling for Chuck's story. He must have laughed long and hard after I signed that contract.

I'm so angry I could spit. I'm also way disappointed in Trip. Does he know how Chuck plans to use *Florida!* to counterbalance the slew of negative publicity coming his way? How could he not? I really thought our high school connection meant something to him. Obviously not.

"Go ahead and say it."

"I'm sorry, Emma."

"I meant 'I told you so.'"

"Hey, you were too close to the whole thing to see clearly. Frankly, I think Gallagher is responsible for this debacle. No self-respecting journalist would have ever let you sign that contract."

Although Richard is a colleague, in some ways he's also my competition. He didn't have to warn me about what's about to happen. Me looking like an idiot only serves to make him a better candidate for Ben's job. "Thanks for the heads-up. Really. I owe you big-time."

"You don't owe me squat. We're friends, right?"

"Definitely." I mean it too.

"So have you seen the boss and his date yet?"

I freeze. This is the exact voice Jackie used to say almost the exact same thing to me. "No. Why?"

"Nothing."

Only I know it's not nothing and I'm about to force Richard to tell me why he and Jackie are so interested in my reaction to Ben's ex, but in that moment I spy Ben. He's at the bar next to Nick and I can't help but compare the two of them. Ben is taller than Nick, although not as muscular. He's wearing board shorts and a T-shirt and leather flip-flops. The two of them shake hands. I look everywhere for Elise, but I don't see anyone who fits the gorgeous-cancer-fighting-doctor category.

Richard also sees Ben and shouts, "Hey! Gallagher! Can you spare a beer?"

Everyone turns to look in our direction. Out of habit, I want to cringe for Richard's sake but everyone seems to find this funny, and amazingly, I sort of do too. Richard and I make our way over to the bar.

"Great party, huh?" I say to Ben. "Looks like you've already met Nick."

Nick and Ben give each other that look that guys do when they think they are one step ahead of you. I introduce Nick to Richard and they shake hands. Becky slides her way in. Soon after, Tony and Lisa join us and we are now a cozy seven-some. Where the heck is Marie Curie?

Out of the corner of my eye I see Jackie emerge from inside the house. She's talking to another woman and they are headed in our direction, and it is in that instant that I realize the woman with Jackie is none other than Ben's ex. Elise is nothing like I expected. Now I know why Jackie and Richard were so anxious to have me meet her.

Ben takes Elise's hand and squeezes it. "This is an old friend of mine, Elise Palmer," he says by way of introduction.

"*Doctor* Elise Palmer. Famous oncologist and all that," adds Richard.

No one says anything for an awkward beat. I don't think Richard has had too much to drink but this seems a little irreverent, even for him.

Elise smiles good-naturedly. "Don't forget world-renowned and tirelessly fearsome. Those are absolute adjectives when describing me."

We all laugh and Ben finishes the introductions but it's obvious that everyone knows Elise is Ben's ex-fiancée.

It does not take long for Elise to become the center of attention. She is in Tampa for another two weeks, wrapping up a research project that involves her working night and day and she's absolutely thrilled to be taking a few hours off to relax and meet Ben's friends. She regales us with stories about Ben's New York days but she's also a great listener and seems genuinely interested in each and every one of us, including Richard's friend Becky, who (much to my shame) turns out to have just graduated from nursing school and is actually a very nice person. Becky is thinking of applying for a job on the oncology floor at Tampa General, but she is afraid the work will be too depressing. Elise reassures her that yes, working oncology is hard work, heartbreaking and demanding, but it's also one of the most rewarding jobs in the world. She ends by giving Becky her business card and the two make plans to have lunch together so they can talk further. Elise can imitate Sarah Palin better than Tina Fey and she knows more about beer and baseball than any woman I've ever known.

Elise is also short and slightly dumpy and has no fashion sense.

chapter twenty-seven

· · · · ·

We are two hours into the party. Nick is with Chris and Jackie getting a tour of the house. When Chris found out that Nick is remodeling a fixer-upper, he got all excited and the two of them started swapping stories about painting and roofing and what insulation materials are best for keeping out the Florida heat. I am on my zillionth lemon drop. I've also had three shrimp. I've tried to eat more, but after five days of almost nothing, my stomach has shrunk and just those few shrimp make me feel bloated.

Who am I kidding? It's the liquor that has me bloated. I need to stop drinking. I make my way to the nearest bathroom. Elise has the same idea and we both reach the bathroom door at the exact same moment.

"You first," I slur . . . er, I say.

"We're all girls here. I'm not shy if you're not." Elise takes my hand and pulls me into the bathroom with her, which is so large that we could both be in here and miss seeing each other if we're not looking hard enough.

Elise begins to fiddle with her hair, which is pulled back in a low bun. She has on no makeup (or at least it looks like she doesn't). She washes her hands at the sink but doesn't primp or even look at herself in the mirror. I finish up and wash my own hands. I check my teeth in the mirror to make sure there is no shrimp residue and reapply my signature red lipstick. I'm really beginning to love this color. I think that even if Parisian women gave up red lipstick, I'd still wear it.

"Everyone here is so nice," Elise says.

"Glad you're having a good time."

"Ben seems to really like it down here and I can see why. Although this humidity must get to be a little too much." Elise makes a panting sound that I think is supposed to make me laugh, so being the polite Floridian I am, I oblige her.

"I guess you've known Ben a long time, huh?"

"We went to Columbia together. His sister and I are good friends."

"Sounds pretty cozy."

She cocks her head to the side and gives me a long look. "Am I what you expected? Because I have to say, you're exactly what I pictured."

"You pictured *me*?"

"Oh, Ben talks about you all the time. Emma *this*, Emma *that*. If I didn't know any better, I'd think you and Ben—well, your boyfriend seems terrific. A really nice guy and all."

"I'm not—" I'm about to tell Elise that I'm not interested in Ben but that's not completely true. "I admit, there was a time when I was pretty infatuated with Ben, but that's over. He never showed any real interest in me."

Elise gets quiet. "Emma, I love Ben. It broke my heart when he called off our wedding. I'll do anything to get him back. He's the one for me. And I think I'm the one for him. I've been offered a job down here, and if Ben gives me the green light, I'm going to take it."

Before I know it, Elise is crying and I've got my arms around her. "I'm sure Ben will come around," I say. "How could he not? You're terrific! Smart, funny, attractive—"

"Don't patronize me," Elise interrupts with a sniffle. "I'm not attractive. Not like you."

I start to laugh.

"What's so funny?" she asks.

There's a knock at the door. I open it to find a friend of Jackie's standing in front of me with what appears to be a fresh drink. I snatch it from her hands. "There are five other bathrooms in the house," I say. She barely has time to look startled before I close the door in her face.

I hand the drink to Elise. "Get comfortable. I have a story to tell you."

We sit side by side on the cool stone tile, our backs against the wall with our legs stretched out in front of us. I tell her all about my crush on Ben and the night at Captain Pete's when Amy called me the ugly friend and everything that's happened since. I even tell her about Nick and how I think he might still be hung up on his ex. We end up hugging and telling each other to "hang in there." Funny, how with just a little commonality you can connect with a complete stranger in just a couple of hours. Adding some liquor into the mix probably doesn't hurt either.

It's after midnight and I'm emotionally drained. I want to go home but first I have to find Nick. I search the pool area but I don't see him. I grab a bottled water from the bar and head toward the dock. There is a slight breeze coming off the water and it feels good against my flushed skin. It's now officially Sunday morning. My Trip Monroe article is due to Ben in twenty-four-plus hours and I have nothing. I check my cell phone again but there's no call, no message from Trip.

"Frazier, what are you doing out here in the dark?"

I whip around. *Great.* It's the person I least want to see right now.

"Contemplating throwing myself into the Tampa Bay."

Ben smiles. "Richard getting on your nerves?"

"Not really."

"By the way, that Nick is one terrific guy."

"Yeah, he is."

He glances toward the house. "Some place, huh?"

"The Trip Monroe article sucks," I blurt.

"You're exaggerating."

"Richard was right. Trip Monroe is a terrible interview. And no matter how hard I try to spin it, it's just going to be a big bunch of blah."

Ben shrugs. "Even a big bunch of blah from that guy is going to sell magazines."

I think about telling Ben about how Trip has checked himself into Betty Ford and how sooner or later every AP agency in the country will know it, only we can't use it because of the contract, but I think it should all come from Richard, since it's his source.

Neither of us says anything for a few seconds and I decide, why the heck not? Maybe I've had too much to drink or maybe my talk with Elise has inspired me, so I'm going to put it all out there. "You know why I offered up that damn interview in the first place? To impress *you*."

Ben shoves his hands into the pockets of his shorts. He turns and stares out at the water.

"You remember that night at Captain Pete's?" I say.

Ben turns to face me. "Sure I remember."

"I wasn't trying to fix you up with Amy. I was trying to fix you up with *me*. But you knew that."

"Yeah," Ben admits quietly.

So, Richard was right all along. I can't help it. I smile in anticipation of what Richard is going to say when I tell him about this
conversation. And I *am* going to tell him because this is one
scenario about which Richard definitely deserves to say "I told
you so."

Ben mistakes my smile as encouragement because he takes a
step forward in my direction. I place my hand in the air to ward
him off. "Stay back."

"Emma, you have to know I'm crazy about you."

I still. "What about Elise?"

"Elise and I . . . that's a complicated relationship."

I frown. "So what happened that night at Captain Pete's? If
you knew I was interested in you and you're so crazy about me,
then why did you blow me off for Amy?"

"I got confused," Ben says, right before he reaches out and
pulls me into him.

I don't have time to think about what Ben means when he
says he was confused because Ben is going to kiss me and I have
about three seconds to decide what to do here.

Do I push him away? It's what I *should* do. I have a boyfriend.
Plus, now that I've gotten to know Elise and have discovered that
I like her, I feel that I'm betraying her too. But I've fantasized
about this kiss for so long, I owe it to myself to see if there's anything between us. I don't want to go the rest of my life wondering if Ben was really the guy for me. That wouldn't be fair to
anyone.

Ben leans down and kisses me. My head is swirling with
thoughts and the crazy emotions behind them. First and overrid-
ing all is a sense of triumph. My instincts about Ben were right
all along. It was that night at Captain Pete's that screwed everything up. I know what Ben means when he says he was confused.

Amy showed interest in him, and like a dolt, I gave up. I let her shove me aside because deep down, I didn't think when given a choice, Ben would actually pick a girl like me over a girl like her.

When Amy called me the ugly friend, it tapped into a well of insecurity that I let take me over. I remember that moment in time, when Amy and Ben were playing darts, and I wanted to march up between them and snatch him away from her. But I didn't. The funny thing is, I know now that it would have worked.

Be good to Nick, okay, Emma?

Tricia's voice snaps me out of my trance.

What am I doing? I was so sure that I could never be like Shannon. That I would never cheat on Nick. But this isn't cheating. It's just a kiss and it's never going to happen again because I realize now it's all wrong. Nothing about this kiss feels right. There's no passion, no tenderness, no anything except a whole lot of regret. I think I needed it, though, to finally get over the last traces of my Ben crush. All the lemon drops I've drunk tonight are roiling around in my stomach, threatening mutiny. Throwing up on Ben was never in any of my fantasies. I break off our kiss.

Ben stares down at me, his eyes a little wild-looking. More confusion? Lust? I'm not sure which emotion I see there. "Are you okay?" he asks.

"Tell me about Elise," I say again. "What happened between you two? Why didn't you get married?"

Ben looks away. "Cold feet."

"Yours or hers?"

"Mine," he admits.

"That's too bad, because I think she's perfect for you."

Ben's head snaps around to meet my gaze. "Yeah?"

"Yeah."

I know why Richard and Jackie were so anxious to have me meet Elise. If I am being brutally honest here, Elise is not nearly as attractive as me. Elise is a five on a good night and Richard and Jackie do not understand what Ben sees in her. In their minds they think I have one-upped Ben by nabbing someone as attractive as Nick.

I think about all the hours I wasted being jealous of Amy. Seeing Ben with Elise tonight, I realize why (despite Amy's many alluring attributes) Ben could never be seriously interested in her. Elise is everything Amy is not. She's a brilliant conversationalist—quick-witted, well traveled. Yet for all her accomplishments, surprisingly modest. But most of all Elise is kind. She is exactly the type of woman my mothers hoped I would one day become.

"Do you love Elise?"

Ben looks startled by my frankness. "Like I said, it's complicated."

"Aren't you the guy who told me to stop overanalyzing? Either you feel it or you don't. You're thirty-four years old, Ben. If you don't feel it, then tell her so she can get on with her life."

A part of me hopes Ben takes my advice and goes back to Elise. But another part of me wonders if he simply isn't good enough for her.

I leave Ben standing at the end of the dock with his hands stuck in his pockets gazing out across the water like some lone romantic figure trying to sort out the meaning of life. The whole scene is like a Nicholas Sparks novel gone bad.

chapter twenty-eight

......

I find Nick deep in conversation with Richard. I would ask them what they are talking about but I'm pretty sure it has something to do with fishing. I tell Nick I don't feel so well and we leave. It's almost one in the morning by the time we reach my place.

"I think we should move in together." Nick hits me with this the moment we walk in the door.

"I don't think that's a good idea." This is one of the first completely spontaneous things I've ever said to him and I can tell he doesn't like it.

"Why not? I'm crazy about you, you're crazy about me, and in a couple of months you won't have an office to go to. You can work from anywhere."

You have to know I'm crazy about you.

This whole night seems surreal.

"Can we talk about this some other time?"

"What's wrong with right now?"

I take a deep breath. Instinctively I know this is a terrible time to be having this conversation, but my encounter with Ben has me reeling. I don't want to play games anymore. "Do you love me?"

"I just said I was crazy about you, didn't I?"

"It's not the same thing."

Nick pulls me into his arms. "Babe, we both know where this is going. We're not kids anymore. Let's take the plunge."

"You didn't answer my question."

"Okay, yeah, sure, of course I love you. Emma, we can have a great life together," he says, bending down to kiss me.

I cannot let Nick kiss me because I'll probably agree to anything he wants and I know this is one thing I'll definitely regret in the morning. I slide out from under his arm. I know what Nick says is true. I could have a happy, satisfied life living in Nick's house by the lake, filling it up with babies (well, at least one or two). I could still work for the magazine, still have a career. It's almost a dream scenario, except . . .

"Nick, am I your dream?"

"Is that like your soul mate or something?"

"Kind of."

"Emma," he says carefully, "life doesn't work like that. It's not all some big romantic sap story. The truth is, you meet someone and if you're lucky it works out. There are no big lightning bolts or fireworks. You just have to be grateful that the important stuff is there. Like trust and respect."

My heart wilts a little at his response. "What if I want the fireworks along with the trust and the respect?"

"Then you're going to end up alone. I found that out the hard way."

For a second I feel like someone has knocked the air from my lungs and I'm going to die. But then I take a breath and my body keeps going. I'm sad, but I'm not heartbroken. I am not Nick's dream. And the truth is, he is not my dream either. Deep down, I think I have known this since the beginning.

Maybe Nick and I should have this conversation tomorrow,

when we've both had time to think. But it seems unfair to keep him dangling when I know in my heart what I have to do.

"Nick, you shouldn't have to settle for me."

"Is that what you think I'm doing? *Jesus*," he swears under his breath. "Okay, I think it's way too early for this, but if you need it, then I'll give it to you. You want to get married?"

Count to ten, Emma.

"You and I . . . we aren't going to work out. I care about you so much and I know you care about me, but this isn't a forever kind of thing we have."

"You're serious," Nick says.

I nod.

His face grows hard. "Does this have anything to do with your boss?"

"What do you mean?"

Nick studies me for a second and shakes his head in disbelief. "No way. You and *Gallagher*?"

Damn my face that gives everything away.

"No, I mean . . . yes, I did have feelings for Ben, but that's in the past."

"Un-*fucking*-believable." He stomps into the bedroom.

I follow him. "Nick, it's not like that."

"Not like what?" He begins gathering up his clothes and stuffing them into his overnight bag. "All this time I've been running around acting like some moonstruck calf and you've been sleeping with your boss?"

"Sleeping with my boss? Where did you get that from?" *On second thought, I think I know exactly where he got that from.* "Nick, listen to me, I'm not Shannon. I didn't cheat on you. I did kiss Ben tonight, but it was more like . . . an experiment. I swear. It didn't go any further."

Nick goes into the bathroom and starts collecting his toiletries. "An experiment? What the hell is that supposed to mean?" He jams his shaving gear into his bag and zips it shut with a ferocity that makes me wince. "Am I'm supposed to be grateful it ended there?"

"I just want to be completely honest with you."

"Thanks, sweetheart, I appreciate it. I have to admit, you got me. I never expected this from a girl like you." Nick starts rummaging through his things. "Where the hell are my keys?"

"What's that supposed to mean? A girl like me?"

Nick looks like he's on the brink of saying something, then changes his mind. I remember what he said to me last weekend in his kitchen. *I have you now, and you're nothing like Shannon.* At the time I thought it was an odd thing to say, but I think I understand now what he meant.

"You never thought I'd cheat on you because you never thought anyone else would want me."

"I never said that." But Nick's eyes give him away. I have to give him credit, he could easily lash out and hurt me with those words, but he's too much of a gentleman. "Emma," he says, gentling his voice. "I'm sorry. I blew everything out of proportion. Let's start over. Baby, I fixed the downstairs bedroom into a den for you, so you can use it as your office. Let me show it to you. Let's drive back to Catfish Cove. Right now."

"Nick—"

"Or tomorrow, we can drive back tomorrow. You're right, we're both tired. I shouldn't have brought up the whole moving-in thing tonight."

He looks at me so hopefully that I can't help but reconsider. What if Nick is my last chance at everything I want in life? A husband. Kids. Family.

But Ben's words come back to haunt me. *Don't overanalyze. Go with your instincts.* My instincts tell me that Nick isn't the one. I think if he listened to his, he'd know I'm not the one for him either. I think Nick fell for me because in his mind I was as far from Shannon as he could get. In time, he'll come to realize that and thank me, but now isn't that time. If you had told me two months ago that I would be the one ending our relationship, I wouldn't have believed it. I was so certain that it was only my heart that was on the line.

"It's not going to work, Nick," I say gently.

He stares at me for a long second and begins picking up his things again. "Where are my goddamn keys," he mutters.

"You're not driving back to Catfish Cove tonight? Nick, it's late and you're tired—"

"I'm not staying here, that's for sure."

He searches my dresser and finds his keys.

I can feel the tears start to flow. I really don't want to cry in front of Nick. "You're upset. Let me have Jason pick you up. If you don't want to stay here, you can stay at his place."

"Fine. Call Jason." Nick stomps off to the kitchen. I hear the refrigerator door open and shut and the sound of a beer-can top pop open.

Jason answers his cell on the second ring. "Hello?" says a female voice I'm positive I know. Did I dial the wrong number? I glance at the screen. It's Jason's number, all right.

"Amy?"

"Yes?"

Good grief. "It's Emma. I'm trying to reach Jason."

"Oh! Emma, hold on a sec."

I hear the rustling of . . . sheets. *Sheets?*

"Emma?" Jason says in a groggy voice.

"Jason, what have you done?"

"What's going on?" Jason asks, sounding more alert.

"I need you to pick up Nick and take him home with you. What's Amy doing at your place? Forget it. I already know what she's doing there. I just didn't think, well, I told her to go for it, but I never thought—"

"Give me ten minutes."

Thank you, Jason. Unlike me, Jason doesn't ask a million questions or ramble like an idiot.

I wait in the bedroom by myself. I can hear Nick pacing. He's on his second beer now. As much as I'd like to go talk to him, I'm afraid it will only make things worse.

Jason arrives. He takes one look at my face and goes straight into the kitchen. I go back to the bedroom, to give them privacy. Whatever Jason is saying or doing calms Nick down because I don't hear him pacing anymore. After about fifteen minutes I go back out to see what's going on. Nick has one hand on his overnight bag and the other one on my front door.

"You weren't going to say good-bye?" I can't help it. The tears are running down my cheeks.

"Sure. Good-bye." He goes to leave, but before he does, he turns to face me. "In the end, everyone settles, Emma. Just remember I was the one who told you that."

I watch Nick walk out the door.

"Don't worry, I'll make sure he's okay," Jason says.

I nod, dazed. How did all this happen?

"Where's Amy?" I ask.

"She drove herself home."

"I hope you know what you're doing."

"Funny. I was just about to say the same thing to you."

I go to bed but I don't fall asleep until almost dawn. *I hope you know what you're doing.* Jason is right to toss my words back in my face, because the truth is, I don't know what I'm doing. I'm flying by the seat of my pants, letting my feelings take me to wherever they happen to land. I just hope wherever that is, it's the right place for everyone.

chapter twenty-nine

· · · · ·

I wake up around noon. My eyes are puffy from crying. I have to get a grip. Tomorrow morning T.K. is expecting a rough-draft copy of my Trip Monroe interview and I have to produce something better than what I've come up with. The thing is, I realized last night that this is the first time I have actually broken up with someone. Usually, it is the other way around, or more often, it's a lackluster mutual parting of the ways. I always thought it would be easier being the one who did the breaking up, but I don't like the way this feels. Not one bit.

I take a quick shower, make some coffee, and call Jason. "How's Nick?"

"We both got drunk. He's still sleeping it off. I'm going to drive him back to your place so he can pick up his car."

I cringe. I'd forgotten about the car situation. "Do you think I should make him breakfast? Maybe he's in a better place to talk this morning."

"I've eaten your cooking and I definitely think breakfast is a bad idea," Jason jokes.

"Is Nick that angry?"

"He's okay. But you have to give him some time."

I sigh and stare down into my coffee. "So what's going on between you and Amy?"

"The usual."

"Jason, if Torie finds out you're sleeping with Amy, she'll never take you back."

"She's never going to take me back anyway."

I think Jason is right, but I don't want to give up hope yet.

"For what it's worth, I think you're the best thing that's ever happened to Torie. And I think one day soon she's going to realize that Kurt is just a passing flirtation."

"Maybe. Maybe not. But I'm not going to be anyone's consolation prize. You know the weird thing? I actually like Amy."

"I'm glad someone does."

"She's a really nice person once you get to know her."

"And of course, she's incredibly hot."

"Yeah, that doesn't hurt either."

Pause. "Hey, Jason? Thanks for everything."

"Anytime. Just because it's not going to work out with Torie doesn't mean you and I can't still be friends."

I pull out my laptop and start the Trip Monroe article over. And then I start it over again. I pace my living room, make myself a sandwich, and pace some more. I glance at my watch. It's almost six. Nick should be home by now. Should I call him and make sure he's okay? That's probably a bad idea. As per Jason's suggestion, I should give Nick more time. I just wish I could forget the last look I saw on Nick's face. The disappointment and hurt were nothing compared to the incredulity. I think in his mind I played him, and knowing Nick as I do now, that was his worst fear. Although technically I never cheated on him, I began our relationship with feelings for someone else and maybe that's even worse than what Shannon did.

I look over my interview notes and pace some more. Screw the Trip Monroe article. It will be finished when it's finished. I pick up the phone and call Torie. Only it goes directly to voice mail. I hang up without leaving a message. I call Kimberly next and actually get a real person.

"Hey," Kimberly says, "how was the party of the century? Did you have fun?"

"Let's see. Ben kissed me, which turned out to be utterly and completely disappointing, and I broke up with Nick, who probably hates my guts right now and never wants to see me again. How's that for fun?"

There is only a moment's hesitation before Kimberly asks, "Ice cream or vodka?"

"Both."

Kimberly arrives forty minutes later, with a tub of ice cream, a bottle of vodka, and two supersize servings of Wendy's french fries. *Thank you, Kimberly.* I start by telling her all about Ben and Elise and the scene by the dock at Jackie's party.

"Wow," she says, dipping a french fry, first into the vodka, then into the ice cream (don't knock it till you try it). "So all this time Ben kind of had the hots for you too."

"*Kind of* being the standout phrase here. I don't think Ben knows what he wants." I then proceed to tell her about Nick.

Kimberly stops her french-fry dipping. "Poor Nick," she says, "it all sounds awful."

"It was."

"Are you sure you made the right decision?"

"I don't know," I admit. "It seemed right last night."

Crap. Am I having second thoughts about Nick? Maybe Nick is right. Maybe in the end, everyone *does* settle.

We finish the ice cream and all the french fries and we're about to watch a movie when my cell phone buzzes. I glance at the screen but I don't recognize the number.

"Hello?"

"Emma? Emma Frazier?"

My heart stops beating. I jump up from my couch and start making wild gesticulating signals with my arms.

Kimberly looks up at me with narrowed eyes. "Are you having a seizure? Should I call 911?"

I take a breath and strive for my calm voice. "This is Emma Frazier," I say into the phone.

"Emma, this is Trip. Trip Monroe." As if I know any other Trips!

"Hi there!"

"Are you busy?"

"You mean right now? No, no of course not."

"Okay, 'cause, I thought this might be a good time to talk. Plus, I have your yearbook. You accidentally left it at my place."

"This is a *super* time to talk. Where can I meet you?"

"Actually, I'm right outside your door."

I run to my front door and fling it open. Sure enough, Trip Monroe is standing there next to the wilted fern I haven't watered in weeks.

He spots Kimberly, who is struck mute by the power of Trip's Sexiest Man Aliveness oomph as she sits on my couch with a partially empty bottle of vodka in her hand. "Are you sure I'm not catching you at a bad time?"

"Positive!" I pull him into my living room. I'd lock the door with my dead bolt if I wasn't afraid the gesture might scare him away.

I introduce Trip to Kimberly, who manages a dazed "hey" by way of salutation.

"Want some . . ." I glance at the empty french-fry and ice-cream containers. "Vodka?" Then I cringe. Trip is basically a Betty Ford dropout and here I am offering him liquor.

Trip gives me the slightest hint of a smile. "No, thanks."

"How about a pizza?" Kimberly chimes in. "We can order a pizza if you're hungry. I'm absolutely *starved*."

"You sure I'm not interrupting? I don't want to get in the way of your girl stuff."

"No, no. We were just going to order a pizza when you called."

"In that case, sure, sounds good." Trip hands me my year-book. "Here you go."

"Thanks, but you didn't come all this way just to return this, did you?" I'm really hoping the answer to this is no.

"My uncle Frank called me a couple of days ago. Asked if I might come talk to you."

Thank you, Uncle Frank.

I offer Trip a seat in my best chair. "I think your uncle is worried about you," I begin gently.

"Frank's a good guy. He's always been there for me when I needed him." He shifts his gaze to the floor. "I also came to apologize. About the night at the Don Cesar."

"Oh, no need." Then I think about it a second. "Wait, yeah, you do need to apologize for that."

"I honestly had no idea . . . I was pretty drunk. Not that it's an excuse for what happened. I'm sorry, Emma. I really am."

"Everyone was really disappointed that you didn't show up at the cocktail party."

He shrugs, embarrassed. "I just couldn't face another one of those swanky parties. Everyone clamoring around me, wanting something. It just seemed easier to stay in my room and get shit-faced."

I'm dying to start shooting off questions but I sense that Trip is like an untamed maverick. One wrong move and he'll bolt. I search for some topic of conversation that seems nonthreatening. Kimberly orders a pizza and brings us all a soda. Trip and I make some small talk and the pizza arrives and we all dig in.

"So did you get a chance to look through my yearbook? I hadn't picked that thing up in years, but I got a big kick out of all the things people wrote."

Trip puts down his slice of pizza and slowly wipes his mouth with a napkin. "I wanted to look through it, but . . . you don't mind? I never ordered one for myself. They were too expensive. Frank would have given me the money, but he'd already done a lot for me, so I didn't ask."

Kimberly and I exchange a look. It never occurred to me that Trip didn't get a copy of his own senior yearbook. "Of course you can look in my yearbook."

Considering our little bathroom scene in the Don Cesar, it's ironic that Trip's good manners rise to the surface for something as tame as peeking through someone's high school yearbook. It's just part of the conundrum that is Trip Monroe. Who *is* this guy?

He opens the book and begins flipping the pages. "I remember him." He points to a picture of Mr. Kazwitz, our junior chemistry teacher. Trip shakes his head and grins. "What a clown."

"I had him too," Kimberly says. "I think he's still teaching."

Trip looks surprised by Kimberly's admission. I introduce

them again, this time making sure to point out what street in Catfish Cove Kimberly grew up on, her brief marriage to Jake Lemoyne, and her current PR position at the Yeager Agency.

"Yeah, Emma gave me your card." Trip looks more relaxed and I take this as a good sign. He continues flipping through pages in the yearbook and then he gets to his own inscription and reads it aloud. " 'Emma, I like your poem. Good luck in the outside world.' " He scrunches his face in concentration. "I remember now. You won the poetry contest. Your poem was called . . . 'The Mommy Burger'?"

" 'The Mommy Sandwich,' " I clarify.

" 'I'm Nobody! Who are you? Are you—Nobody—too?' " Trip recites.

Kimberly clears her throat and looks at me.

"Emily Dickinson, not Emma Frazier," I say, just in case Kimberly doesn't recognize the opening line to one of the most famous poems of all time.

"Emma and I were partners for an English project," Trip explains. "We had to take a poem and dissect it, line by line, discover the meaning of it, that kind of stuff."

I'd remembered Trip and I were partners for the English project but I'd forgotten the specifics. It all comes back to me now. How we paired off two by two, one boy and one girl, the way you do in PE class when they make you learn how to square-dance, only no one wanted to be Trip's partner, because he wasn't particularly cute and he didn't stand out as this great student either. So when it came my turn to pick someone, I noticed him slumped down in his desk, avoiding eye contact, and it occurred to me that if it was the guys who had been doing the selecting, this would be me, hoping beyond hope that I wouldn't get picked last. So I picked Trip as my partner and we drew the Emily Dickinson poem. We worked on our project the rest of the week after school in the library and we both got an A-plus.

" 'I'm Nobody! Who are you?' " Trip recites again, but this time there's an edge to his voice. "Well, I'm a fucking somebody now, aren't I?"

"You sure are," I say softly.

And then it all comes spilling out. How he wanted to quit racing after his crash at Talladega but he was just starting to make the big money then and how stupid it would be to quit. He tells me about the races and how with each win he felt more reckless and more out of touch with himself. How giving away money made him feel better at first, but then it didn't, and the booze and the women made him feel better. And now they don't.

"The weird part is that after a while I didn't even know where I was going or what I was doing. I just got behind the wheel of my car and drove. That's the part that felt good. The driving fast," he says. "But the rest . . ."

He tells me about how Frank tried to get him to slow down. To take a year off racing, but Chuck was against it. "He said we should keep striking while the iron was hot. But the truth is, I'm tired."

"Is that why you dropped out of the circuit this year?"

"I got in my car and froze. I think it scared Chuck. Plus . . . I have this problem."

"You checked yourself into Betty Ford," I say.

Trip looks surprised that I know this, but he nods.

"What do you want to do?" Kimberly asks. She's been so quiet, I'd almost forgotten she was there.

"I want to fix cars. I want to fish. I want to retire from racing for good."

Trip keeps talking and I keep listening. I'm not taking notes.

I don't have to. I don't think I could forget any of the things he's saying. Plus, I'm not sure how much of this Trip wants me to write about. If he tells me he doesn't want any of it to end up in the article, I'll defer to his wishes. This isn't about getting the scoop of the decade anymore, it's about being there for someone who needs a friend. I guess that's what makes me saddest of all for Trip. I don't think he has any real friends.

It's past two a.m. when we all fall asleep. Me in my bed, Kimberly in the guest room, and Trip on the couch. The next morning I wake up to the pop, crackle, grease sound of frying bacon. I stumble out to my living room and follow the smell to the kitchen.

"Good morning!" Kimberly says cheerily. Her blond hair is pulled back in a ponytail and she's wearing last night's clothes but she still looks gorgeous. She's also scrambling eggs. Trip is stirring a pot of grits. "Don't oversalt those," she warns him. I don't know who looks more in love with her right now, Trip or me.

"If you tell me you've made coffee, I'll be your slave forever."

"There's cream and real sugar too, just like you like it." Kimberly's Catfish Cove twang is back and in full glory.

"When did you have time to go to the grocery?" I ask, because since I've been starving myself, I don't keep things like bacon or real cream in the house.

"We woke up around eight," Trip says.

"Eight? What time is it now?" I look at my kitchen clock. It's nine-thirty. Crap! I've missed the Monday-morning staff meeting. I scoop up my cell phone and dial the office. Richard answers.

"First off, before you say anything, I'm sorry about the donuts."

"You okay?" he says.

"I'm fine. About the donuts—"

"Don't worry about the damn donuts. I was just about to call your cell and make sure you weren't in an accident. Do you realize in the six years you've worked here you've never once been late?"

"Why are you yelling?"

"You think this is yelling?" He pauses. "So where are you?"

"I'm . . . sick. Yeah, please tell Ben I'm calling in sick."

"On a Monday after a party? Don't you think that's a little suspicious? I mean, it essentially gives you a three-day weekend."

"It's definitely suspicious."

I swear I can hear Richard smile over the phone.

chapter thirty

· · · · ·

Kimberly calls in sick as well and the three of us decide to spend the day playing hooky. Even though it's nearly a million degrees outside, we head to Busch Gardens theme park. Trip wears a baseball cap and sunglasses, but despite his "disguise" he still gets some long looks. A few from excited fans, but mostly from women who can't help but check him out, because let's face it, any guy who looks like Trip is going to get stared at. We ride all the scary rides, drink a quart of soda apiece, and eat more fast food than the average Parisian sees in a year. By the time we get back to my place it's after seven and we're exhausted. But even though I'm physically tired, I'm mentally exhilarated. I want to start writing this article. Ben texted me three times today asking me where the article was. I sent him a reply after the first text telling him "I'm working on it," and have ignored the other two.

Trip asks if he can spend the night at my place again.

"Anytime," I tell him.

Kimberly gives Trip a big hug and says "she'll call him later" then heads home. What that is about I'm not sure, but I wouldn't be surprised if those two got together, which brings a smile to my face. Trip Monroe definitely one-ups Jake Lemoyne.

I change into something more comfortable, make a big pot of

coffee, and get out my laptop. I set up "office" on my kitchen table and begin typing. Trip falls asleep on the living room couch but I don't get up from the table until I see the sun shine through my kitchen window. I don't make eggs or bacon or grits but I do make another pot of coffee. Even though I'm running on almost no sleep, I feel more awake than I have in weeks. I wrote down everything Trip told me—the good, the bad, and the ugly. And believe me, there is plenty of ugly here. I'm not going to edit the article yet. I'll let Trip tell me what he doesn't want me to include and go from there.

Writing up this article from my kitchen table has got me thinking. No interruptions, no telephones ringing. Maybe working from home isn't such a bad idea. I could turn my guest room into an office and sit around all day in my pajamas. Richard and Jackie and I could carpool to Orlando for the Monday-morning staff meeting. We could eat the Krispy Kremes on the drive over and catch up on what's going on with one another's lives. It actually sounds kind of fun.

I print out the article and hand it to Trip.

He looks at me funny. " 'I've Been a Bad, Bad Boy'?"

"That's not really the title," I say quickly. "It's more there as a placeholder."

Trip makes a grunting sound of skepticism and begins reading. Occasionally he frowns, grimaces once, and laughs twice (although I think it's sarcastic laughter). He tosses the pages on the coffee table in front of him. "Yeah, you pretty much nailed it."

"So what parts do you want me to cut out?"

"None."

"But—"

"It's all true and it's all going to come out anyway, so you might as well be the one to write it."

"So . . . you're okay with all this? I mean, it violates the contract I signed."

"Screw the contract; that was Chuck's idea and I already fired him."

"You did? When?"

"Yesterday, when we were at Busch Gardens."

"You fired Chuck over the *phone*?"

"Yeah. I did it right after we rode the Scorpion."

The Scorpion is one of those roller-coaster rides that takes you around in circles, which means a lot of the time you're basically hanging upside down. I really hope all that blood didn't rush to Trip's head and lead him to make a hasty decision. Not that I don't think Trip firing Chuck isn't the best thing ever, but I don't want Trip to regret any part of the last two days.

"Are you sure that's what you want?"

"Positive. I'm only sorry I didn't do it a few years ago." Trip notices my hesitation. "Don't worry. I've already got my lawyers negotiating with his. Chuck is getting a hell of a nice payoff to go away quietly. You were spot-on in that article, Emma. I'm tired. I want to go home. I want to be a regular guy again."

"Home? To Naples?"

"Home to Catfish Cove. I'm going to stay with my uncle Frank until I build my own place. And I'm going to start a nonprofit, one that's going to benefit underprivileged kids. Kimberly is going to help me set it up, do all my PR, that kind of stuff."

"You're signing on with the Yeager Agency?"

"Nah, she's going to leave them and come work for me full-time."

I'm practically speechless. But not quite. "That's fantastic! But what about . . . you know, the Betty Ford thing?" In the two days Trip has been at my place he hasn't touched a drop of alcohol. I admit, I've been a little worried about all that.

"Betty Ford was Chuck's idea. Personally, I'm more of an AA guy, myself."

"Oh, okay, well, great!"

Trip chuckles. "It's all right to talk about it, Emma. I have a drinking problem, but I'm not the guy who needs a drink every day. My problem is more situational. I have to learn to deal with stuff that stresses me out in healthier ways."

I give Trip a hug. "I know you can do it, Trip. If you ever need anyone to talk to, I'm here."

"Thanks."

Trip and I make plans for dinner and I leave for work with Trip sitting on my living room couch watching *Good Morning America*.

I can't believe I did it. I have scored the biggest interview of my life! Ben will be thrilled and T.K. will probably throw me a party. Kimberly is happy and Trip is on his way to getting there. I bet even Uncle Frank is pretty pleased with me. Other than the fact that I feel crummy about the Nick situation and that my moms have been engaged in a thirty-two-year conspiracy against me, I should be ecstatic.

But strangely, I'm not. The funny worm feeling has come back to my stomach, which makes absolutely no sense at all.

I toss my tote on top of my desk and automatically head to Ben's office, but before I knock on his door, I find myself making a detour back to my cubicle. Jackie is at her desk, drinking a cup of coffee.

"Nice tan," she says to me.

I don't bother lying. "Thanks, I went to Busch Gardens yesterday."

"You missed a hell of a staff meeting. Ben finally announced the big move to Orlando. Among other things."

"So you knew about the move to Orlando too?"

"I think he pretty much told everyone in confidence."

"What are you going to do?"

"Work from my home. It's a dream come true. What about you?"

"The same, I guess."

She raises a brow. "We'll see."

"What's that supposed to mean?"

"Nothing." But I can see from the gleam in her eyes that she knows something I don't, and she's enjoying it.

I briefly consider having Jackie read the Trip Monroe article and then just as quickly dismiss the idea. I know exactly what she will say. She'll tell me to march my jiggly fanny right into Ben's office and give it to him ASAP. Why I don't do just that, I'm not sure, but it has something to do with those nasty worms. My article, as written, will definitely put a blush to Trip's mama's cheeks. Something I already promised Uncle Frank I wouldn't do. But Trip has read the article and given me his blessing, which pretty much negates my promise to Uncle Frank, doesn't it? I have somehow managed to fulfill the spirit of that stupid contract, which gave Trip final editing privileges.

It should be a journalistic slam dunk.

I slide my chair around to Richard's desk and toss the article in front of him. "Favor?" Before he can say anything, I add, "And no, I haven't read your manuscript yet. I've been too busy writing the story of the decade."

Richard looks up from his computer screen. "So, despite the

fact that you continue to blow me off, you expect me to drop everything and read your article yet again?"

"Well . . . yes."

"All right."

Richard takes my pages and tells me to get lost. I guess he doesn't want me staring at him and I don't blame him. I will interpret every nuance, every eyelid flutter or hint of expression, as a potential reaction to the whole piece. I suppose I can be a bit annoying that way. I roll my chair back around to my cubicle to wait it out.

It seems like forever before he leans over to place his arm on the back of my chair. "It's the best thing you've ever written."

My shoulders slump. Richard is right. It *is* the best thing I've ever written. Every word is true but it's going to expose Trip as this weak-willed man-ho who uses booze and sex to get over the pain of his so-called horrible life that half the world would give their right arm to live.

"What's wrong? You don't look happy."

"It's just . . . I don't know. I hate to think what this might do to Trip's image."

"His image? Baby, it's a little late to get a conscience here. You went after this story because you wanted to impress Ben and T.K. You wanted to write what no one else could about this guy. And you did. It's going to sell a lot of magazines, so congratulations."

"You make me sound mercenary."

"It's what journalists do. They take a story and wring the truth out of it. Only you could write a piece like that and feel *bad* because it's going to hurt someone's feelings." He shakes his head. "I'm actually going to miss that about you."

"Just because we won't be working from the office anymore

doesn't mean we won't be seeing one another. There's still the Monday-morning staff meetings." I tell Richard about my carpool idea, making sure to include the part where I still get the donuts.

"A tempting offer, but no can do. I quit the magazine last week. Ben announced it at the meeting yesterday."

"*What?*" I think I must have heard wrong. "Why?"

"I'm going to focus on my writing career."

I'm expecting something more, something funny or boastful, but nothing comes. Richard is *serious* about this.

"That's . . . that's great!"

"You think I'm crazy."

"Maybe, just a little. Not that I don't think you couldn't make it writing genre fiction, you know, with some plot help and all, but what are you going to do about money?"

"No worries about that, thanks to Gallagher. It just so happens his blackjack method is spot-on. I made almost fifty grand a couple of weeks ago in Vegas. Together with the rest of the money I've won, I have enough socked away for about two years, if I'm careful with my money, buy cheap beer, stuff like that."

"Fifty thousand dollars? You won fifty *thousand* dollars playing blackjack?"

"Can you just shout that out a little louder? I'm sure the IRS would love to hear you."

"Richard, please tell me you plan to the pay the taxes on that money."

"Rule Number Two: Never pay the IRS today what you can put off until tomorrow."

"I really hope that's a yes."

"Don't worry. I got a guy watching my money. He's on top of it."

"A guy? You mean like an accountant or a business manager? Fifty thousand is a lot of money, but are you sure it's enough to last you through two years?"

"I told you, I plan to buy cheap beer."

I give Richard a look.

"Okay, I also have a nest egg."

"I thought only grannies had nest eggs." Pause. "This nest egg of yours . . . the money is all legit, isn't it?"

Richard laughs. "God, I'm really going to miss you." At the dubious expression on my face, he says, "Relax. No one's going to jail here. It's the dough I made from royalties on my e-book sales. You can really rack it up if you get a following."

Lisa happens to walk by just then. "Aren't Richard's novels wonderful?" she gushes. "I've read *Steve Danger Goes to Washington* three times now and I still haven't figured out how he's going to get away from Dr. Hatchett's evil snakes."

I whip around to face Richard. "Steve Danger? Isn't that going to be your pen name?"

"Maybe, maybe not." He shrugs. "I'm keeping an open mind on that."

"*Emma!*" says Lisa. "Steve Danger is the name of Richard's spy character. You know? The one in his novels."

"Novels?"

"Yeah, the novels he published himself on Amazon." She gazes at Richard with open admiration. "That's why he goes to Vegas every month. So he can win enough money to write full-time."

"*That's* why you call in sick every fourth Friday? You go to Vegas to *gamble*?"

"Aw, Emma, you *were* keeping tabs on my sick days. What? Were you worried about me?"

I snort. "In your dreams."

"Every single night."

I feel like Richard and I have wandered out of the friends zone and back into fake flirtation mode, only it doesn't feel fake.

Lisa must have picked up on it as well because she looks at me and then at Richard. Her eyes widen. "I think I'll just leave you two alone."

"Not necessary!" I call out after her retreating form.

Jackie comes over to Richard's cubicle. "Can you two keep it down? I'm trying to get some work done here."

"Did you know Richard was going to Vegas every month to gamble? And that he's got a bunch of novels out about some spy named Steve Danger?" I demand of her.

"It's not like he kept it a big secret."

"Did Ben know too?"

Richard shrugs good-naturedly as if to say, *Yeah, everyone knew but you.*

"Show me," I say to them.

Jackie goes to my computer and punches some keys to get to the Amazon Web site, where Richard's author page pops up. She then shows me his Facebook page. Richard now has four thousand nine hundred and forty-eight "friends," most of whom I realize are not friends at all, but fans. I cannot help but smile because this is just so Richard to pull my leg about Steve Danger being the name he plans to publish under. Or maybe he does plan to pub under an alias, since his vampire/werewolf novel is probably very different from these spy books everyone on his Facebook page is raving about.

I go back to the Amazon link provided on his page and check out the books. He's got four spy novels at bargain-basement prices. Being the supportive coworker and friend that I am, I purchase all four books and download them to my e-reader.

"Thanks," Richard says. "If you like them, make sure to write a review."

"Of course," I say, smiling brightly, but inside I'm less than ecstatic. Not about buying the books. But I don't like the fact that everyone at the office has known about Richard's double life all along and that I was totally clueless. How could I have sat less than ten feet away from him for the past six years and never known this most basic thing about him? The whole thing makes me feel self-absorbed.

"I think it's great. I wish you the best of luck. Really. I mean that."

"Thanks." Richard stares at me a little too long and I feel myself blush. *Blush*?

"So how long has this been going on?"

"The Steve Danger novels? I put the first one up on Amazon back in January."

January is when Ben came to work for *Florida!*, so I guess that explains why I was out of the loop. I was too busy crushing on Ben to pay attention to what was going on right under my nose, or rather, on the other side of my cubicle.

"So it looks like it'll be just you and me, Emma," says Jackie. "Lisa's only staying until Ben makes the move to Orlando, but regardless, he won't need her then. He'll have *Abby*."

The way Jackie says Abby's name makes me blink. Surely, she isn't hinting that there is something between Ben and T.K.'s assistant Abby? "Ben is taking T.K.'s job?"

"He announced that yesterday too."

"Jeez. You miss one Monday-morning staff meeting and the whole place falls apart."

"So," Jackie says to Richard, "we need to plan a going-away party for you. I'd do it at my house but—"

"How about we make it easy? Beer and wings at that new place in Ybor?" Richard says. "Everyone pays their own tab."

"Captain Pete's?" Jackie says. "Perfect. When's your last day?"

"This Friday." Richard turns to me. "You'll be there?"

"Of course. I wouldn't miss your going-away party."

Richard winks at me and although his wink does not constitute a reply, I somehow feel like it does. Surely there must be something I can pull out of my hat to equalize the playing field again.

But there is nothing.

Richard, three.

Emma, zero.

I gird my loins and march into Ben's office.

He looks up from his computer screen. "Where's the article?"

I haven't seen him since our kiss by the dock. I would think we'd both be a little embarrassed. It appears he's not, so I shouldn't be either.

"Well, hello to you too. Didn't you hear? I was sick yesterday."

"You look pretty tan for someone who was sick yesterday."

"Really? You think I got a tan?"

Ben gives me a hard stare.

"I don't get it. Richard calls in sick every fourth Friday and you never give him a hard time." Ben goes to say something but I head him off at the pass. "Okay, I wasn't sick. I was at Busch Gardens with Trip. So technically, I was working."

"Why didn't you say so? We could have sent a photographer."

"It was a spontaneous kind of a friends' thing."

"Friends? Let me get this straight. You're now friends with the guy who practically accosted you?"

"It's not like that. Trip is very sorry for what happened that night at the Don Cesar."

"I can't wait to hear all about it," Ben mutters. "I hope that's going to be in the article."

It is *all* in the article, but I've just made up my mind. I don't want Ben to read it. Not yet anyway. "Remember that little contract I had to sign? It expressly forbids me mentioning the events at the Don Cesar."

"Damn contract." He indicates with the wave of a hand that I sit down. "I need that piece by next Monday. *No* extensions."

"Sure," I say, "no problem." I sit on the edge of his couch and wait.

"You've probably already heard I'm taking T.K.'s job."

"Sounds like I missed a big meeting."

"And you heard that Richard has quit?"

I nod.

"Lisa has also turned in her resignation, but I was expecting that one."

"It looks like the staff of *Florida!* is dwindling down to zip."

Ben sharpens his gaze. "I hope you're not jumping ship as well."

"What? Me? I never even thought about it."

"Good, because T.K. and I want you to take over as editor."

"Honest?"

"No, I'm kidding. Of course, honest." Ben gives me a lazy smile. "Haven't you figured out I've been grooming you for this for a while now?"

"Grooming me?"

"Sure, all those late nights, helping me with articles, the trip to Orlando. No one knows this magazine better than you. You're perfect for the job."

"I kind of thought all those late nights had something to do with the fact that you're crazy about me." I probably shouldn't be saying this, but I can't help myself.

He clears his throat. "I admit it'll be hard, separating the private from the professional, but I think we can manage."

"I'm a little confused here. Exactly where do we stand?"

"I don't know. There's the matter of your boyfriend for one."

"Oh, don't worry about that. Nick and I broke up last weekend."

The color drains from Ben's face. "I'm sorry to hear that."

I know I'm giving him a bit of a hard time, but honestly? Ben needs to own his actions.

"Really? Okay, well, that's confusing. Did I imagine it or did you not kiss me at Jackie's party?"

"I think we both got a little carried away that night. We'd both been drinking and—"

"Yeah, yeah, whatever. Are you getting back with Elise?"

"Elise is going back to New York. It just isn't going to work out between us," he says with a sad face.

"That's too bad." Although I cannot help but feel that Elise has been given a reprieve. I was right, Ben doesn't deserve her. I think about how accomplished Elise is and then I think about Amy, and her Harvard Law degree, and something occurs to me. Is Ben intimidated by successful women?

"So I can count on you, right? You're taking the job?"

"Would I have to move to Orlando?"

"It would be tough to do the job from Tampa. You could commute, but I think that would get kind of old."

"In that case I'm going to have to think about it."

"Seriously?"

"Yes, seriously."

Ben sighs. "Okay, but I need an answer by Monday."

I leave Ben's office feeling a mixture of dazed and disgusted. Dazed because I really wasn't expecting to be offered the editor job so soon. Obviously Jackie knew, though. It's what she was hinting at when she said I might not be working from home. I'm flattered and excited by the possibilities the job offers, but I also know that I don't want to move to Orlando, which seems silly, but there it is.

And I'm disgusted. Mainly at myself. How could I have ever thought that Ben *got* me? Richard was right. I hate to say it, but Ben did get off knowing I was crushing on him. Just like he gets off having Elise dangling on an emotional string. It boosts his ego (or whatever) and that speaks very poorly of him.

I think I also understand Jackie's remark about Abby now. Abby shows all the same signs that I must have once exhibited. The lingering looks, the admiring sighs. I wonder if Ben has been subtly encouraging her too? Poor girl. I almost wish I could warn her but I don't think she'll listen. I know I wouldn't have.

Richard is right about something else too.

Ben is definitely a schmuck.

chapter thirty-one

· · · · ·

That night, Trip, Kimberly, and I go to dinner, where Kimberly regales us with the story of how she marched into Murray's office and turned in her resignation. According to Kimberly, everyone at the Yeager Agency is shocked, and Kimberly is thrilled by their reaction. I had no idea she hated her job this much, but I get it. I really hope this thing with Trip works out for her.

Kimberly and I are in the restaurant bathroom and I take advantage of our moment alone to ask, "So what do you think? You and Trip?"

"Me and Trip what?" She pauses in the middle of touching up her lipstick. "You mean, me and Trip as in a *couple*? No way. It's strictly business and friendship between us."

"Oh, okay. I thought . . . well, never mind."

Kimberly is obviously just as smart as I always knew she was. Mixing business with pleasure is never a good idea, something I should have already known.

We finish dinner and the next morning Trip drives home to Catfish Cove. I spend the next two days editing down the article but it still reads like something out of a cheap tabloid. The week goes by quickly, and before I know it, it's Richard's last day at work. Lisa decorates the office with balloons and signs wishing

Richard GOOD LUCK. Jackie, Lisa, and I take off after lunch for a girls' only afternoon. We get manicures and pedicures at the mall and Jackie talks me into buying a new dress for tonight's going-away party. The dress is red, a color I rarely wear. Jackie phoned Kimberly, who dashed over with the same four-inch red stilettos she wore to the celebrity cocktail party at the Don Cesar, and the three of them convince me to wear them tonight.

"You look great," Jackie says as we approach Captain Pete's. A second before I open the door, she reaches over with both hands and pulls down the bodice to my dress, which effectively pushes my boobs up.

"Hey!" I joke. "Hands off."

"Think of it as a going-away present for Richard," Jackie says.

"I don't see the two of you exposing *your* cleavage."

"It's not our cleavage he wants to see," Lisa says. She exchanges a look with Jackie and I freeze.

"Oh, come on," I say.

"For someone as smart as you, Emma, you sure are dumb," says Jackie.

Lisa shoves me inside the door and once again I'm hit with the myriad of emotions that a crowded bar always evokes in me. Only this time add confusion to the list. Jackie and Lisa are insinuating—no, they are *blatantly* telling me that Richard is interested in me. I have to admit, I've been wondering about that myself. But that can't be possible. Wasn't it just a couple of weeks ago that he said I was like a little sister to him?

We zigzag our way through the crowd. Ben arrived early to hold the big table in the back so that we would have plenty of room for our party. Richard is deep in conversation with Lisa's fiancé, Tony. Jackie's husband, Chris, is here too, along with a few of the sales guys from Orlando who have driven over for the party. I notice Richard has not brought a date. I choose a seat as far away from him as possible, which puts me between two of the sales guys, which is a big mistake, because they both immediately start talking about the Trip Monroe article.

I try my best to fend off their questions, alternating between pretending to check my cell phone and stealing glances at Richard.

Richard looks really good tonight. He has obviously just shaven, because by this time of the day he is usually sporting a pretty significant five o'clock shadow, and that isn't the case this evening. He's wearing jeans and a blue oxford shirt with the sleeves rolled back to his forearms. Even from across the table I can see that the blue in his shirt brings out the blue in his eyes. Richard has the kind of eyes that can appear either blue or green, depending on the light. Not that I've ever stared at them or anything. I'm just stating a fact here. Other than an initial greeting in which he playfully ogled my chest the same way he would anyone else who practically had their boobs hanging out, he has not singled me out in any way. I definitely think Jackie and Lisa are playing a joke on me.

I glance up and see that Kimberly and Torie have arrived at Captain Pete's. They come over to wish Richard good luck in his new endeavor. I can tell the sales guys want Torie and Kimberly to join us but they decline, saying that they don't want to "crash" our good-bye party, and since the majority of the conversation is dedicated to talking about work, I don't blame them.

Torie takes me off to the side. "Have you seen Jason lately?"

"Not tonight," I answer truthfully. I think about telling Torie about Jason and Amy but decide against it. This is news she needs to hear from Jason himself.

"Where's Kurt?"

"Who? Oh, Kurt," she says with a roll of her eyes. "Yeah, he and I are through. Turns out he was a jerk."

I give her a hug. "Sorry."

Torie's eyes are bright with unshed tears. "Live and learn, right?"

"Right," I say, mustering up as much supportive enthusiasm as possible. A part of me wants to tell Torie "I told you so," but as her best friend, I'm sure this is not what she needs to hear from me right now.

Torie and Kimberly take off to mingle at the bar and our party resumes.

We're on our umpteenth pitcher of beer and our third tray of hot wings when I spot Amy and Jason walk through the front door. I immediately tense.

Richard looks at me with a question mark in his eyes.

"What's wrong?" asks Lisa.

"Nothing!" I raise my beer mug in the air in an act of faked cheerfulness.

It's now time for everyone to make toasts.

Ben goes first. "I remember the first time I met this guy." He nods at Richard. "It was my first day at work and I walk into my office and there's this dude sitting in my chair with his legs propped on my desk, his cell phone in hand."

We all start to laugh because I remember this day clearly. There was a one-week interim between the time that Stuart left and Ben arrived. It had seemed a shame to let a perfectly awesome office go to waste, so Richard, Jackie, and I drew straws to see who would use the boss's office. Richard won, although I clearly remember accusing him of cheating and he never denied it.

Ben continues his story. "So in between texting he glances up at me and asks if I remembered the egg rolls. Now I ask you, do I look like the delivery boy from First Coast China?"

We all laugh again and everyone takes a drink in honor of the memory.

One of the sales guys goes next, and then Jackie regales us with a story about the first time Richard and she did a story together. They were driving to interview a guy who lived out in the middle of nowhere (literally). On the drive over they got lost but neither of them wanted to stop for directions. It is funny but, at the same time, poignantly sad because it is just occurring to everyone that stuff like this will never happen again. Jackie actually has a tear in her eye as she wishes Richard good luck.

It's now Lisa's turn. "To Richard," she says, raising her glass, "and his awesome Steve Danger novels. May you hit the *New York Times* bestseller list!"

The table claps in approval. Richard grins sheepishly. Our gazes meet for a long second and I feel my cheeks burn. What sort of friend am I that I haven't yet read Richard's manuscript? Yes, I've been incredibly busy, but who hasn't? I should have found time to work it in somehow. It's the least I owe him after all the help he's given me with the Trip Monroe article.

"Emma!" Jackie shouts. "You're up next."

"Toast toast toast!" everyone chants.

In anticipation of tonight's party, I have prepared this great ditty recalling the time Richard did a story about a new ride at Universal Studios. We went together to preview the ride, and when Richard saw that it was basically a giant roller coaster, he insisted on holding my hand. He squeezed it so hard I thought it was going to fall off. The idea of big bad Richard being afraid of a little roller coaster is hilariously funny. I know the sales guys are going to get a big kick out of it. But when I go to speak, nothing comes out.

Maybe I should simply say that I'll miss him, but after all our years of bickering it almost seems disingenuous. It occurs to me that this may very well be the last time we are all together and the truth is I'll miss everything about our Tampa office. I'll miss the drive every morning with the bustling traffic on Howard. I'll miss my tiny cubicle with the chair that wobbles, the daily interaction with Ben, who, despite everything, is still a great editor. I'll miss Lisa's giggle and Jackie's intenseness. And yes, I'll even miss Richard's raunchy jokes, the blare of his hard-rock music, and the way he always challenges everything I say. Although it makes no sense, in some ways, I think, I'll miss him most of all. But that must be because he has been here the longest. He is a part of everything I equate with *Florida!* and all that's about to end and a new era will start, and despite the fact that's it kind of exciting, it's also sad.

I stand and raise my mug in the air. "To Richard. I . . . best of luck."

Everyone waits for the rest of the toast. I take a sip of my beer and this signals everyone to follow suit, except Jackie, who says, "That's *it*? That's your toast?"

I shrug, too embarrassed to say more, so I excuse myself to head to the bathroom. I go into one of the stalls and swipe the tears from my eyes. I think everything has just hit me at once. My breakup with Nick. Mom's secret marriage to Frank Monroe (which I've yet to get to the bottom of), the pressure of getting the article in, and now the pressure of trying to edit it so that everyone will be happy, the decision whether or not to take the job as editor and having to move to Orlando, and now the office breaking up. You know how much I like Mondays? Well, it's like the Friday of my life has finally arrived. I tear off some toilet paper to dry my cheeks, when I hear the sound of familiar voices.

"I can't believe you'd go behind my back like this!" It's Torie.

"Jason is a big boy," I hear Amy say. "He can make his own decisions."

"You know, when you tried to steal Ben from Emma, I thought you were a bitch, but now, *wow*, this really cements it. It's no wonder you have no friends, Amy."

I hear Amy sniffling.

Sigh.

I open the stall door. Amy and Torie turn their gazes on me. Talk about déjà vu. Was it really just a couple of months ago I overheard another conversation between them in this exact same manner? Only this time I'm not pretending I didn't hear it.

"Leave her alone, Torie."

Torie stands there, hands on her hips, looking more intimidating than any playground bully. "Can you believe Amy has been seeing Jason behind my back?" she says to me.

Amy looks at me with her big blue eyes, but she doesn't give me away. While I am no fan of hers, I still have to do what's right here.

"Jason's not your boyfriend, Torie, so how could anyone be seeing him behind your back?"

Torie looks like I've just slapped her in the face. "You *know* what I mean."

"No, I don't."

"Jason is . . . well, no friend of mine would ever go after him, that's all I'm saying."

"What if he went after her?"

"Whose side are you on? Don't you remember what she did to you? She practically stole Ben right out from under your nose!"

"And she ended up doing me a favor. Look," I say more force-fully, "Jason and Amy have every right to see one another, whether or not you approve."

Torie's jaw drops. "You *knew* about this?"

Uh-oh.

"I . . . not exactly. Amy asked me what she thought about Jason, so I told her Jason is a terrific guy and that she should go for it."

Torie looks at me like she's never seen me before. It has just occurred to me that she has been doing the same thing to Jason that Ben did to Elise. Through her subtle flirtation she has kept Jason dangling on a string in the hope that they will one day get back together again. She's been keeping him around for "just in case." I want to add that I'm glad Jason has moved on to Amy, but I don't think that will go over too well just now.

Amy looks between me and Torie and senses that it's best to get out while she still can. She mumbles something and slips out the bathroom door.

"I thought you were my best friend," Torie says in a voice that almost breaks my heart.

"I *am* your best friend and that's why I'm going to tell you that you're wrong here. I told you Jason still had feelings for you. I tried to warn you that you were going to lose him, but you told me it was over between you two. Torie," I say, gentling my voice. I go to touch her arm but she steps out of reach. "You can't keep Jason in the wings like some consolation prize. He deserves bet-ter than that. Believe me, I know how much it hurts to let some-one you care about go. You were right about Nick. He was like some . . . trophy boyfriend for me because my ego was hurt when Amy called me the ugly friend. But I had to break up with Nick because it wasn't fair to keep stringing him along when I knew he wasn't the one for me. You have to do the same for Jason. You have to just let him go and move on."

Tears run down Torie's face. I'm torn between wanting to shake her and wanting to pull her into my arms and console her. I go for the latter, but once again she pulls away from me.

"I'm never going to forgive you for this, Emma. *Never*."

I stare in numb silence as she walks out the door. After a minute a couple of girls walk into the bathroom and begin chatting. I text Kimberly and briefly tell her what happened. She texts me back. She and Torie are on their way to Torie's apartment and she'll keep me in the loop. I wish I could go with them and console Torie. Just like the night they followed me out of Captain Pete's and we all got drunk on Absolut and stayed up talking till the wee hours of the morning. At times like this, a girl needs her friends. Only knowing Torie the way I do, I know she will not want to see me right now. I do my best to pull myself together.

I walk out the bathroom door and run smack into Richard. The hallway leading to the barroom is narrow, so I scoot back against the wall to let him pass.

Richard takes one look at my face and says, "Have you been crying? Emma, I had no idea that my leaving would be this hard on you."

Despite my misery I manage to smile. "Your ego is unbelievable."

"Is it the cop? Is that why you're crying? I noticed you didn't bring him tonight."

"Nick and I broke up."

"Oh yeah? You or him?"

"Me," I admit.

Richard takes a few seconds to think this over. "Is there someone else?"

"Nope. There's no one else."

"Rule Number Three: You never break up with someone unless you have someone else waiting in the wings."

"Thanks. I'll keep that in mind for next time."

Richard drops his smile. "Hey, listen, I'm sorry. I really liked the guy."

"Me too."

"Maybe it's not too late to get him back. Especially if you're willing to debase yourself with some sexual tricks."

"Sexual tricks?"

"Yeah, you know. Hanging from a chandelier. Dressing up like Darth Vader. The usual stuff."

I laugh. "Thanks for the advice, but it's not going to work out with Nick." I decide this is a good time to fill Richard in on the events of Jackie's housewarming party, my long conversation in the bathroom with Elise, and my "talk" with Ben on the dock, including our big kiss.

"So was it everything you dreamed it would be?"

"It was actually pretty disappointing."

Richard tries to hide his smile but fails.

"Where's Becky? I thought you'd bring a date tonight."

"Becky's not my girlfriend."

"Oh?"

"She's just the kid sister of a friend, Emma."

"Oh."

I catch a whiff of Richard's cologne. It's the same one he wore that day he leaned into my cubicle to ask me about the Trip Monroe interview. Was that really only a couple of weeks ago? I start to feel a little dizzy.

"Have you thought about what you're going to do about Ben's job?" he asks me.

"Not yet. I've been so busy trying to edit down my article on Trip that I haven't had time to think."

"You haven't turned the article in yet?"

"Nope."

"Then you're not going to," he says flatly.

"How do you know that?"

Richard sighs heavily. "You're a bleeding-heart, environmental, *sensitive* soul. You write about beach erosion and manatees falling in love with each other. You don't write about guys who get so drunk they can't remember how many girls they've done in one night. Not guys you like, anyway. And you *like* this guy. It shows in the article, which is the only weak spot because it shows your bias. On the other hand, it's also brilliant because your obvious like of the guy also shows how conflicted you are and gives the article a nice balance."

"Wow. Is that a compliment?"

"What do you think? Take Ben's job. You'll be great editing the magazine. Hell, I might even start reading it."

There is something in the way he says this that makes my breath catch. If I didn't know any better, I'd think that Jackie and Lisa are right and that Richard is interested in me. I thought Richard was jealous of my professional relationship with Ben. Which of course, was all wrong. Richard was never interested in furthering himself at the magazine. Which can only mean that Richard was jealous of Ben because—

"Richard, that day of the Facebook fiasco . . . you said you did it to teach Ben a lesson." I shake my head. Maybe I've had too many beers tonight or maybe I'm still reeling from the scene with Torie. "I'm confused. Tell me why you did it again?"

At first Richard doesn't say anything. Then he leans in close and I find myself trying to back away from him, only my back is already up against the wall, so there is nowhere for me to go.

"I've always liked you, Emma."

My heart starts to thump wildly. As crazy as it sounds, I'm pretty sure Richard is going to kiss me. Do I want him to kiss me? The answer is—

"There you are!" At the sound of Lisa's voice Richard and I jump away from each other like guilty teenagers. "Everyone's starting to leave."

We go back to the table and it takes another hour for everyone to say their good-byes. Since I drove with Jackie, she and Chris offer to take me home. Chris was on call tonight, so he hasn't been drinking. Ben says that he's already called a cab for everyone else and we all agree this is a good idea. I hug Richard and wish him well. His hug is quick and efficient and I'm left disappointed, because somewhere in the past hour I've come to the conclusion that, yes, I wanted Richard to kiss me.

chapter thirty-two

· · · · ·

I'm too wound up to sleep. Tomorrow I'm driving to Catfish Cove to confront Mom and that's a scene I'd love to put off even longer than I already have, but I can't. I've been checking my cell phone every few minutes to see if Kimberly has an update on Torie, but my phone is frustratingly silent. So I decide to read. I know I should read Richard's manuscript, but I just can't do the werewolf-vampire thing right now, so I turn on my e-reader and start my first Steve Danger novel. By five a.m. I'm finished and begin to read book number two.

The novels are campy (cheesy really) but they are also humor-ous, well paced, full of intrigue, and sexy. I am totally hooked on Steve Danger and his cast of misfit rogue spies who end up saving the world from the evil Dr. Hatchett (no joke). There is even a romantic subplot involving Steve's long-suffering techno-geek assistant, Bridget. Despite the fact that every other woman in these novels practically falls into Steve Danger's arms (and his bed), Bridget is stubbornly immune to his chiseled good looks and James Bond–ish charm. Bridget also wears glasses and has an hourglass figure that Steve secretly lusts after. Humph.

I finish novel number two, and as much as I'd like to go on to the next one, I have to get some rest. I sleep till three p.m. and wake up with the horrible worm sensation again. Although my instincts tell me not to reach out to Torie until she's had a chance to cool down, I give in and text her anyway. She doesn't text back. I have a feeling this Jason-Torie thing is going to be an even bigger mess than the Great Tuna Fish Incident. But surely, we are more mature now than we were eight years ago and in a short time she will see how pointless it is to stay angry at me for something beyond my control.

At least I hope so.

I call on my way up to Catfish Cove and tell my moms I have something important to talk to them about. Mom tries to wheedle it out of me on the phone but I stick to my guns and tell her she's going to have to wait to hear it in person. I pull into the driveway at eight. My moms are watching a show on the Discovery Channel about how the world is supposed to end in the next three days. Which, if true, means I won't have to worry about turning the Trip Monroe article in on Monday. Still, I'd kind of like the world to keep going as is. I'm a half-full-glass sort of person, and even with all our global problems, I hold out hope for mankind.

My moms envelop me with their hugs.

"What kind of sandwich are you today?" Mama J asks.

"Fried liver and onions."

When I was a kid, Mom made me eat fried liver and onions one night for supper. I made such a fuss about not liking it that she never made it again. Ever since then, the fried-liver-and-onion sandwich is code for "something is wrong in Whoville."

Mama J steps back. "Oh no. Did you and Nick break up?"

"Actually, yes, we did."

Mom throws her arms up in the air. "I knew it was too good

to be true. Guess this means we won't be getting the family discount at Louie's."

"Nope," I say, "you are most definitely not getting the family discount."

"So this is what you wanted to talk to us about? To tell us you and Nick broke up?" Mama J asks.

"I think we should all sit down first," I say.

"Uh-oh," Mom mutters, "here it comes."

She and Mama J sit back down on the couch. I sit on the edge of the coffee table to face them directly. "I want to talk about Mom's marriage to Frank Monroe."

Mom's eyes widen. "How—"

"Frank Monroe told me."

Mama J uses the remote to turn off the television. She slips an arm around Mom's shoulder. I tell them about coming up to see Frank Monroe to ask for help with Trip and how he told me about his marriage to Mom.

"When was this?" Mom asks.

"Last weekend."

"And you've kept this secret for a whole week?"

"One week of secrecy seems pretty tame compared to thirty-two years."

Mom purses her lips.

Mama J sighs. "I wanted to tell you that day at the store, when you told me about trying to contact Frank, but it's not my story to tell." She gives Mom a stern look. "So tell her now, Sheila."

Mom squirms around on the sofa. "Frank Monroe was my high school sweetheart and we dated off and on through college. Then I went to med school and he came back here to Catfish Cove and opened his auto shop, and later, when I came back to work with Daddy, Frank and I got married."

"I already know all that." Pause. "But why?"

"The usual reasons. I loved him and he loved me."

"Oh . . ." I glance between their faces and wait for more. But I might have to wait a long time, because getting Mom to open up is like twisting the top off one of those childproof medicine bottles. *"And?"* I prompt.

"And I didn't tell you before because I didn't want you to be confused," says Mom. "Plus, you know, there's the whole drama thing."

"Well, I'm confused now."

"In case that expression is what I think it is, let me put your overactive brain to rest. Frank Monroe is *not* your daddy. I would never keep something like that from you."

"I already know that too."

"So what's the problem?" Mom asks.

"What's the problem? What's the *problem*? You don't think keeping a little secret like the fact that you were once married from your own flesh and blood is a problem?"

"Don't raise your voice to me, missy. I don't care how old you are, I'm still your mother."

I count to five and say in a sweetly false voice, "Let me get this straight. You didn't tell me about your secret marriage because you didn't want to confuse me?"

"The marriage only lasted a few days. And no one except our families ever knew about it."

I give Mom my best glare.

She sighs. "Life isn't always black and white, Emma. You of all people should know that."

"Well, of course I know that."

"I wanted to tell you. A couple of different times, but . . . when you were younger, I truly *was* afraid I'd confuse you. And then you got older and high school was so hard for you. I didn't want to add anything more on your plate. Then later, well, it was all so long ago it just seemed silly to bring it up after all this time. But you're right. I should have told you. I'm sorry."

I don't think in all my thirty-two years I've heard Mom admit she was wrong about anything or even admit that things weren't always easy for me. Sometimes a girl needs a little sympathy instead of Mom's standard "Buck up, little cowgirl!"

"I knew the whole thing was a mistake a couple of days in, but I didn't have the courage to be honest with Frank, so I told him I didn't love him anymore and I wanted a divorce." Mom starts wringing her hands the same way I do when I get nervous. I've never seen her do this before and it fascinates me. "He fought it at first, but he agreed to a trial separation. Then I got pregnant with you."

"Let me get this straight. You were married to Frank Monroe, you got a separation, and then while you were separated you went out and found a sperm donor and got pregnant?" This is essentially what Frank said to me, but I guess I had to hear it from Mom's lips before it truly sank in.

Mom nods.

"He must have been—"

"Mighty pissed off," Mom supplies. "If we were still married when I had the baby, Frank would be listed as the daddy on the birth certificate and he knew darn well that wasn't the case. The situation forced his hand."

I'm not sure what to say to all this. Mom notices my silence and continues.

"I might not have wanted to be married to Frank, but I always knew I wanted a baby. Emma, you were my . . . my one anchor during that time." Mom's eyes turn misty. "I've never been good at expressing myself and I didn't know how to tell my family the things I was feeling. I was worried—no, more like petrified about how they would react when they did find out. After I announced my pregnancy, of course, everyone thought the baby was Frank's. It gave me the opening to tell Daddy the truth about everything. Susie had already guessed, but Mama, well, she cried for two days straight. Eventually, though, the world tilted back on axis and everything went back to sort of normal."

"Did you and Frank ever make up?"

"He didn't talk to me for five years. Then I met Jenny and I *had* to see him. To tell him how Jenny was going to move in with me and how everyone in town would know then, but I wanted him to be the first. I owed him that much, and more," Mom admitted.

"What did he say?"

"He'd had five years to cool off, so he was pretty good about it. We talked some and he wished me luck. We're never going to be great friends, he and I, which is a shame, because he's a real decent man, but a part of him probably won't ever forgive me."

I remember what Mama J said to me that day in the park. That sometimes we hold on to the people we love even when we think they've betrayed us. I recall that unfriendly phone message Frank left me back in June and have to wonder if a part of him is still holding on to Mom. I'd like to think that maybe meeting me has now given him some kind of release. It's obvious he and Julie have something going. I'd really like to see them together in a permanent way.

I think what had me so upset about this whole thing was the fact that no matter what was going on in my life, the one constant has always been the love of my two mothers. To find out they have purposely kept something from me all these years made me feel like an outsider. But after listening to Mom's story, I can't be upset with her. I'll be honest, I don't know how I would have reacted to the news of her marriage at seventeen. Mom can joke all she wants, but the truth is, I was like most teenage girls, full of drama and angst, trying to figure out where I fit inside this great big world. One more piece of baggage might have set me over the edge. Mom made the best decision she could under the circumstances.

It's easy to start to believe as you get older that your mom is your friend and that you are equals. But that is all an illusion, because the fact is, I realize now that no matter how old I am, my moms are not my equals. To them I will always be their little girl. They will always want to protect me, always champion me, and thank God, always forgive me. Maybe being the parent of a teenager is just as hard as being a teenager yourself. I can only hope that I'm lucky enough to find out one day.

"I loved Frank and a part of me still loves him," says Mom. "But he wasn't my *dream*. I always knew there was someone out there, someone just for me. Someone I could love with all my heart and soul and feel completely myself with. And I found her." Mom looks at Mama J with wet eyes. "Jenny was my dream. And I'm hers."

I've never heard Mom speak so freely about her emotions. How strange is it that she has just used almost the same exact words I used when I broke up with Nick? I can't help myself, I start to cry. And then something truly unexpected happens. Mom starts to cry as well.

Mama J just shakes her head and wipes away her own tears. "Here comes the drama," she says with a laugh.

I take my yearbook to bed with me and begin flipping through the pages.

In the days that followed the Dixie Deb Ball, I was probably the most miserable teenager in existence. Although my moms forgave me for being a shit, I couldn't forgive myself. Around this same time I was also waiting to hear back from colleges. I'd applied to the two big state colleges in Florida, as well as a couple out of state. I got accepted everywhere, which should have thrilled me, but I was still too miserable to be happy. In the end I chose the University of Florida, because that's where Mom and Grandpa George went to school, and being a Gator was just about the most important thing in his life. I figured it was a tradition I shouldn't mess with.

I remember the day our English teacher gave us the poem assignment. Trip and I had already done the Emily Dickinson project, so my senior portfolio consisted of the project and two original short stories I'd written. The poem was the only task left. As seniors, we were exempted from finals if we completed all our assignments with a passing grade, so I wasn't about to not do the poem.

Although I've always loved poetry, I'd never written any myself. I sat at my desk for hours, crumbling paper after paper of fumbled attempts. In the end the poem was ridiculously simple and kind of bad. But it was written with all the emotion (as Mom would put it) of an overly dramatic seventeen-year-old girl and that was good enough to win the contest.

> *Arms that surround me, soft and white,*
> *Keeping me safe throughout the night.*
> *There's no daddy in this mommy sandwich . . .*

I could read on, but you get the point. I'm no Dr. Seuss, that's for sure.

I already told you that I never meant to win the poetry contest, because honestly, I never thought I had a chance. But my English teacher submitted it and then, miracle of miracles, it got top three. She called me to her classroom and told me the news. The next day at the senior awards program, it was announced that my poem had won. As I walked to the podium my knees shook so bad I was convinced everyone could hear them knocking. I reached the mike, and looked down to see my poem neatly typed out with a blue ribbon tacked on top of the paper. My gaze darted around the stuffy gymnasium until it settled on my moms. I cleared my throat and began reading.

If you haven't figured out by now, Mom has always been the kind of person who shuns the limelight. She hates being the center of attention and I know that once I began reading, people were probably turning to look at her and Mama J. It isn't that everyone didn't already know they were a couple, but no one talked about it openly. As I read, I kept my gaze on them. I think a part of me was afraid to look away because I've never been particularly good in the spotlight either. I just know that as I kept reading, my voice grew louder until it almost seemed like I was shouting. When I looked back later at a tape of the ceremony, my voice sounded surprisingly normal. Weird, huh? How you remember something different from the way it really was.

I just know that the smiles on my moms' faces that day made up for the look I saw on their faces the day of the Dixie Deb Ball. After the awards presentation, people kept coming up to me and congratulating me and my moms. A few people went out of their way to avoid me, but overall it was the best day of my teenage life.

I turn the page in my yearbook and run across an unposed picture of Shannon and Nick taken at a pep rally. They are both smiling and look incredibly young and happy. The more I think about it, the more I'm convinced that Nick deliberately kept that box from Shannon. I like to think that maybe my relationship with Nick will be a step toward his healing. Even though we were together for all the wrong reasons, I hope he'll eventually see that I was right and he was wrong. I wish I could make Nick see that he deserves the fireworks *and* the trust and respect. We all do. He just doesn't think it's possible, and maybe it's not possible for everyone, but I think I'd rather be alone than not have it.

Not everyone settles.

Mom didn't. And I don't plan to either.

I turn to our senior-class pictures and find Trip's photo. Beneath his somber face is his full name, Thomas Alexander Monroe. I read his senior quote and smile. Trip quoted Dr. Seuss.

Sometimes the questions are complicated and the answers are simple.

I look back and think about how much Trip and I had in common. We were both outsiders, both different, and both desperately trying to fit in. In some ways we still have a lot in common. Just like Trip, I'm still trying to be someone I'm not.

The fact is I'm not Parisian. Strange things pop into my head at the weirdest times (and I'm okay with that). I'm an ordinary girl from Catfish Cove, Florida, who was raised by untraditional parents. Sometimes I speak with a twang. I'm twenty (okay, maybe twenty-five) pounds overweight, and to be honest, unless something really drastic happens, I don't think I'll be losing any of that extra poundage soon. My favorite author is Jane Austen and my favorite movie is *Little Women* (the version with Winona Ryder).

Oh, and I suck at moderation.

Yes, I am different.

But then, isn't everyone?

chapter thirty-three

. . . . .

Once again it's Monday morning, and despite there being no editorial staff meeting and that it will just be me and Lisa and Jackie, I still bring in the Krispy Kremes. A dozen donuts split three ways. Lord help us.

Ben is spending the day in Orlando with T.K. but he's already texted me twice asking me where the article is and whether or not I've made up my mind to take the editor job.

This particular Monday is unlike any other Monday in my career at *Florida!* magazine. For one thing, I circumvent my old cubicle and head straight to Ben's office, or as I am now calling it, *my* office (at least while we still have a lease on the building). Yep. I'm taking the editor job. But I'm not moving to Orlando. I whip out an e-mail to Ben, copying it to T.K., accepting the job with the condition that I work from my home. I am willing to travel to Orlando for any necessary meetings, but I foresee that most of what I have to do I can do from the sanctity of my den (Jackie has volunteered to help me feng shui it for utmost productivity).

The next thing I do is send Ben a copy of the Trip Monroe article. The new title is "Zero to Hero to Starting Over." Richard was right. I was never going to turn in the previous version of my article on Trip. I think the new piece is a sympathetic story about a guy who basically started from nothing and became a huge superstar and gave away bundles of bucks, only to discover that same stardom has cost him plenty of personal angst. It doesn't sugarcoat what's going on in Trip's life, but I left out all the embarrassing stuff. Let another magazine cover that. We have an exclusive from Trip himself and that will have to be good enough.

Richard was right about something else too (I guess I should just say that Richard was right about a lot of stuff). I hate celebrity interviews. I prefer writing articles about marine life and beach erosion. If I ever go to law school, I don't think I'd want to be a kick-ass prosecutor like the ones in *Law & Order*. I'd want to be a kick-ass environmental attorney who makes the corporate litterbugs of the world cringe.

Ten minutes after I send the article, Ben calls. "Good work," he says.

"Really?"

"You sound surprised."

"Just relieved that's it over."

"T.K.'s reading it now. We're sending Ike Johnson up to Catfish Cove tomorrow for a photo shoot."

Ike Johnson is *Florida!*'s best photographer. He did the photos for my manatee article and I couldn't have asked for anyone better.

Ben's voice turns melancholy. "I'm glad you're taking the job, but I think you're making a mistake staying in Tampa. Are you sure you want to do all that driving?"

"One hundred percent sure."

"It's just, well, hell, I'm going to miss you, Frazier."

But you'll have Abby now, I almost say. "It's not like you aren't going to see me fairly often."

"I know, but it won't be the same."

Thank God for that.

I e-mail a copy of the article to Richard (because I think he'll get a kick out of the new version) then meet Kimberly for lunch. I hand her a printed copy of my article and sit back while she reads. I figure that as Trip's new PR person, she should get an advance copy.

"Emma, this is terrific. But are you sure?"

"Yeah, I'm sure." Pause. "So how's Torie?"

"She's still mad at you but I think deep down she knows she only has herself to blame. Don't worry, she'll come around."

"I don't get it. Does she want Jason back or not?"

"I don't think it matters anymore. Jason told to her bugger off. Not in those words. He used the American version."

"Ouch."

"Yeah, but totally deserved."

Sigh.

"So tell me about your new job with Trip. What's going on there?"

"I'm temporarily moving in with my folks until I get my own place, but I'm going to be so busy I won't have time to think. I have to get office space, hire staff. This whole thing is really going to be great for Catfish Cove." Kimberly fidgets with the edge of her napkin. "Emma, I know this is kind of premature, but I wanted to run something by you."

"Shoot."

"Do you think, in like, maybe a couple of months when things cool off and it wouldn't be terribly weird, would you mind if I asked Nick out?"

"Nick? *My* Nick?"

"He's not your Nick anymore. Unless . . . you've changed your mind about breaking up?" she asks anxiously.

"No. Of course not. Kimberly! I think that would be great."

"The thing is, I ran into him while I was in town moving some of my stuff and we got a cup of coffee. At first all he wanted to talk about was you, but then . . . well, I think maybe there might be a spark there. But I'm only cool with it if you are."

"Of course I am!"

We talk some more about the article but my mind keeps wandering back to Kimberly and Nick. The idea of them getting together actually makes me feel good, and if that isn't a huge sign that I did the right thing, then I don't know what is.

I'm back in the office when I get Richard's text.

Great article. I knew you could make it work.

I text back. *Thanks! Hey, I read your first two Steve Danger novels. I am now officially a fan.*

I wait for Richard's next text, but nothing comes. Not that my response required a response from him, but still, I guess I'm a little disappointed.

I'm almost done for the day and am ready to shut off my computer when I decide to play around a bit. Jackie mentioned posting pictures of Richard's going-away party on Facebook, so I log into my account. It's been too long since I've been on Facebook. The first thing I do is take myself out of my "relationship" with Nick. I can't help but smile as I remember the day of the "Facebook fiasco." It still amazes me that Richard set that whole thing up.

Jackie has a slew of pictures on her page. There are photos of her house in every stage of the building process, as well as pictures from her housewarming party and Richard's going-away shindig at Captain Pete's. There is a very nice photo of the five of us—Jackie, Lisa, Ben, Richard, and me. I'd really like a copy of it to frame and put on my desk. Sort of a reminder of days gone by. I ask Jackie where I can get a copy of the original.

"I'll send it to your e-mail," she says.

"Thanks." I start to go back to my office, but something has been niggling at the back of my mind ever since I read that first Steve Danger novel, and I turn around. "You've read all of Richard's spy novels, right?" I ask Jackie.

"Of course I've read his novels. Why?"

"Don't you think Richard should concentrate on these spy novels instead of going off in the vampire direction? I mean, vampires just seem so overdone these days."

"Vampires? What are you talking about?"

"You know, Richard's one-hundred-and-eighty-thousand-word vampire-werewolf novel? The one no one in the office wants to read?"

"Emma, I have no idea what you're talking about."

"Richard didn't ask you to read his manuscript?"

"If he had, I would have read it. So no, I can definitely say that he has never asked me to read anything of his. I offered to edit one of his Steve Danger novels once and he practically bit my head off."

"Oh . . . I guess I misunderstood."

Jackie and Lisa leave the office promptly at five. I leave a few minutes later and grab some takeout on the drive home. I can't get Jackie's words out of my head.

I know what Richard said and I didn't misunderstand anything.

I go to my laptop and hook it into my printer and find the e-mail Richard sent me all those weeks ago. I download the attachment and start printing. I'm afraid I'm going to run out of paper, but after awhile the printer stops and I see that the entire document has printed out and it's only about 250 pages. No way is this a 180,000-word manuscript. Obviously, Richard was playing with me and I fell for it. I glance at the first page. The novel is titled *Curveball,* which seems like a strange title for a paranormal novel, but, oh well. Richard has proven to be a terrific friend these past few weeks and I owe it to him to finally read this manuscript. I grab up the papers and a red felt-tip pen and start reading.

The traffic on Kennedy is blissfully slow. Of course it's not even seven a.m. yet, so that's probably the reason. I grab a dozen Krispy Kremes and two large coffees and drive to Richard's. I spot his red Ford Explorer parked in the driveway of his town house and park my little car behind it. I'm still wearing my pajama bottoms and an old T-shirt that I threw over my camisole top. I didn't sleep a wink last night but I'm more awake than ever. I ring the doorbell, and for the first time since I came up with this harebrained idea, I begin to panic. What if Richard isn't alone?

I take a settling breath.

If Richard isn't alone, then that's okay. This isn't a romantic visit (if it was I would have primped just a tiny bit maybe). This is a professional call, colleague to colleague. Richard asked me to critique his manuscript and that's exactly what I've done.

After a couple of minutes I hear shuffling behind the door. Richard blinks the sleep from his eyes and looks down at me. He's wearing boxer shorts and a T-shirt. "What time is it?"

"Six thirty-seven." I offer up the donuts. "I brought Krispy Kremes. And coffee."

Richard snatches the coffee and ushers me inside. It appears he is alone and I'm relieved because I realize that it would *not* have been okay to find someone here with him. Which means . . .

"I read your manuscript."

Richard sits on the sofa. I sit next to him. He takes a long swig of his coffee before he says, "And?"

"And it took me about three pages to figure out this isn't a vampire novel."

"Smart girl."

Just then an insanely large cat jumps onto my lap, startling me into almost dropping the box of donuts.

"Whoa." Richard saves the day by grabbing onto the box. "Watch where you're going, Fat Boy."

"Fat Boy?" I get a better look at the cat. It's the same cat Ben adopted from the shelter. The same one Richard called Animal Control to come take away. "Is this Ben's Lucky? I thought Lisa had him."

"Turns out Tony is allergic to cats."

"Oh. But . . . what happened to him? Richard, he's huge!"

Richard pulls a donut from the box and shrugs. "Guess he doesn't have my metabolism."

"Richard, please tell me you're not feeding this cat human food."

"What am I supposed to feed him?"

"Ever heard of Meow Mix? Friskies? Fancy Feast?"

"Are those cat-food brands?" At the look on my face, Richard grins. "Relax. I'm feeding him cat food."

"How often?"

"I dunno. Whenever the bowl is empty?"

Sigh. "So about your novel. It's really good. As a matter of fact, if I wasn't afraid you'd get a big head over this, I'd tell you that it's almost kind of brilliant."

"You really think it's brilliant?"

"I said *almost.*" I hand him the manuscript. "I made a few notes. On the sides. Not much really."

Richard's manuscript is not normally the type of novel I would buy, based on the subject matter, but I totally loved it. It's about a guy who dreams of being a professional baseball player (a pitcher) and his journey through baseball only to be denied his big chance to play because of an injury. There's also a romantic interest, a woman who turns out to have his son, whom the main character then reconnects with later in life.

"This isn't autobiographical, is it?"

"You mean is this guy me? Yes and no." He sees the expression on my face and elaborates. "I don't think I have any kids out there, if that's what you mean."

"Okay, just checking."

Richard points to my pajama bottoms. "Instituting a new dress code on your first official day as boss?"

I ignore his question. "I'll have you know I stayed up all night reading your book. I've even started the third Steve Danger novel." I stroke the back of Lucky—er, I mean Fat Boy's neck. "Hey, is Steve ever going to get together with Bridget?"

"Now, that would ruin everything, wouldn't it?"

"How so?"

"Emma, the point of a sappy romance that never gets off the ground is to keep the reader anticipating that it will one day happen. Once Bridget and Steve get together, then the tension will be gone."

"Not necessarily."

"Are you trying to tell me how to write my novels?"

"You're the one who was practically panting for my opinion."

He goes to say something then clamps his mouth shut. We stare at each other for a few long seconds and my throat goes dry. Who am I trying to fool? Richard is more than just a colleague. More than just a friend. Ever since his going-away party I've thought of nothing else but our almost kiss. When did I start having romantic feelings for him? Maybe it began that day just a few short weeks ago when he rolled his chair next to mine and asked me how the Trip Monroe interview went. But I don't think so. I think it was earlier than that and I just never wanted to acknowledge it. I'm not sure. The one thing I know is that I'm not going to overanalyze it.

"So . . . that night of your going-away party. You said you liked me."

Richard slowly nods.

"How so? I mean, do you like me as a friend? Or do you like me as a girlfriend? Or—"

Richard then does something totally unexpected and yet totally natural. He knocks the Krispy Kreme box to the floor and pulls me onto his lap.

"I like you like *this*."

And then he kisses me.

And I kiss him back.

epilogue

•••••

It's been a year now since I've officially been the editor at *Florida!* magazine. I still live in Tampa, and although I end up having to drive to Orlando at least twice a week, I really don't mind. Ben has proven to be a fantastic publisher. He has raised our profit margin, instituted a bonus system, and, overall, improved office morale. He and Abby got engaged a few months ago, but then out of the blue, she called it off. Smart girl.

Kimberly is still working for Trip. His nonprofit agency has really taken off. I had dinner with him a couple of weeks ago. He's been dry since that day he and Kimberly and I ate pizza at my town house, and I'm incredibly proud of him.

Kimberly and Nick dated a few months, broke up for about a week, and then got back together again. Their relationship resembles that roller-coaster ride from Universal Studios that Richard was so leery of. It's constant fireworks but there's also trust and respect. I think Nick is still a little skeptical of the whole thing but I have every confidence that Kimberly will prevail and get her man this time.

Jason and Amy broke up when Amy was offered a big position in her firm's Miami office. Torie didn't speak to me for almost two months. But then she invited me to dinner, and over some wine, she began to cry and asked me to forgive her. Which of course I did. Torie is far from perfect but she's still my friend. If I don't forgive her her faults, then how can I expect to be forgiven when I screw up too? I'm still holding out that maybe one day she and Jason will end up together. I know it's a long shot but the romantic in me won't give up on them.

A couple of months ago Frank Monroe married Julie Williams in a small ceremony in his backyard. The wedding took place just as the sun set over Otis Lake while a string quartet played "My Girl" in the background. The whole thing was horribly romantic.

Trip was there, of course, along with a small handful of friends, including me, Richard, Mom and Mama J. I cried like a baby the whole time. So did Mom. I guess the drama gene can go dormant for a while, but once it's been awakened, there is no telling when it will surface.

As for Richard and me, well, we've been together ever since that crazy kiss on his couch. My moms adore him. I've met his family and I'm pretty sure they like me as well, which is good because things are getting awful serious between us and it really helps if you have family behind you.

I guess it's way past time I told you about Richard.

Richard is the kind of guy who can sit ten feet away from you for six years and yet you know nothing about him. Not the stuff that counts, anyway, because he's intensely private. But over time I've come to discover all the little things I love about him. He likes to play tough guy but he's the biggest softy I know. Despite hating cats, he has given Lucky aka "Fat Boy" a home. He dislikes sushi and his favorite food is the good old American hamburger. Medium rare, onions and ketchup. No mustard, please. Most of his jokes border on the raunchy but I find them all incredibly funny (at least most of the time I do). His favorite movie is *Casablanca* (yes!) and his favorite writer is Stephen King.

I even know his favorite word.

We'd been dating about a month. We were sitting on the couch, my legs draped across his lap, watching the Tampa Bay Rays play the Yankees. The Rays were down two runs.

"I hate those Yankees," Richard said.

"Yeah, me too." *See?* I told you I could hate the Yankees if I thought about it enough.

Then I turned and asked him what his favorite word in the whole wide world was. He never took his gaze off the screen as he answered, "Home run." Thank God he doesn't allow me to take myself too seriously.

Last night we talked until three a.m., discussing the plot of his latest Steve Danger novel. I still think he should stop teasing his audience and get Steve and Bridget together, but Richard disagrees (he is also incredibly stubborn). There is a fancy literary agent who is interested in his novel *Curveball*. He asked Richard for some revisions, which Richard is happily doing. I keep my fingers and toes constantly crossed that it all works out.

So, back to last night. I told you we brainstormed till three in the morning, but we didn't actually go to sleep until a couple of hours later. What we did in between the brainstorming and the sleep, well . . . some things a girl likes to keep just to herself.

But there is one more thing I will tell you about Richard.

He is everything I ever dreamed of.

And more.